Deep
Grass
Roots

a novel

The Adventures
and Challenges of Two
Women Homesteaders

Marcia Neely

Deep Grass Roots

a novel

The Adventures
and Challenges of Two
Women Homesteaders

Marcia Neely

Beaver's Pond Press
Minneapolis, MN

Edited by Angela Wiechmann and Nancy Overcott
Front cover art by Doug Pederson

ISBN: 978-1-59298-687-3
Library of Congress Catalog Number: 2018906857
Printed in the United States of America
First Printing: 2018
22 21 20 19 18   5 4 3 2 1

Book design by Athena Currier

Beaver's Pond Press, Inc.
7108 Ohms Lane
Edina, MN 55439–2129

(952) 829-8818
www.BeaversPondPress.com

To order, visit marcianeely.books.com or
email marciakgarden@gmail.com.

Dedicated to the memory of
Tillie Hagenstad and Bertha Amundson

Journey from Watson, Minnesota, to Homestead Land in North Dakota

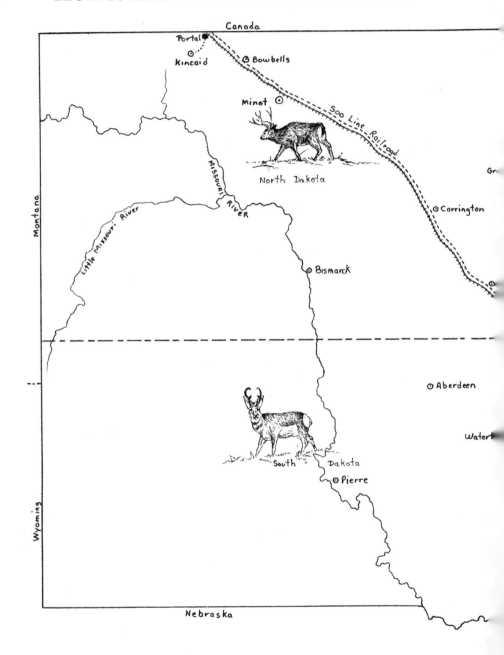

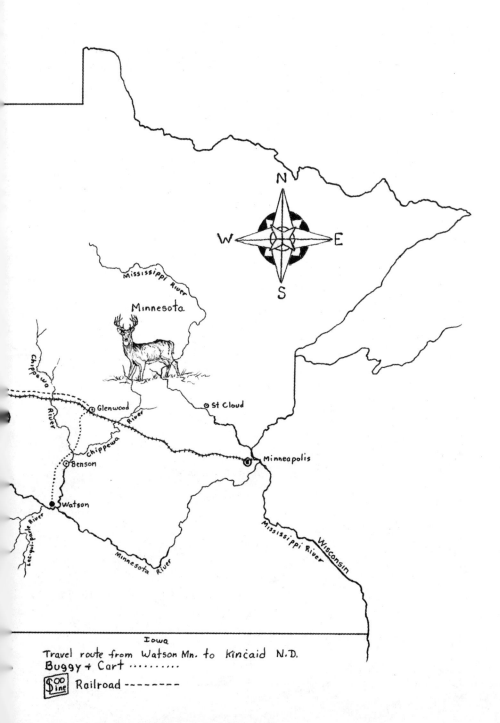

Travel route from Watson Mn. to Kincaid N.D.
Buggy & Cart ··········
[SOO Line] Railroad --------

Preface

True events in the life of Tillie Hagenstad Stoen, the mother of my adopted father, inspired this novel. As young women, Tillie and her friend Bertha Amundson, both from near the village of Watson, Minnesota, journeyed to the northwestern tip of North Dakota. As the twentieth century dawned, they each filed claims for homesteads in Meadows Township, Ward County, which eventually became Burke County. They were among the 14 percent[1] of single women homesteaders who made claims in that county.

I first visited Tillie's homestead land in 1990 while on a motorcycle trip to Alaska with my husband. Even then, ninety years after Tillie and Bertha's first sighting, the land looked foreboding, especially on a cold, gloomy, and windy day in early June. Seeing the site gave me the utmost respect for the grit it would have taken to spend even a year on that land in the early 1900s. I felt deep admiration for the courage and tenacity of Tillie Hagenstad, who died before her son became my adopted father when my mother married him after being widowed.

I'd been told that Tillie and Bertha primarily used coal to heat their small shacks in winter and cooked with cow chips in the summer, making do with the offerings of nature and the Dakota land.

---

1   H. Elaine Lindgren, *Land in Her Own Name* (Norman: University of Oklahoma Press, 1996), 52. (Original copyright: The Institute for Regional Studies, North Dakota State University, Fargo, North Dakota, 1991.)

Tillie and her friend stayed on their homesteads about a year and a half and then returned to Minnesota. To "prove up" on land and receive homestead rights for free land required a residency of five years. Thus, I assume Tillie paid one dollar and twenty-five cents per acre, costing a total of two hundred dollars for one hundred and sixty acres, giving her homestead rights after staying on the land a minimum of fourteen months, as the law at the time allowed. Tillie owned that acreage during her lifetime, deeding it to her two sons, Ernest and Manfred Stoen, both deceased, of Big Bend, Minnesota. Duane Essen, who grew up on a farm next to the homestead site and now lives in Battleview, North Dakota, purchased the land in 2006 and still owns it.

Even though my visit to the homestead land was short, it fueled the belief I've had most of my life that I was born a century late for my spirit. Perhaps that thought was first stimulated when, as a child, my grandmother, Synneva Saue Pederson, told me stories of Per Hansa while she was reading *Giants in the Earth*, Rølvaag's classic novel of pioneer life on the plains of Dakota.

For more than twenty years, I'd think of Tillie during quiet, reflective moments as her story percolated within me. Finally, I began this novel, which is dedicated to Tillie and her friend.

The novel uses the names Tillie and Bertha as the central characters, but it does not portray the real lives of Tillie Hagenstad and Bertha Amundson. Instead it fabricates the story of two young women proving up by spending five years on their homesteads. Although a few of the incidents in the novel are based on stories I heard of the real Tillie, such as using a broom to sweep away snow from the inside walls of her tar paper shack and surviving a grass fire by plunging into a nearby small lake, the actions and thoughts ascribed to the two women in this novel are purely fictional. Yet, I attempted to create a sense of the time and place and to be true to historical facts, modifying small aspects only as needed to create compelling fiction. I hope my narrative captures some of the experiences and thoughts of the intrepid North Dakota homesteaders.

Below are photos of the two women whose homestead experience inspired this novel:

Bertha Amundson and Tillie Hagenstad in Tillie's shack.

Visitors arrive at Bertha and Tillie's shacks.

Dakota Beckons

1900

The farewell drew to a close as the eastern sky began to lighten, bringing cattle into silhouetted view on the distant pasture. Aunts, cousins, and neighbors watched silently. Tillie hugged her mother while tears full of sadness, joy, and anxiety streamed over reddened cheeks.

Tillie's father, Jens Melbakken, who homesteaded in Minnesota after emigrating from Norway in 1868, hitched two horses to the buggy, strapped two trunks into the cart, then climbed into the buggy and took the reins. Lifting her skirt, Tillie stepped in next to him.

Bertha gave a final hug and kiss to her younger sister, Hilda, holding her tightly, as if she didn't want to release her. Tears trickled from their eyes and a sob emerged from Hilda. Bertha hugged Hans, her younger brother, tears dampening their faces, although Hans tried to conceal his. After a kiss on the cheek and a *"Lykke til"* from her grandfather, Bertha stepped up into the buggy.

Snow had melted on the prairie, leaving occasional mounds along a fence line or within a grove of trees as the *clop, clop, clop* of the horses sounded on the dirt road. Those hoofbeats would be

1

the last sounds some family members would hear of the two young women as their adventure began. Neither looked back as the buggy left the farm near the village of Watson, Minnesota, with Tillie's brother, Peter, driving a cart behind them.

With penetrating eyes, a strong mouth, dark brown hair parted in the middle, and full cheeks, Tillie was striking. Fear and excitement fought for dominance in her expression. Bertha looked rather teacher-like with spectacles framing her large eyes with heavy brows. Her cheeks were rosy, her lips full. She wore a small ivory-colored bow near the front of her brown hair that curled atop her head and framed her comely face.

Both women were fit. Their years milking cows, feeding pigs, butchering chickens, helping with haying, as well as performing the womanly chores of gardening, canning, and sewing, would serve them well as they embarked on a journey to a life that would challenge not only their skills, but their deepest emotions.

The *clop, clop* continued to Benson, where the four ate lunch at the Pacific Hotel, then resumed until midafternoon when they reached Glenwood, where the Soo Line Railroad had the closest depot to Watson. Here the two friends picked up land-seeker tickets, costing one cent a mile, to take them on a nearly five-hundred-mile journey to Portal, North Dakota.

Tillie heard the train coming toward the station, the *roar*, the *hiss*, then the *clanking* of the wheels becoming a *chugging*, the whistle sounding three times. She swallowed, elation and apprehension leaving her unable to speak. She looked at Bertha, whose face exhibited similar emotions. Their eyes met, their mouths opened a bit, but no words flowed.

After Jens and Peter loaded the trunks into the baggage car, and after the first boarding call, the two women stepped into the train that would eventually take them to the far northwest of North

Dakota. Jens handed Tillie the sturdy wooden travel box he'd built to store food and other items they'd need during the trip; then he threw her a kiss, his face stern and solemn, yet not without care. Tears tried to form in Tillie's eyes, but didn't spill onto her cheeks.

The train chugged along slowly as it left the station, then picked up speed as it headed northwest. Sitting in the passenger section, Tillie thought about the contents of her trunk. She wondered if she'd packed the right sort of things, if she'd find some items useless and hunger for others she'd left behind. Her trunk contained a quilt in a log cabin pattern her mother had made for her journey, her shotgun wrapped in a quilt she'd made herself, simple skirts and blouses, a nicer skirt and a couple of fancy blouses, bloomers of course, a couple of sunbonnets, work shoes, and boots. She had a hammer, saw, and screwdriver, a small spade and hoe, her bake kettle and cooking pots, as well as an embroidered tablecloth to set an appropriate table, and a locket to wear for church, if one existed, and for other affairs—Christmas celebrations? Dances? Weddings, perhaps? As prized possessions, Tillie had packed her coffee grinder and the maple rolling pin, made by her father, to roll out *lefse* and *flatbrød*. Then too, there were beans and other seeds gathered from last fall's harvest, a number of photographs of family, and candles that would hopefully bring some light into her simple hut on the spacious plain of Dakota.

Both young women wore long dark skirts, plain blouses, and hand-knit woolen sweaters. Tillie had an American Waltham watch pinned to her blouse. She and Bertha were bundled in their warm seal-plush coats, a fake fur popular at the time, even though the weather was moderating. Both wore high-topped boots.

Several people, including Bertha's grandfather, had warned Tillie and Bertha about robberies on trains or in hotels. So the women had sewn a number of silver dollars into their bloomers and the lining of their coats to minimize the risk of losing their cash if they were robbed.

They carried Wells Fargo traveler's checks in their handbags, having learned there would be Wells Fargo agents in most towns and that they each should have eight hundred dollars to get started on their homesteads. Tillie had saved more than seven hundred dollars from her teaching days, since she lived at home the whole time. Her father provided the rest. Bertha had saved about six hundred, but her grandfather advanced her the additional funds.

They planned to buy many of the supplies and provisions they would need in the small settlements of Bowbells and Portal.

———

The homesteading idea had started as a lark just over a year earlier. "Let's head out west and stake us a claim," Bertha had said in jest.

"Think we could?" asked Tillie.

"Well," said Bertha after hesitating a moment, "probably not, and Lars wants to get married next year."

The jest kept festering in Tillie's mind, though. She and Bertha were completing their first year of teaching and were planning to teach a second year. Bertha taught country school in Big Bend Township, east of the village of Milan, and Tillie conducted classes for twenty-one students near Watson. Both had completed ninth grade, then attended Moorhead Normal School from which they received teaching certificates after two years' study, practice, and an extensive test that required knowledge in astronomy, mathematics, geology, US and world history, civics, geography, horticulture, anatomy and physiology, English, grammar, and elocution.

Teaching challenged not only their intellectual skills, but their ability to handle the rough boys. Tillie had a stern teacher's voice, which she used regularly. Bertha's voice was weaker and the boys in her class took advantage of it.

It was after complaining about those boys that Bertha had suggested staking a claim, but she'd been planning to marry Lars and have children of her own. She was sure, she said, that any of her own boys would behave better than some of those in her class. Boys who taunted the girls, dipping their braids in ink and tripping them during games. Boys who occasionally used ugly language and talked back to their teacher, even knowing she'd switch them with a ruler. "I wonder how their parents control them, if they do, but then I guess I'm a little softer than you are, Tillie," Bertha remarked. "One stern look or word from you and they'd likely behave."

On a Saturday afternoon a month later, Tillie had asked Bertha if she and Lars were going to the barn dance at Torgerson's that evening.

"Lars didn't say anything about it last Saturday, so I asked him and he said, 'Well, maybe,' so I suppose he'll call for me."

Tillie noticed her friend's somber expression. "Is something wrong?"

"Well, he's been acting strange lately, like maybe he doesn't want to get married, though he hasn't said that. He even mentioned he might want to enlist in the army." A soft tear rolled down her cheek.

"Oh, Bertha, I thought he was being so sweet to you."

"Well, he used to be, but lately? I don't know," Bertha said while putting on a stoic face. "Maybe it's just my imagination."

A couple weeks later, Bertha told Tillie that Lars hadn't called for her the night of the Torgerson's barn dance. "I think he's about ready to jilt me."

"Oh, Bertha, love can be so complicated. I feel badly for you. And men! I sometimes just don't understand them," Tillie said. "But if Lars is seeming kind of reluctant, how about seriously considering getting a homestead? We could have such an exciting adventure. Just think about getting your own land in a far-off wonderful place. I've always dreamed of it. It would be thrilling, wouldn't it, Bertha?"

"Sure 'nuf," Bertha replied. "It sounds so thrilling and maybe it would give Lars some pause. I'll think more about it."

A month later, Lars enlisted in the US Army and was immediately sent to the Philippines to fight in the uprising of Filipino insurgents that followed the Spanish-American War. He told Bertha that his patriotic sense and manliness demanded army service when he thought his country needed it.

Bertha's limited news of the war had convinced her it wasn't a necessary one. To Tillie, Bertha wondered out loud what her country wanted with far-off lands filled with likely uncivilized people who spoke some strange language. "Why can't we leave the Filipinos alone in their own country?"

She'd kept these thoughts from Lars, although she'd tried to talk him out of enlisting, to no avail.

Not long after that, the young teachers let the dream of going west turn from fantasizing to shaping a plan. "I bet we could even teach school out there and earn a living," Tillie said.

"Quite an adventure it would be. Building ourselves little shacks, maybe getting a horse and a milking cow, planting gardens, breaking land for crops," Bertha said. "Hopefully getting some of the men to help with that," she added with a bit of a smirk. "We'd make new friends, sure, sure. Bet there'd be creatures a'plenty to shoot. Likely some to fear as well." She didn't admit to Tillie, though, that she'd told her grandfather that, although she felt exhilarated by the idea, she wasn't convinced the adventure was wise, a thought he'd readily acknowledged.

"Well, fears or no fears, I've always imagined going west," Tillie said. "In my dreams, I see beautiful green grasses rippling in summer breezes and flowing golden in autumn. Pristine and magnificent. Let's do it."

"Well, we can at least find out more about the possibilities. We should check with Mattie Larson about how to get in touch with her brother who's out there."

After checking with Mattie, the two friends composed a letter to Hans Larson, who had filed a claim in northwestern North Dakota. Before he left, he'd lived on a farm near Montevideo and, while Tillie and Bertha didn't know him, his older sister Mattie attended Zion Lutheran Church in Watson where their families attended services. Hans had joined Henry Berge, also from near Montevideo, on the Dakota adventure.

Dear Mr. Larson,

We are two teachers from Watson and have attended Zion Lutheran Church, where we know your older sister, Mattie. We are desirous of coming west to file homesteads. We may be interested in coming to the area where you now have a homestead. We are wondering what might be the best way to travel and what we should think about in planning such an undertaking. We would most appreciate any advice you might give us as we consider our dream of going to northwestern Dakota.

Very sincerely,
Miss Tillie Melbakken and Miss Bertha Harstad

A few weeks later, his reply came. The Norwegian community south of Portal was growing and they'd welcome Tillie and Bertha, should they decide to undertake the adventure. *"Be sure you have the strength and stamina for it. It's a good, but hard life,"* he wrote. His advice was to get information from the United States General Land Office in Minot and to take the Soo Line Railroad the whole way. He and Henry had taken a wagon, but he didn't think that was wise for two girls. His wife Helen came later, but her brother had traveled with her by train as far as Minot. They'd taken the Milwaukee Road from Montevideo to Valley City, North Dakota. From the Milwaukee Road Station they had to get to the Soo Line to travel to Portal. Getting Helen's trunk to the Soo depot had been tough. *"Think it'd be too hard for a couple of girls. Better to make the journey to Glenwood and get on the Soo Line there,"* he wrote.

Just before school resumed in September, Tillie sent a letter to the Minot Land Office questioning where land might be available and how a young woman with a teaching certificate might proceed to procure it.

Tillie filled her mind and taxed her body preparing lessons, teaching the children, and helping her family with the harvest, as well as bringing in eggs, milking cows, carrying slop to the pigs, and occasionally helping with cooking and baking. Yet a rare day passed without Tillie assembling fantasies of a life in Dakota and hoping for a letter from the Minot Land Office, which would take weeks to come.

Bertha did much the same, although she did as much of the cooking as she could manage, since she and her younger sisters had normally prepared meals ever since their grandmother passed. She stopped by the Watson Post Office once a week and always looked first for Lars's handwriting, but only received one small note from him that fall.

Dear Bertha,

Hot and muggy nights keep me awake most the night. Daytime heat is awful. Moved to a new camp a few days ago and are so busy putting up our tents, finding wet wood to try to cook our meals, creating camp, and dodging the dam mosquitoes, so I don't have much time to think. Monsoons haven't even hit yet, but some of the guys have dysentery or malaria. Guess Minnesota winters weren't so bad.

Lars

"Didn't even sign the note *love*," Bertha said with a petulant look when she told Tillie about the note. "And he spelled *damn* wrong." Her expression changed and, after a big sigh, she'd looked as if she might cry. "Didn't say anything about missing me. I miss him, though, and feel sorry for him being there. Sounds awful." Then she slowly nodded her head.

"Probably he's too tired to write much, or even feel much," Tillie said softly.

"We'll see. Grandpapa tells me to be patient, that men in war don't write much, but it feels like Lars doesn't really care. Probably'll never get married. Reminds me . . . There's the Iverson wedding next Friday. Want to go with me? I might start bawling when seeing other people get married."

"Sure, we'll go together," Tillie said. "Wear that pretty white blouse with the ruffles you made last summer and your bright calico skirt. It'll brighten your spirits. But bring a hanky. I will too."

In early November of 1899, Tillie finally received a letter from the Minot Land Office, which provided information about where homestead sites were available in the northwestern part of the state and described the procedures and laws regulating staking a claim. A seeker could locate one's own land, but more commonly a home-steader would seek the assistance of a land locator who could be found in most settlements, including Portal near the area where many sites were available. The law stated: " . . . any person who is the head of a family, or who has arrived at the age of twenty-one, and is a citizen of the United States, or who has filed his declaration of intention to become such, . . . and who has never borne arms against the United States Government or given aid and comfort to its enemies . . ." would be entitled to one quarter section. The letter also outlined the application and filing requirements and declared that, once a person made application, to receive homestead rights that person must settle on the land, make improvements including cultivation and building a dwelling, and reside on such land for five years with no absence to exceed six months.

Tillie rode her horse to Bertha's the following Saturday morn-ing. Bertha's face beamed with excitement as she reviewed the letter. "Well," she said, "you're already twenty-one and I turn twenty-one in April. We meet that one. We're both citizens and I surely never took up a gun against the government. Did you?"

Tillie laughed and the two friends' dream began taking shape, blossoming into a plan, creating images of summers of gardening and raising chickens, canning produce, and going to barn dances, and winters of quilting, reading, and hopefully teaching home-stead children. "I might even find myself a suitor," Bertha laughed. Then, in a serious tone she added, "But I keep thinking Lars might just need a little adventure before he settles down, so I shouldn't be thinking of suitors."

In spite of Hans's advice, the friends considered getting a wagon to travel through the wild land. Both of their families kiboshed that idea, upset enough already about the young women's dangerous adventure without added worry about Indian attacks on the trail, not to mention the ravages of young men of any race, as well as wild animals, storms bringing torrential rains or brutal winds, and wagon trouble while alone in the wilderness.

Train travel was a safer option. The Soo Railroad had put in lines through the northwestern corner of North Dakota, lines reaching to Portal, an outpost on the Canadian border not far from the land opened for homesteading just a couple of years earlier. Tillie and Bertha's families also felt some comfort knowing that other Norwegians, though mostly men, had already settled in the area and apparently some of the men had wives. Neither Tillie nor Bertha, nor their families, knew of any single woman who had staked a claim. That didn't stop the young teachers, enticed as they were becoming by their imagined adventure.

In January, another letter arrived from Hans Larson.

Dear Tillie and Bertha,

We had us a bad December in Dakota, the worst anyone can remember. Just now can get out a letter. Wasn't as bad here as south from here. Heard that some homesteaders abandoned their shacks and caught the first train going east that they could. Trains didn't run for a week. Lots of cattle died, probably some folks too. So, can be a rugged life. Great life for me and the wife Helen, but don't think it's an easy life. Let me know if you decide to come. There are homesteads available here in the Norwegian section. We'll help out.

Hans

"Tillie, my girl, have you any idea how awful life can be out there, alone on the prairie?" her father asked when Tillie reluctantly shared the letter with him. The letter sobered Tillie's anticipation. Sleep stayed away most of that night.

When she and Bertha talked about the letter over the next few weeks, Bertha said, "Y'know, Tillie, we ought to reconsider this idea, maybe see if your brother might come with or even bring young Hans along, though he's just thirteen. Or maybe," she'd said, not looking at Tillie, "we should give up the idea." Bertha occasionally expressed her fears as well. "I wonder how we'll manage the homesickness, don't you?" Another time she admitted lacking confidence in her ability to confront the blizzards and other adversities.

"Oh, Bertha, there'll be neighbors, of course, and we'll have each other and we've both already endured hardships galore." Yet, especially at night, Tillie sometimes doubted her own confidence and wondered if she had allowed her dreams to so stifle thoughts of reality that she was being foolish.

But a few days later, the friends received a copy of the *Bowbells Tribune*, which had published its first edition on November 24, 1899. The newspaper talked about the rich, dark loam soil in the area and the excellent water in wells just twenty feet deep. "*Coal in abundance is available for one dollar a ton. Wheat, flax, and vegetables cannot be excelled in quality or quantity anywhere,*" the newspaper promised.

So, serious planning resumed. Tillie wrote to Hans again to say she and Bertha were making plans to travel to Portal by train when the spring thaw came. Just a few weeks later, Tillie received a letter back. Hans wrote that a small general store, with basic provisions, had just opened in the settlement called Kincaid in the coal-mining area, which lay about three miles northeast of the area where he and other Norwegians had filed claims. He told Tillie to look up John Miller, the land locator, when she and Bertha got to Portal. "*Get him to take ya out to the Norwegian section. Tell him to stop at Kincaid General Store on the way. Get someone to fetch me and Henry. We'll not tarry to find ya when we get the word. We'll help ya make a hut to start you settling in,*" he wrote.

So, the young women began making final preparations for the adventure.

Tillie's mother didn't outwardly oppose Tillie's plan and told her friends that she was proud of her daughter's strength of mind. She also admitted that she worried a great deal about Tillie's safety and could hardly bear to think of the loneliness she'd feel when Tillie left, especially if she didn't eventually return to Watson or nearby. "You don't know how hard it might be to manage in Dakota, my Tillie. I fear for you."

While Tillie understood her mother's caution, she was determined to follow her plan to homestead. "I think women are tougher than men when it comes to seeing things through. I must go. Feel like I'm being called to do it."

As the train picked up speed and the adventure was upon her, Tillie wasn't quite as confident of her toughness. She didn't voice her misgivings to Bertha, but rather spoke of her excitement. "Two weeks or less and we'll see our land. Can't wait to see my very own land, can you?"

"No, but I must. Planting a stake will be the most exciting thing I've ever, ever done," responded Bertha. "Course I've not had all that much excitement in my life—until now." A moment later, though, her face grew grim. "I wonder if I'll ever see Lars again."

"Well, Bertha, you might just rope yourself a husband out in Dakota; then Lars can really know what it feels like to be left behind."

Bertha's eyes turned upward and she raised her left eyebrow, but formed a silly smile.

Traveling in the passenger section, the women had limited comfort for sleeping. The train took them through Valley City, North Dakota, where they departed the train for a welcome two-hour reprieve from traveling. The station offered hot vegetable soup and fresh bread, nourishing and welcome tastes to the friends, considering they had finished most of the nuts, dried fruit, and flatbrød their families had prepared for them to eat on the trip.

Reboarding the train, the women watched the landscape as they traveled toward Minot. Even when traveling at nearly fifty miles per hour, the plains of Dakota seemed endless and desolate, some places with patches of snow, some gray and black with accumulated dirt, others green with emerging grass stretching on and on.

Tillie and Bertha came from land where prairies bordered woodlands. Large stands of woods edged the Minnesota and Chippewa Rivers near Watson and most early settlers had planted rows of trees as shelter from the wind. Those trees softened the travelers' familiar landscape, but as they traveled north and west, trees became sparse. "*Uff da*," said Bertha, "looks endlessly barren out there."

Tillie agreed. "But I bet out where we're going there'll be trees galore." As she viewed the landscape, though, her words belied her feelings and a sense of foreboding invaded her thoughts.

A short time later, while walking back to her seat after a trip to the privy, Bertha felt a tap on her shoulder. Jerking around, she saw a fellow passenger with a rugged, pockmarked face, a scar running across his cheek, and small eyes. "Where ya headin'?" he asked with a snigger.

"I'm going to Portal," she stated matter-of-factly.

"What'cha going there for?" he queried.

"I'm staking a claim," she said. "Umm . . . my brother's out there already."

"Always willing to help out a damsel in distress. Cockamamy idea it is for girls to homestead," he said. "Bet you sure could use some manly help." He produced a lecherous smile.

"She's not in distress and her brother will give us all the help we need," said Tillie, using her teacher voice, as Bertha reached her seat and sidled in. The man, leering at them with a shocked yet menacing look, moved on.

Both young women were quiet for some moments. "He made me nervous," Bertha eventually acknowledged.

"For good reason, I think," said Tillie. "We must be careful. That was a good lie about your brother."

Bertha smiled wanly.

The train traveled on, the *clackety-clackety* of the wheels melting into an undulating rumble. Tillie read her Bible as the hours passed. She happened to open the Bible to Deuteronomy. A particular passage caught her attention:

> *Be strong and of a good courage, fear not, nor be afraid of them: for the Lord thy God, He it is that doth go with you; He will not fail thee, nor forsake thee. (Deuteronomy 31:6)*

She thought about the passage. Did she have the courage to confront what lay ahead? Would God be by her side and keep her safe and strong in mind and spirit? While she certainly believed in God, she wasn't as convinced that he would be there to help if a grass fire raged outside her hut or a snake, be that a reptile or a man, attacked. She knew she would face daunting challenges, not only physically and emotionally, but also spiritually. She had had little reason to question God's presence and guidance when she was in the comfort of her home, although when she'd learned about little children who died from diphtheria or scarlet fever or when a mother died in childbirth, she couldn't quite believe the common expression that God wanted them with him. That seemed rather mean to her. She'd been told never to question God, but heading toward the reality of life in Dakota, she could no longer suppress her worries and questions. Still, she kept most of her thoughts to herself.

As night fell, the friends slept as best they could, slumbering through the whistles and rumblings and conversations of fellow travelers. They fell asleep for short periods during daylight, as well. They were among the few women traveling, and the only women on board traveling without a man.

Dawn always provided energy and hope and excitement. "Can you really imagine having land in your own name?" asked Tillie for the tenth time.

"Wellll," said Bertha, "we just might get land in our own names. *Namen,* though, five years. Quite a challenge we face. Hope I'm up for it."

"Can't imagine what awaits us. Just getting some sort of a hut put up will be first, then a thousand other trials, but both of us have strong backs and strong wills. And Hans said there would be men to help, but we don't want *that* guy," Tillie said, moving her thumb in the direction of the man who had accosted Bertha the previous day.

"Yup. Natural to be a bit afraid, sure, sure. Maybe even scared stiff. But I know we both have courage and determination and a better person to do this with I could never find," Bertha said, turning to look directly at Tillie. They both smiled.

"When I was a little child," Tillie said, "I would dream about going west in a covered wagon. And, here we are. This isn't a covered wagon, I give ya and I think I'm glad it's not, but you and I are heading to our own land in the West."

On toward Minot the train rumbled, with the occasional deep bass whistle blowing three melodious tones as they came to a crossing and the *clackety-clackety* becoming a *chug, chug, chug*. Tillie and Bertha were the talk of the car. Along with many men, there were three couples and one family with children. The teachers, of course, spent time talking with the young ones, tutoring them some, checking their arithmetic skills, and giving tips on how to remember multiplication facts.

At Minot, a city of nearly thirteen hundred residents, all of the occupants got off the train for a welcome stop. Scents of cooked meat and baked pies drifted toward them even before the girl homesteaders-to-be saw the café next to the station. A kerosene lantern hung by the hand-painted sign. "Good Food," it proclaimed. Inside, they found a room with enough lanterns that they could see the white painted walls. After they seated themselves at the counter, a plump woman with cheerful dimples offered pot roast with mashed potatoes and gravy, along with buttermilk pie and coffee, for twenty-five cents.

"I've stuffed myself full. Every morsel was delicious," said Tillie after almost gobbling down her meal.

After using the outhouse, in a hushed voice, Bertha said, "It was decent, almost nice. Didn't stink as much as the one in the Valley City station." On the train, their bodily wastes simply drained or plopped onto the tracks, but the privy, in a tiny claustrophobic area, was stinky, nonetheless. Tillie had her monthly sickness and had to use knitted pads she'd brought with in her handbag and travel box. "I can hardly wait to get to our own land with wide-open spaces and no one around to observe our womanly necessities," said Tillie with a wry smile.

Then, with the boarding call, they were back on the train for more days of rolling on the rails toward Portal. After Minot, the landscape improved. In the lower spots, trees dotted rolling hills and the newly growing grass already flowed in undulating waves. "It's like a green ocean, deep and vast!" exclaimed Bertha.

"Beautiful, isn't it?" remarked Tillie quietly. The landscape gave her hope and anticipation that their land would be even more picturesque.

Near Kenmare, the land flattened and the women could see a river to the south. As the evening darkened, Tillie remarked, "It looks kind of like home, though not as many trees." Again, a barb of homesickness hit her and the certainty of a wonderful adventure hit a wall of nervous insecurity.

Staking a Claim

When the train's whistle sounded and the conductor called out "Portal!" Tillie and Bertha looked at each other. "I'm so excited," beamed Tillie.

"Me too, but a little scared too." Bertha tried to smile while she bunched up her eyebrows.

Tillie tried to rein in her excitement so as not to appear childish to the townspeople. They stepped onto the platform in the tiny town and the porter handed Tillie her wooden travel box. Then they arranged to store their trunks temporarily. Once they found some land and made plans for transporting their goods, they would come back to claim them.

Bertha stopped and turned around as if she were looking for something. "That must be north, must be Canada," she said, pointing. "Imagine how close we are. Could walk right into Canada from here, sure."

"Let's not do that right now," laughed Tillie. "I'm exhausted. I'd rather see a bed than Canada."

Tillie, with Bertha smiling behind her, inquired at the station about a hotel or sleeping place. The man hesitated. "Well, there's the Müller Hotel up the street by the café. Or ya might find a sleeping room above the general store. Might be more to your likin'."

They proceeded to the hotel, went inside, looked uneasily at each other, and overheard the clerk saying something they couldn't understand due to his heavy German accent, maybe something about a couple of cots in the women's room. Bertha nudged Tillie toward the door, and exiting, she murmured, "Looks pretty seedy, don't ya think? And it smelled like foul-tasting sauerkraut or somethin' worse."

Tillie nodded. "Yeah, and sounded like it might be a dormitory maybe, not a single room."

They proceeded to Portal General Store where they met Berdina, the plump shopkeeper who had a smile that twitched at one corner of her mouth. She showed them a small room. "*Schuppen* is out through the back door." The girls took this to mean the outhouse.

They looked at each other and nodded. "Reasonably clean," whispered Bertha after they closed the door.

The next morning Tillie volunteered, "Sleeping on hay would have been more comfortable than what this place calls a bed."

"Ya betcha. Then again, better appreciate what we have. This bed might be better'n what we'll have for a while when we find us some land . . . if we do." She raised her eyebrows as she looked at Tillie over the top of her spectacles.

"Well, maybe we can have someone drop off some hay in our huts, assuming we have them, until we get proper beds," said Tillie with a phony smile.

With that, both women started giggling. Their emotions surfaced with a deep, guttural sound and soon they were sobbing, sobbing that turned into laughing, then sobbing again.

"Oh, my tummy hurts," cried Bertha.

Eventually their laughter and crying subsided. They ate a good breakfast at the Portal Café—eggs, sunny-side up, side pork, toast with currant jelly, and a good cup of steaming black coffee. "Might be one of our last good meals for a while," quipped Bertha. With that, the giggling started again, although they tried to restrain it for fear of looking ridiculous or worse.

Once the laughing jag was over, the young women, always called "girls" by the locals, were in good spirits when they found John Miller, the land locator. He was a tall, firm-looking man, rounded in the middle, with a face red, roughened, and rugged from the wind and maybe from drink. They told him they were hoping for sites in the Norwegian community that Hans and Henry had written them about. He nodded. "Still some sites out there."

They made plans to leave the following morning for nearly a half-day's journey to see some likely sites. They'd return to Portal after locating their land.

"Sounds like there's still some available land near Hans's and Henry's," said Bertha as the women walked back toward their room. "Been worried 'bout that, tried to hide my fear."

Tillie smiled. "Neither of us veiled our concerns very well."

"You did better'n me. I kept thinking you had lots of confidence in this whole adventure. Gave me enough assurance to come."

Tillie kept her thoughts to herself while ruminating on whether or not Hans and Henry would show up when notified or whether someone would even try to notify them.

John arrived at Portal General Store promptly at eight o'clock the next morning as promised. Bertha and Tillie climbed into his cart with anticipation showing on their radiant faces that were red from a little pinching, but mostly excitement. It was a cool but sunny morning with a moderate wind, a wind they would come to know as a constant companion on the plains. John's long auburn hair flew this way and that in the wind. "He reminds me of a rather pudgy scarecrow," Bertha whispered to Tillie as the journey began.

The emptiness of the land gnawed at Tillie. Still, the new growth of prairie grasses appeared tinged with gold as they rolled in the sunlight, and the sight of it gave her some hope. The first part of the journey to the possible sites was pleasant, although the roads were rough. Wagon ruts had created deep craters and each hump or hollow felt like a cavern since they were sitting on thin blankets on unpadded seats. A few dark clouds began building in the west as the journey continued through rugged territory, with not a lonely tree to break the barren landscape.

As they approached the Kincaid area, Tillie saw a shack on the horizon and nudged Bertha, pointing. Bertha pointed to another shack. "Them there are Danish shacks," said John. "Your sites'll be in the Norwegian section, a'course."

The young women were quiet as they gazed at the land, but John kept talking. "It's a tough life out here. Those who manage it get more robust, y'know. Develop a cheerful attitude in time. Builds character, y'know. You girls must have a bunch of that to be out here. Don't see too many girl homesteaders, though there's been a few come through."

Tillie wasn't quite as sure about her character as she usually was. Nonetheless, she knew, believed, or maybe just hoped that the adventure would be worthy of the fortitude it would entail. "Hard things always offer the most reward," she acknowledged. Bertha nodded her head.

"Know a couple girls up by Portal took the hardships in stride, they did, maybe better'n the men," added John. "Oh, and just a couple'a weeks ago, two stocky girls, not so pretty as you two, got sites with the Norwegians, if I remember."

"Really!" exclaimed Bertha. "Imagine that, two other girl homesteaders here."

Making his way through the tiny settlement called Kincaid, John stopped at the general store, really just a shack with an extra room. "There's a couple'a girl homesteaders here checking out a claim," he said to the woman at the counter. "Lookin' for some men named Hans and Henry. You know 'em?"

"Sure do. They told me some girls might be comin' along."

"We're headin' out to the Norwegian section now. Will be back here in an hour, two at the most. Can ya send word to the men?"

"I'll have someone fetch them or at least one of them," said Eleanor the shopkeeper, "and tell 'em to find you out there and, if they don't find you there, to meet you back here."

John climbed back into the cart. "Someone'll go try to find the men."

Tillie sighed, letting out her breath.

The only other buildings in the settlement were three little shacks. Continuing down the trail past the village, if it could be called that, John turned off at a path. It was well trodden, but smaller than the trail. "There's a shack back there," John said, motioning at a little rise. "Sometimes men gather there. I'll go check. See if Hans and Henry might be there. You girls just stay here, now. I'll be back soon." With that, he stepped out of the cart and walked toward the rise.

Behind the little hill stood a shack, but only the tip of the rooftop poked up behind the hill covered with greening grass. As minutes elapsed, both women fiddled with their skirts and coats and kept looking in the direction of the shack. They breathed in as a couple of men came around the elevation on their horses. The men slowed as they approached the women, offered greetings, perhaps in Danish, and drove on.

Bertha chattered, unable to contain either her nervousness or her excitement. "Soon this will be our little village. John'll be back in a minute or two, sure. We'll find our own land. Hans and Henry will help us, a'course. We'll soon meet their wives. They'll be a big help, sure 'nuf."

Tillie answered mostly in monosyllable. But, after a time, she began seething with anger. "I'm going to go get him. If Hans and Henry were there, they'd come out. We might miss them altogether if John doesn't get out here."

"Better wait just a bit longer, Tillie; then I'll go with you. Whatever's back there is probably not a place to go into by yourself."

John sauntered out of the shack just a little later with no word on the men, but in a relaxed mood. *A little too relaxed,* thought Tillie when he jumped back into the cart. She knew North Dakota was a dry state, unlike Minnesota, but John's face had reddened and he spoke more slowly. Tillie thought he could have been drinking whiskey or some kind of spirit.

A few miles southwest of Kincaid, John pointed out two adjoining sections of land available for homesteading, each sixty-five hectares, with a small lake lying at the northeast corner of one of the sites. John pointed at the lake. "You can use the lake for washin' up clothes, washin' up yerselves, for cookin' and drinkin', at least until you get yerselves a well. Look. Even some bushes, scrubby though they are. Best I can offer, I reckon. All the Norwegian shacks are nearby. Suppose this'll do ya?"

The women looked at each other, raised their eyebrows, smiled rather weakly, disembarked, walked a few feet onto the land. Bertha looked at Tillie again and raised her eyebrows as if asking a question.

While feeling a gurgle of uncertainty in the pit of her stomach, Tillie formed a slow smile. "This could be it," she cried as she twirled around and threw up her skirt. Bertha joined her and they joined hands and twirled again.

"Yes," cried Bertha, with Tillie smiling her assent. It wasn't exactly the idyllic land suggesting bountiful harvests that the newspaper wrote of, nor that she had dreamed of. Yet it was land with Norwegians nearby and it could be *her* land, and she couldn't turn back now. Hand in hand they walked back to John, nodding their heads rather slowly.

John checked the surveyor's posts in the middle of each section. He told Tillie: "Yer's is the southeast quarter of Section Seventeen in Township 162 North. This here's Vale Township in Ward County." He marked it on his map to be sure he'd write down the right information for the women to make application for the appropriate parcels at the Minot Land Office. "And yer's," he said to Bertha, "is the northeast quarter of Section Seventeen."

John showed them about where the two sites came together, demonstrated how to plant a stake, then gave the stake and sledge-hammer to Tillie. Each woman pounded a stake into her own land, which was mucky from recent rain. Bertha took a piece of brightly colored cloth from her coat pocket. "Let me tie this around the stake," she shouted. She looped it around the stake, tying it as securely as she could in the wind. Tillie did the same on her stake.

"We did it, Bertha. We just staked a claim," Tillie yelled, acting more excited than she felt. She twirled again, making her skirt a kite and her hair a dancing dervish, large strands having freed themselves from her bun.

Bertha looked around at the stark, treeless land, then gazed toward the other shacks. "Wish I'd see some movement over there. Wonder if Hans and Henry headed into town already, if they intend to help us at all."

"Or maybe nobody really went to get them." Tillie wanted to feel thrilled at finally getting to what would be her land, but she felt agitated instead.

"We ought to head back toward Portal," John called before climbing into the cart.

Slowly the friends turned toward the cart. Just when they had stepped into the cart for the return trip, they looked again toward the closest shacks and noticed two horses coming toward them at full gallop with four arms waving in the air like flags in a Dakota gale.

Tillie and Bertha stepped back out of the cart, both of them beaming at the men who whoaed their horses to a stop. Goose bumps raised on Tillie's forearms.

"*Hallo, hallo, velkommen* to Norwegian Kincaid. I'm Hans and that t'ere's Henry," Hans motioned with his hand. "You got to be Tillie and Berta."

Tillie didn't think a Norwegian-sounding word had ever sounded as good as Hans's *hallo*. Hurrying toward them, she held out her hand. "*God å se deg,*" she shouted.

Bertha moved forward, held out her moist and soiled hand and shook Henry's hand first. "*Jeg er så glad for å se deg.*" She hadn't known these men, but they had come west nearly three years earlier when the western Dakota land was just opening. Now they were both nearly halfway to proving up their claims. And both had wives, Hans having sent for his flame from near home and Henry finding Belle, a woman who had come west from Illinois with her brother and tried to prove up on her own land, but instead got hitched to Henry and joined his effort.

Both men exhibited stocky builds, Hans a little rounder than Henry, and both wore bib overalls caked with dirt or maybe manure. One of Hans's straps had come loose from the button. He was a tall man and the pants of his overalls were too short, Tillie noticed. Henry had a jovial, reddened face with a shaggy beard while Hans displayed a few days of stubble on his face with heavy black eyebrows framed by his poorly cut dark hair.

The men said they'd get started right away to put up a temporary hut. "Should be done in a few days, ya betcha. It'll give you brave girls a place to sleep and put yer belongin's while we make plans to put up yer shacks," said Hans with a grin.

"*Tusen takk, tusen takk,*" said Bertha with a shakiness in her voice as tears formed but didn't spill.

John, scowling at the western sky where ominous clouds were building, demanded that the girls get back in the cart. "Now!" He pointed at the sky.

"*Ser deg snart,*" called Henry. The women nodded and Tillie shouted, "*El par dager.*"

As the cart began bumping along toward Kincaid, Tillie said, "Hans and Henry are pretty weather-beaten and prairie-worn, but they sure were a welcome sight, weren't they?"

"I was so glad to see them I almost peed my pants. Feared they might not show up. Their looks are nothin' to pee in your pants about, I give ya, but they looked so good to me I wanted to hug them." Bertha said this quietly, hoping John wouldn't hear in the whipping wind.

As the trio hurried through Kincaid, not even stopping to thank the woman they would later come to know as Eleanor for sending the men, which the women wanted to do, a light rain began to fall.

John spurred the horses, trying to outdistance the thunderstorm but not succeeding. With the thunder and lightning came heavy rain. With the horses almost at a gallop, the seats wet from the pouring rain, Tillie and Bertha had to hold onto the sides of the cart to keep from bouncing out. They spoke not a word.

By the time the cart pulled up to Portal General Store, they could only imagine the bruises on their behinds. John said he'd be there midmorning the next day to give them needed information about their sites. They disembarked quickly, thanked John for all his assistance, and hurried into the store, entering with their soggy shoes squeaking, their stockings and skirts seeping.

Jostled from the ride through rain and ruts, both women expressed appreciation for the comfort of a dry and reasonably warm room in Portal. Even though the beds poked straw from the mattresses, which were stained with "who knows what" as Bertha exclaimed, the women slept well.

———

The next day, the two women waited for John. Though they tried to act cheerful, troubled expressions clouded their faces and they kept glancing in the direction from which they thought he would arrive. "Said he'd he here midmorning! He's probably sleeping off a drunk," lamented Bertha with a pout.

He finally arrived just after noon. After he wrote down the correct numbers for the location of their homestead parcels, which they'd need to bring with them to Minot to fill out their applications, they paid him his fee of fourteen dollars. "That fee includes transportation back to yer claims with yer belongings after you return from Minot," he told them.

After a quick lunch, Tillie and Bertha spent much of the remaining afternoon considering the provisions they'd need without overstocking their lodging place, whatever that might be for a time. They purchased the supplies at the general store: canned vegetables, dried beef, dry milk, a couple cans of Borden's condensed milk, ten pounds of wheat flour, five pounds of brown sugar, a couple pounds of hard cheese, four two-pound cans of Chase & Sanborn coffee beans, Quaker Oats, salt, soda, flatbrød, lard, vinegar, a gallon of molasses, kerosene, and a supply of friction matches. Tillie picked up some Fleischmann yeast cakes, then put them back. "Won't have a decent way of making yeast bread for a while."

"Yup," said Bertha. "Soda bread'll have to do us for a spell, or maybe salt-raised bread if we have the time."

They told Berdina they'd be gone a couple of days and she allowed them to store their provisions in the room at half her usual price. "Likely won't be anyone coming along to want the room, anyway," she said.

The following morning, the almost-homesteaders boarded the train back to Minot. "Can hardly believe we're headed back east already," grumbled Bertha, "even though I know I'll feel such glee when I sign the application. At the moment, it feels like I've had enough travel for a lifetime."

Tillie agreed. Both of the women were tired, more from the emotions of their endeavor than from physical exhaustion, which they would face later.

The next morning, after sleeping poorly in a dormitory room, they found breakfast, then arrived at the land office just before it opened.

Tillie's hands shook from excitement as she handed the clerk her property identification numbers and he produced an application form for her to complete. Bertha did the same. Then the clerk went behind a wall to search the records to determine if anyone else had claimed the land.

They waited. Too much time went by for Tillie to remain calm. "What do you suppose is taking him so long? Must be some problem with our claim," she whispered with concern as the two awaited his return.

Eventually he returned with a smile on his face. In his hand he held claim forms that he gave to each woman.

After signing, they handed him the completed forms and twelve dollars each, and then he signed the papers. The clerk said, "Your sites are documented as being reserved for you should you meet all of the requirements for proving up." He reviewed the requirements in detail, then shook hands with Tillie and Bertha and wished them well on their homestead adventure.

"He actually seemed to respect us. Acted like it was normal for two young women to be filing claims," stated Bertha with a radiant smile as she and Tillie walked out the office door.

"Well, maybe it is." Tillie did a little two-step in the street.

Their mission was done before midmorning, which made it possible to catch the late morning train for Portal. On the trek back to the train station, they stopped to admire fashions displayed in a shop window. "Nice looking," said Tillie, "but doubt we'll have use for any such fancy dress."

"Gosh, I'm weary," admitted Bertha. "Let's get to the station and see if we can find a place to sit and rest."

Back at the station, Bertha left Tillie alone while she went to the privy. Half-dozing on the bench, Tillie thought she heard Bertha shriek. She bolted up and hurried toward the privy, where she found Bertha in tears, looking this way and that. "Whatever happened?" asked Tillie on joining her friend.

At first Bertha was too distraught to explain; she just motioned with her empty hands. "My ticket," she eventually said, trembling. "I'd taken my ticket out of my handbag to check the departure time again and a man grabbed it right out of my hand."

"Did you see where he went?"

Bertha shook her head. "Maybe that way," she said, pointing. "Happened so fast I hardly knew what he had done till he was gone."

Tillie, with Bertha trying to wipe away her tears beside her, went up to the station agent and told him the story, but the man said he wasn't able to help since Bertha couldn't provide a description. "Likely he's long gone or hiding somewhere. Sorry for your trouble, Miss. Best the two of you stay together. We get all sorts of tramps in here."

Tillie looked at the man. He was one of the oldest people she had seen in Dakota. *Fifty, maybe,* she thought. Although he didn't smile, he didn't look stern or hard-hearted.

"He took her ticket," said Tillie. "Can't you give her another one?"

"Sorry, I'll have to charge you for it. Get so many in here claiming somethin' like this. Never quite know the truth, though I believe you two girls."

"We're girl homesteaders," piped up Bertha, having regained some of her composure. "We've just been to the land office to claim our sites."

With that, the station agent appeared to soften. "Don't tell anyone I'm doing this," he said, as he handed her a free ticket.

Both shook their heads. "We won't," said Bertha, "and thank you, thank you so much."

The two returned to the bench, waited until they heard the rumble, then the whistle, and then they got up to board the train to Portal. They sat across from two people who seemed to be together, and, when asked, said they were homesteaders from near Portal. Tillie beamed. "We're homesteaders too. Just were at the land office to file our claims."

"Good for you!" said the person who Tillie thought was a woman, but who wore pants stained with grease, with a ratty shirt the color of which Tillie wasn't just sure. As she and Bertha chatted amiably with the couple, Tillie determined the person in pants was indeed a woman.

"A year ago we left Milwaukee, Wisconsin. Both of us worked at the Milwaukee Iron Company making rails for trains. After we got to Dakota, we put up a shack and now got a few chickens and a couple'a pigs. Homestead life suits us. Hard work, harder'n making rails, but it's our own work. No boss telling us what to do," said the man.

"We know there'll be grueling work, but I think it suits our spirits too. Hope so," said Tillie in a sprightly voice.

———

The conductor called, "Portal." Stepping down onto the platform for the second time did not elicit the excited trepidation of the first occasion. Bertha ventured, "It almost feels like we're returning home."

"Well," said Tillie, "not home exactly, not yet anyway, but familiar."

After eating beef stew and custard pie at the Portal Café, the homesteaders returned to the general store and interrupted Berdina's preparation for bed. She wore a plaid nightshirt that clung to her full body and her light brown hair with hardly a sprinkling of gray hung in long ringlets, giving her an air of being half eye-catching young woman and half tired-out matron. "So sorry to have interrupted your evening. Yet we are so proud to announce that we're official homesteaders now," declared Bertha.

Berdina returned her bright grin. "*Gratuliere!*"

The friends slept well that night. The next day, they found John the locator again and made plans to set off for their claims the following morning. At the general store, they bought a pitchfork, scythe, a good shovel, a washtub and scrub board, nails, and a couple of buckets. Tillie asked Berdina about well digging and she assured them that she knew a water witch and men who could dig a well.

Berdina had staked a claim nearly two years earlier. "Wit my man, a'course. I give you *mädchen* credit *für herkommen*," she said with a huge smile. Partly by motioning, she told them to buy a tin box for their provisions "so's to keep da *Geschöpfe* away till ya have decent hut." Although Tillie didn't know just what Berdina meant, she reckoned Berdina gave good advice and bought the box.

Land of Their Own

Before setting out for their staked property, Tillie and Bertha each sent a telegram to their families with the good news that they had safely arrived, found their land, and connected with Hans and Henry.

John arrived at the appointed hour, this time driving a buckboard wagon that would accommodate the trunks and provisions. The realities of homesteading had sobered the women's moods and they spoke little as the wagon bounced along.

When the wagon pulled onto their adjoining properties, they found Hans and Henry finishing up the hut's construction. Before John would allow Tillie and Bertha to examine their new quarters, he pointed out where to plant stakes on each of the three unstaked property corners. Along with Hans and Henry, he then helped the girls load their belongings into the shelter, not much more than a tent. "Well, I got other matters need attending," he said and stepped onto his wagon.

The hut was a lean-to, held up with timbers in the corners with several boards spanning the space between the timbers. A large tarp, smelling of mildew, covered it, with an opening flap in the front to allow entering and exiting the dwelling, if one could call it that. It was eight-by-six feet and just high enough toward the front so the women could stand upright. With their trunks inside and provisions on top of the trunks, there was barely room to lie down. "It ain't a decent place," said Henry, "but I t'ink it'll do ya till we can get suitable shacks put up for you girls. We'll get them up soon as we get some plantin' done. Busy time, y'know." He shrugged his shoulders and raised his eyebrows as he grinned.

The girl homesteaders nodded. Tillie felt grateful for any shelter from the wind, which that day was moderate by Dakota standards. She knew the hut was as good as she could expect, though the wind caused the tarp to beat like a drum. "Thank you so much. Tusen takk, tusen takk," she said with a genuine smile, although her voice quivered a bit, whether from anxiety or excitement she wasn't sure. "Here," she said after reaching into her handbag and retrieving two silver dollars. "Has to have cost you something for the lumber and all."

"Aw," said Hans. "Keep da money. Just used leftover stuff we had and can use da tarp when you're done with it. Just glad to help ya a bit."

The men brought hay for sleeping quarters and dumped it into the tiny hut, at which the two young women glanced at each other, each displaying a slight grin. Tillie tried not to giggle.

"You girls sleep good tonight. We'll check on you *i morgan*," said Hans with a chortle.

Tillie gave a wan smile back. Bertha said, "We'll be fine."

When the men left, the friends scanned the hut. Tillie noticed a few holes in the tarp. "Looks like mice used it for a home and made some holes to provide us with a wee bit of light," she said.

"Smells like it too."

They arranged their meager belongings in hopes they could find what they might need, and sat on the trunks silently for a few moments. "It's rather dark and dreary in here," mentioned Bertha.

"I feel a bit like a child dropped off at an orphanage, not quite knowing what to do or how to act."

"Or like Pilgrims having made it to Plymouth Rock," said Tillie with a somber expression on her face. She looked around the bleak hut. "Y'know," she said, brightening her features, "I think I could use just a thimbleful or so of that Vin Mariani. Might bring a bit of relief from this dark hut. Help us celebrate having a place to sleep out here on our own Dakota land."

They had indeed accepted a bottle in town before they left. Berdina insisted they take it as a gift from her. Although North Dakota was a dry state, Portal was right next to the Canadian border and men regularly brought in liquor of various sorts by crossing at spots other than the main entry, where the guard checked. "Rumor has it he can be paid off, if ya got the money," Berdina had said.

Vin Mariani was touted as a tonic and had taken the country and the world by storm. In fact, it was Bordeaux wine mixed with ground coca leaves. Berdina made Tillie and Bertha understand it might be best not to tell anyone where the wine came from. "The early settlers wanted to *halten* us *Deutschen* so made no *schnaps* in Dakota. Course we figured a way to deal with that and *kommen* anyway."

Neither Tillie nor Bertha had drunk wine or any other non-medicinal alcohol apart from a swallow or two at Christmas. They had been reluctant to accept it, but Berdina had insisted, saying, "You'll put it to good use. Medicine for the body or soul or both. You'll see." Then she'd chortled loudly.

Now, it seemed it had been an excellent idea. Tillie dug in her trunk and found some appropriate glasses—not wine glasses of course, but they were crystal and would serve the celebratory cause.

"We'll go outside," declared Tillie. "I'll find us some flatbrød and cheese to have with the wine."

The Dakota wind had lulled to a breeze. The sun was setting in the west. No trees to diminish its effect, no clouds to block its intensity, it riveted their attention. A deep golden globe, the bottom flattened by the horizon, surrounded by a pinkish-orange sky, a few light clouds brilliant in the reflection. "Have you ever seen such a beautiful sunset?"

Tillie shook her head and sat down on a bale of straw the men had left. "It's like we imagined." For some moments they sat quietly, listening to the silence that slowly grew sounds—mourning doves cooing, last year's dry grass rustling, a faint whistle-like call.

"Maybe that's a ground squirrel whistling," said Bertha. "Sweet-looking little creatures."

"Kind of sweet looking, I agree. Mama's never liked them in the garden." Tillie sniffed her new habitat. "Doesn't smell like home here, but can't quite say what's different. Maybe the lack of trees, maybe different critters around."

Bertha opened the wine, then inhaled its aroma. "This tonic, or whatever it is, isn't quite like anything I ever smelled either." She laughed. "I feel like some kind of barmaid or maybe a loose woman."

Tillie tittered. "That'll be the day!"

"Well, this isn't exactly legal, y'know."

"Don't think there's much chance of us getting caught," remarked Tillie. "Yet I feel a bit guilty." Her mouth, though, turned up at the corners as she displayed her dimples. "*Skål.*"

"Skål, and may our efforts prove worthy."

After a sip or two, both women erupted in laughter and soon dissolved in tears. After the crying jag, they sipped on the wine, more than a thimbleful. "This tastes a bit like vinegar," Tillie laughed as she took her last sip. "Better save the rest for medicine."

"I think I won't write home about this," quipped Bertha, still teary from the laughing and crying.

The two imagined out loud the lives they would have, both sobered and energized now that such lives confronted them. Not next month, not on the morrow, but at the moment. They sat in silent reflection as the sun dipped below the horizon and the air grew chilly. Eventually Bertha remarked, "Seems like evening goes on forever here. Stays light later than at home."

But soon the sky became dusky-blue. The wine and the day's intensity produced yawns. "Well, let's hit the hay," Tillie giggled.

Within minutes, even though darkness was just settling on the land, the friends curled up near each other on the hay and covered themselves with a quilt that Tillie took from her trunk. Even though they had each confided to the other of their fear that a coyote or skunk could get into their abode, and had shoved a trunk in front of the opening flap, the deep breathing of sleep soon filled the hut.

The next morning, the chill of the air and the thrill of being on their own land energized the women as they stood out of doors on their homesteads. "Let's dub this the 'B&T Estate,'" said Bertha, and thus it would forever be known, sometimes shortened to just "the estate."

Raising Shacks

Three days later Hans helped the girl homesteaders purchase dimensional lumber for framing, roughhewn boards about six inches wide and six or eight feet long, and eight-foot slats, along with nails, tar paper rolls, and such. They arranged to get it hauled to their claims. Tillie knew what quality lumber looked like and noticed there was hardly a straight two-by-four in the bunch and the large boards had sizable cracks and knotholes. She said nothing and assumed that everyone used inferior materials for shacks. *Or maybe*, she thought, *this far from where trees grew in abundance, the lumberyard could only get poor-quality lumber.*

Two days later the time came to construct two twelve-by-fourteen shacks. Most of the neighborhood men gathered for the raising. The newcomers met Willie, a very genial man; Herman, with sparkling blue eyes and a knobby nose; Orlo, quiet, but pleasant; and Halvor, who seemed not only quiet, but brusque. For Tillie and Bertha, it was their first involvement with building a dwelling, although back at home they'd gone to barn raisings and helped construct chicken coops and sheds. For the neighbors, shack raising had become almost routine.

By nightfall the first day, even with a noon break for "a light lunch"—which all Norwegians knew was *not* light—and a late afternoon supper, which Han's wife, Helen, brought, the structure on Tillie's land was more or less complete. The double two-by-fours in the corners had been set about three feet into the ground as footings. The men had hung a door and left an opening for a window. Knotholed boards with large cracks visible between many of them covered the frame and roof. Bertha whispered to Tillie, "Looks sturdy even though the lumber is poor quality. Wonder how we'll stay warm in winter."

"The men are good carpenters," Tillie acknowledged while wondering about trying to live for years in the tiny structure.

Inside, a rough wooden floor was ready for a multicolored rag rug, put together hastily by Helen. Tillie felt grateful for a wooden floor, knowing that many shacks made do with dirt ones, and she much appreciated the rug that would add needed color to her drab abode.

"I really like Helen," said Bertha. "She's probably not a lot older than we are, but with her matronly figure and demeanor she almost seems like a warm grandmother."

"For sure, and I love her braids that she piles on top of her head. She'll likely be a good friend."

The next day was Sunday and everyone took it off. Most of them gathered at the home of Orlo Larson to give praise to God. Inspired by the community spirit they already felt part of, Tillie's and Bertha's voices carried above the rest of the gatherers as they sang "*Takket vaere Gud, takket vaere Gud.*"

On Monday the men returned to help build Bertha's shack. In fact, the men did most of the work, with Tillie and Bertha doing some of the nailing. The men likely would have preferred to have the women watch instead of help, but Bertha had declared, "Some of our own work must go into this."

The two homestead shacks were built about sixty feet apart. Each had one door and one window, the windows facing each other.

By late afternoon on a day that started out frosty, but ended toasty, the neighbors finished framing up Bertha's shack and sheathed it over with the boards.

"Bertha and I will put up the tar paper," asserted Tillie.

"That there tar paper roll is damn heavy," said Hans. "Pardon my language, sometimes forget ladies are around. You best have a little help with it for the roof, at least."

"Bertha and I have strong backs. I'm quite sure we're capable," Tillie insisted.

Although all of these Dakota men were used to their wives and other women doing heavy chores, Tillie's response left a couple of mouths gaping.

"How 'bout dem windows? You girls know how to frame-in glass?" asked Henry.

"Helped my grandfather put in windows," said Bertha, smiling. "Think we can manage it just fine." She later told Tillie that she hoped she'd sounded more confident than she was.

Henry made sure the girls knew how to wrap the tar paper and use slats to nail it down, and how to cover the roof, as well. By that time, some of the community wives had arrived, bringing liverwurst sandwiches, gingerbread cake, and cookies, along with fresh milk and lukewarm coffee. The most interesting visitors were two other women homesteaders, sisters Anna and Olga, who had come just a few weeks before Tillie and Bertha.

"Oh my," said Tillie. "Two other girl homesteaders, as they call us. It's so good to meet you. *Velkommen* to our homestead. And what brought you two out here?"

"Vell," said Olga with her thick body and even thicker Norwegian brogue, "Nels done left me for some floozy he found at the bar so I tell my sister, 'Let's get us a claim. Hell, it can't be much verse than stayin' here and wallowing in the pain of his leavin,' so we headed nort'west from Brookings and found us this spot. My shack's a helluva lot better 'n the dump he left me in Brookings."

"Oh," said Tillie. "Quite, I'm sure."

"And I said, 'Sure why not?' Must be a better life than in Brookings," put in Anna, whose hair was cut very short. (*And not too well,* thought Tillie.) She had a very broad nose and quite small eyes, making her face appear rather peculiar.

Knut, a slender man with a personality bouncy like his music, had brought his accordion and Hans his harmonica. Square-dancing began with Willie doing the calling. He had only started after his move to Dakota and missed calls from time to time, but the dancers simply filled in with their own movements. Square-dancing continued until the light began to fade; then it was time for a few waltzes. Tillie and Bertha danced most of the square dances and took turns waltzing with neighborhood bachelors, Ole and Orlo. Halvor, the other bachelor, didn't participate. When the dancing ended, Ole said to Bertha, "Ve'll be seein' you around."

"Sure," acknowledged Bertha as he smiled, displaying his dimples and lifting his cheeks so his eyes became slits.

Since rain was nowhere in sight, the women again assured the men they were perfectly capable of nailing tar paper to their shacks and eventually lining the inside walls with the blue tar paper. That paper cost more than the black stuff, and it was thicker, a little sign of upper crust for homesteaders. Hans had confided that last bit to Tillie. She wasn't sure if "a little sign of upper crust" was a good thing or not, but she liked the color and recognized it would provide a little needed insulation. When Hans said again that they could "sure 'nuf help," Tillie assured him that she and Bertha truly wanted to do these tasks themselves.

As dusk deepened, the two women reviewed the day. They fell to laughing as they talked about Olga. "Vell, it vas hell," laughed Bertha.

Tillie erupted in giggles, especially because she and Bertha had hardly ever uttered a swear word, both having grown up in strict Lutheran homes.

"She was coarse, of course, but I liked her," said Tillie. "Sure has some character and ya don't need to vonder vat she t'inks."

As deep darkness descended, they retired to the hut, admitting to each other they hoped they'd need only spend a few more nights in the tiny structure. With no window, it didn't have the moon or the heavens to bring a bit of mysterious glow into their nights and their thoughts.

Sleep came easily for Tillie and so did dreams. She had occasionally dreamt of flying just above the treetops, and it was this flying dream she remembered as she woke the first time. In the nether land before sleep hit again, she was transported to a cornfield near Watson and her first kiss. The community had gathered for a barn dance and, after a few waltzes, she strolled with Jergen out toward the cornfield and then wandered just within the camouflage of corn. She was nineteen years old. Jergen was twenty. It was a kiss on the lips, without depth or passion, but it lingered for many seconds as each of them savored the experience.

Waking again, she was unsure whether the thought of Jergen was a sleep-induced one, or her semiconscious mind at work. She hadn't given him too much thought back at home, though she remembered the kiss with fondness and had hoped he'd call for her. He lived north of her, near where the Chippewa River meandered in the township called Big Bend. He was a farmer, as were most Norwegian men. Since that kiss, they had seen each other on some occasions and even danced together. He had looked into her eyes with warmth, maybe tenderness, but Jergen had never again encouraged her to leave the group with him and maybe, she thought, he'd not been comfortable being alone with her. Although

Jergen looked at her as if he might wish to court her, as least so Tillie thought, he hadn't come to call. In fact, Tillie hadn't had any real suitors, Bertha telling her she was too serious and gave off an air of overconfidence. "You're a bit of a stick-in-the-mud sometimes," Bertha had said.

But Jergen, having heard of Tillie and Bertha's planned adventure, had stopped by the Melbakken farm the evening before their departure. Again, he had a look that Tillie would remember—longing perhaps—as if he wanted to hold her, not let her go. Tillie thought she had looked back at him with affection, perhaps even yearning. Yet Jergen simply clasped her hand tightly, gave her a wistful look, wished her well on her journey, and pecked her on the cheek.

Sleep came again and the first edges of dawn were apparent as Tillie arose from an uncomfortable dream of a wolf approaching her on a full run, a wicked snarl spread across its face. She had come up from the depths of sleep before it attacked.

The next day Bertha admitted that it had taken her a while to fall asleep, perhaps because her thoughts kept returning to Ole. "It was nice to have someone look at me in a special way, like I was almost a gift," said Bertha with a shy smile. "He's not so much to look at, I give ya, but he seems of good stock. Has a rough kind of charm to him."

"Oh, for heaven's sake. You haven't got past thinking that Lars left you. You don't have any real idea what will happen with Lars, do you?"

"Not really." Bertha's expression soured and she looked at the floor.

Tillie thought she might have hurt her best friend with her words. Softly, she said, "I'm sorry. Sometimes I'm a little unfeeling with my words. Ole seems like a sweet man and . . ." She didn't know what else to say.

"It's okay, Tillie. I still have feelings for Lars, of course, but I enjoyed being looked at by a man."

"Of course."

———

Life on the Dakota plains was busy from dawn until nightfall for the two homesteaders. Tillie helped Bertha nail tar paper to her shack, then Bertha helped Tillie nail tar paper to hers. Putting it on their roofs was harder than they'd imagined, but they'd never admit that to the men. There was water to gather from the little spring-fed lake and food to prepare, which was a bit of an ordeal on an open fire, especially since wood was scarce and they could only use it for kindling to start their coal or dried cow dung that their neighbors left with them.

The women usually shared simple meals in one of their shacks or on the ground, after spreading flour sacks down. "Not quite so fancy as some meals we made at home," said Tillie, "but it sure does taste good out here where we can see for miles. Yet the only things to see are the sky, grasses blowing in the constant wind, an occasional creature scurrying past."

"And some tar paper shacks off a little ways," added Bertha.

Tillie made soda bread in her bake kettle over the open fire. It didn't turn out too well, although it was edible. Barely. "We need to find ourselves some stoves to cook on and keep us warm," she said.

Bertha laughingly agreed after eating some of the bread, scorched and concrete hard. "Yup. Need stoves, sure, sure. Hope they don't cost too much. Keep worrying about whether my funds will manage."

"Somehow, 'spect they will."

Using a small walking plow they had borrowed from neighbors, the women opened a little garden stretching between their two properties, planning to open a much bigger one the following year. On the still morning, the air heavy with evaporating dew, the soil exhaled a rich, earthy aroma. In awe, Bertha, exclaimed, "How beautiful it is! I've always appreciated a newly turned garden, but here . . . oh my, the contrast with the green grasses and clear blue skies simply shouts perfection."

They planted beans, carrots, beets, and potatoes. Then, of course, they needed to water the seedlings regularly. Hauling water from the little lake was a daily task, one of many.

Bertha wrote a letter home to her grandfather, sister, and brother, telling of their accomplishments and the good neighbors. Although she told them that she sorely missed them, most of her letter was cheery and bright. She also wrote a letter to Lars.

Dear Lars,

I wonder if and where this letter will find you. Tillie and I have made it to northwestern Dakota where there is nothing but the flat plain for miles around, only broken by small rises and occasional shacks, including ours. The community men helped us get our shacks up. The routines of getting our little farms in order have settled in. We haul water from a little lake nearby and collect some of the minimal rain that falls.

Perhaps next year we'll get a well put in. There are water witches around to help, of course. I've heard much of the water here is alkali and gives people the trots, especially

*newcomers, and that affliction—called the Dakota trots—
has come upon us. Both of us are exhausted at the end of
each day, just from the necessities of life. It is a good life,
hard and lonely, yet exhilarating.*

*I think of you often and hope you are safe. When life feels
rather hard here in Dakota, I sometimes think of you in
the Philippines or wherever you are and imagine your
life being so much harder. When I complain of the trots, I
think of you and worry about malaria and dysentery and
know I have little to complain of.*

*I remember the special time we had together before you left.
Of course, I also remember all of the good times we had
dancing and sitting on the swing and going for walks and
picnics and holding hands. I miss you and hope you think
of me with fond memories.*

Med kjaerlighet,
Bertha

The letter would go out from the Kincaid General Store, now an
unofficial post office bearing a painted sign. If a neighbor were
going by the B&T Estate, he would stop to check with the women
to see if they had things to post and might return later in the day,
or the next, with mail for them. Letters from home were cause for
celebration, like rain in a drought.

A Party on the High Plains

Soon after the arrival of two box cook stoves, along with smoke stack materials and a pile of lignite coal, Hans and Henry helped move the stoves into Tillie's and Bertha's shacks and then put up the chimney pipes. They cut holes in the roofs and fed the pipes through. "Now," asked Henry when they were done, "ya got some tin cans?"

"Have a few."

"Need quite a few. Got some at home. I'll get 'em for ya. Need to flatten 'em and cover the edges where the roof and pipe meet to keep the pipe away from the wood and keep out rain and snow. Ya know how to do that?"

"Sure," said Bertha, "and Tillie and I'll come over and pick up the cans. Give us a chance to see your wife again."

After the men left, Tillie asked Bertha if she really knew how to use the cans to keep out the weather.

"Well, no, but I like to pretend I know how to do most everything. And it can't be that hard, can it?"

"Probably not. We'll manage."

A few days later, after burning a couple loaves of bread and leaving muffins gooey in the center as they got used to controlling the temperature in their ovens (and their shacks, which became almost as hot), the two women planned a party.

It took a few more practice runs, but on the day before the community gathering, Bertha baked several loaves of bread and Tillie made three pies, one of which was filled with wild gooseberries she'd gathered in the bushes near the little lake. The opaque-green berries were still hard and tart, but with enough sugar, they were good for pie. Later, when they sweetened, she could harvest more for jelly and fresh eating.

Just before guests began arriving, Bertha and Tillie finished nailing together a makeshift table for the food. As was the custom, everyone would bring something to share, along with dishes on which to eat and something to drink. For women and children, the drinks were usually fresh milk, buttermilk or, occasionally, berry juice made from whatever berries could be gathered, along with plenty of sugar. For some of the men, drink meant whiskey or some type of home brew.

The day dawned sunny. Later, a few wispy clouds floated in the western sky. The morning gale had diminished to a balmy breeze by midafternoon. "This calm, sunny day is a good omen for our lives here," Bertha remarked while they readied the estate for company. "I believe in omens and trust that our adventure will turn out to be the best of our lives."

Tillie moved her eyes slightly upward and to the left as she considered. "Well, there'll be wonderful times like this, of course. Likely terrible times, too, with storms and drudgery and maybe some calamities. Hope we'll become stronger and maybe wiser. And today is indeed a good sign."

A party on the high plains was always festive, if simple. Any gathering that broke the routine of arduous and dirty work was welcome. Yet Tillie thought the hard work, tiring her so she fell into her quilt each night, was more rewarding than any work she had ever done, even more gratifying than teaching. She savored creating her own space on her own land even while longing for the comfort and familiar companionship of home.

As guests arrived, Tillie recognized she had already become a part of the community. Seeing Olga and Anna; Knut and Eleanor, the shopkeeper with her sparkly eyes; Ole; Hans and Helen; and Henry and Belle was almost like seeing old friends. And other people she'd not yet met were there, more men than women. Children came, too, so it was the first time Tillie spent with the homesteading children in the community.

Little Brunhild, Ellen and Frank's daughter, was four years old and had a brother Karl, aged three. Their older brother Sven was eleven and already labored along with the men. Hildegaard with her long pigtails, daughter of Henry's Belle who'd been widowed, was five, and would be turning six, she said, the next month. Josie and Earl's daughter Sharon was eight. Jens, Gunner, and Nels, sons of Arne and Emma were eight, seven, and six, respectively. Susan, ten; Gustav, four; and Mildred, three, were the children of Herman and Millie.

Tillie met Elizabeth, whose mother was Eleanor the shopkeeper. Erik introduced his brother Lars. "My *mor* and *far*," he said, pointing to Nels and Helga Iverson, "brung us here last year. Came by wagon. Was so exciting!"

"I bet it was. Bertha and I came by train. Exciting enough for us."

Tillie asked the older children about school. Peter, Susan, Sven, and Erik had gone to school before they came to Dakota a year or two earlier, but since then there had been no school. "Mor gives me lessons from the Bible," chirped Peter.

"Well, we'll have to see what we can do about some schooling," said Tillie.

Bertha glanced at Ole as he walked toward the group. He smiled, displaying his dimples, and nodded his head. She nodded back, smiled politely, then turned away before her smile widened. Helga told Bertha about the family's wagon journey from near Minneapolis. "I was scared stiff some Indians would attack us," said Helga, "but our only encounter was a friendly one. Can't make no sense of what they say, a'course, but they seemed excited to see us. I heard they were of the Assiniboine tribe. Think that's how to say it. Most people call them the 'Assinines.' Must be well provided for on the reservation."

"Perhaps," said Bertha. "I fear them, too, yet I wonder how they fare, kind of cooped up a bit like chickens."

"Well, I wouldn't worry much about how they feel," said Helga. "They're not quite like us, y'know. Kind of barbaric."

"But they must be capable of some feelings, even if not as developed as our own," she replied.

"Well, I suppose." Helga gave a little frown.

At that Bertha went to tend to the food, though she stood at the table staring at all the dishes, doing nothing for some moments, which Tillie noticed.

Ole came up behind Bertha and said, "Hallo."

She jumped. "Oh, hallo, Ole. I didn't see you come up. So good to have you join us. How've you been?"

"Sorry to have scared ya. I been just fine. Got the winter wheat in now, the little we had of it. Hardly worth plantin' it out here. Hope we get a bit a'rain this summer so's we have a decent crop of the spring wheat come fall.

"This here's Willie and Winnie," he added when the couple walked up with their young boy. "Live between me and you on the nort' side of the lake . . . and this here," he said to the couple, "is Berta, the pretty girl homesteader I told you 'bout."

Color rose in Bertha's neck as she greeted the couple. "So good to meet you, Willie and Winnie. Can't say how much I appreciate having you all so close. Should be able to remember your names—Willie and Winnie—just substitute an 'n' for an 'l.' And how long have you been here?"

"Almost two years it is now," said Winnie. "Took a bit gettin' used to, but wouldn't trade this place for nuthin'."

"It sure 'nuf felt lonely when I first came," said Bertha. "Like I didn't know how to act or what to do, but quick enough the work put an end to worrying about that. Get too tired to think of problems."

"And you'll find it gets better'n better at least till the winter comes stormin' in."

"Think I'll try to put off thoughts about winter for a bit," said Bertha with a laugh.

She turned back to Ole who'd struck up some conversation about crops with Willie.

"Well, and that's good that da wheat is in, sure Ole," she said, falling into a brogue, "I'll go check on the food. Must be near ready. Again, so good to meet you, Willie and Winnie. I'll talk wit you later."

They had food galore, including *rommegrøt*, which tasted like the best fare Tillie had ever eaten, so reminiscent was it of home. The adults slowly ate the butter-slathered sandwiches, beans, pies, and cakes while the children gobbled them and then returned to their games.

Soon Knut took up his accordion and Hans his harmonica and they began playing some of the old tunes. The mood turned merry, especially after one of the men took a bottle from his pocket and passed it around.

"Here's to homesteading," shouted Tillie. "Thank you all for joining us in this celebration. We're so happy to be here and to have all of you as neighbors." At that, she twirled her skirt and Halvor, who Tillie would later learn tended to be taciturn, jumped up and asked her to dance, surprising most everyone. Halvor was a rather coarse man, given to swearing, Tillie had noticed. He was prone to spit right on the ground in front of ladies and burp without excusing himself. Dark brown stains from spittle caked the corners of his mouth. When he smiled, though, it was with a sweet, childish grin. Tillie accepted the invitation and found that he danced well. They chatted amicably about life on the plains.

"Last summer," claimed Halvor, "geese fell right out of the sky hit by the verst hailstorm I done ever see."

"My goodness."

"Life out here can be kind of tough, though," he said and then spit. "You girls got to have some kind of character to be here."

"Well, I guess we hungered for some kind of adventure and sure 'nuf found it. Maybe it's the hard work needed here that builds character in time."

"It does that," he said. "Least for most it does. Some crack up and hop a train back."

Soon Ole came and bowed to Bertha. "You'll dance?" he asked shyly.

"Why, sure 'nuf, Ole."

With the drink, Knut and Hans soon turned into clowns and the music grew louder and rowdier. Frank turned into a badger, callously yelling at Sven for not hitting a ball and arguing with Arne about some chickens. Tillie noticed that the other guests were ignoring Frank and she did likewise, but wanted to tell him to be nicer to his son.

As the sun fell halfway through the distant horizon, Knut and Hans put down their instruments, dancing stopped, and community members started to depart. Soon only Tillie and

Bertha were standing, watching the puffy pink clouds in the western sky turn mauve.

"What a day this has been," said Tillie. "Don't think I've ever felt so alive as out here. Gives me a feeling that this is what God intended me to do."

"It has indeed been a good day. Can't say there has ever been a better day."

As they started cleaning up, Tillie asked Bertha what she'd been thinking about when she stood at the table staring and Ole made her jump. "Oh," said Bertha, "guess I didn't realize I'd been staring. I was bothered by Helga's belief that the Indians have no feelings. I know I can feel sorry for anyone, maybe too sorry. And I know Indians can be savage, but I remember what I learned about the Dakota Indians slaughtering the settlers near home back in '62, then the soldiers massacring the Indians, and kind of think we can all do awful things when frightened."

Even though Tillie wondered at her friend's belief, she didn't completely disagree with her. "Maybe, but I'm afraid of them too. Sometimes at night I imagine I hear Indians whooping in the distance."

"Well, I fear them too, but I haven't heard of any attacks around here and sure haven't seen any Indians."

As dusk was deepening toward darkness, Tillie said, "Well, we better finish getting this place cleaned up so we can be back to chores in the morning."

———

Tillie's encounter with the school-aged children dominated her thinking as she hauled water the next morning, heated the water to wash clothes on the washboard, and pulled weeds away from the bean and carrot seedlings in the glaring afternoon sun. She continued to ruminate about schooling when she swept away dirt tracked into the shack by her neighbors and gave the floor a good scrubbing. By nightfall, she had a plan. "Let's put out word we'll teach the neighborhood children come October. Could do it in our homes this year."

"Sure, sure," said Bertha. "Been thinking along those lines too. Shame to let our training go unused and these children could use some teaching, sure; and a few extra dollars for us, if there are some, won't go to waste."

"Let's check with the Department of Public Instruction, in Bismarck I believe it is, about what we might need to do to get started. Maybe see if we can get a school built come next year."

That evening, Tillie and Bertha, with some quarreling over word choices and paragraph organization, composed a letter to the superintendent of schools at the Department of Public Instruction. Tillie, whose penmanship was better than Bertha's, wrote the letter. But, with corrections that Bertha insisted on, including a misplaced comma, she had to revise it. She deplored wasting a sheet of perfectly good paper, but agreed it was necessary. Before she finally finished the letter, she needed to light a kerosene lantern.

My Dear Sir:

We are teachers new to North Dakota: Miss Tillie Melbakken and Miss Bertha Harstad.

Each of us recently filed claims for homesteads in Ward Country in Meadows Township, near the settlement of Kincaid. We are in the Norwegian section and understand from men in the community that the school section, number sixteen, is next to our homesteads.

Settlement in the community began nearly three years ago and there is no school yet. We have met many of the community children who receive no schooling apart from that their parents might provide.

Both of us received teaching certificates after attending normal school in Moorhead, Minnesota. Miss Melbakken taught school for two years in District No. 4, Tunsberg Township, Chippewa County, Minnesota, where the school board president was Mr. William Torgerson. Miss Harstad taught two years in District No. 35 in Big Bend Township in Chippewa County where Mr. Sven Pederson was school board president. O.E. Saunders, superintendent of schools for Chippewa County, visited our schools at least once a year.

We are hoping that by this fall we could begin providing instruction for the twelve school-aged children now living here. There are also three younger children who'll be ready for schooling in a year or two. Perhaps there will be even more youngsters by fall since the community is growing.

We respectfully request that you provide information to us to assist us in proceeding to teach the children, which we can do in our own homes this coming year. Miss Harstad could teach the younger children and Miss Melbakken the older ones. You may deliver such information to us at Kincaid General Store.

We thank you kindly for your assistance.

Most respectfully,
Miss Tillie Melbakken
Miss Bertha Harstad

Routines of homesteading propelled the women and didn't allow much time for reflection, at least not during the day. The constant demands—finding sharp-tailed grouse or jackrabbit to shoot for dinner, or even some ground squirrels for stew, building a little hut for a chicken coop and other storage, tending the garden, preparing food, making curtains, washing clothes, and hauling water—kept worries and fears at bay.

The two friends wanted to buy laying hens, but they were not to be found, so they decided to order chicks for next year and buy eggs from their neighbors until they could get a small flock going.

They discussed what to do about breaking up the sod. "Ole said it would take months to do it by ourselves with a little plow, even if we had one," Bertha told Tillie. "He said the roots of the grasses here are really deep, lots deeper than at home, apparently 'blankety-blank tough to break.' Plus there's usually lots of rocks to dislodge and move. Better plan to have one of the men do it and share crop, don't ya think?"

"You're probably right, Bertha, especially with plans coming up for schooling. We'll have more than enough to do. Hate to admit I might not be able to do it, though."

"Think you sometimes forget you're a woman. I'll talk to Ole and see if he has any ideas," said Bertha.

"Yeah, okay. If I have a chance I'll check with Orlo or Hans, perhaps."

When Bertha asked Ole two days later, he suggested that Hans and Henry would likely be willing to break up the sod and plant flax the following year. "Best to plant flax the first year, wheat the next," he told Bertha.

"That would ease some of my burden, Ole. I so appreciate all your advice. Hardly know what I'd do without you already." She looked away from Ole to try to hide the color that began growing on her face.

"Oh, you girls do quite well for yourselves, sure do. Can see that."

"Well, we're getting used to it all. Have settled in pretty good. There are mornings I wake up and wonder what in the dickens I'm doing out here; other mornings I wake up to the glow of first light coming through the window and think how lucky I am."

"Took me some gettin' used to, too. Now? Wouldn't never go back."

Ole was a soft-spoken man with a genial laugh. He had a bulbous nose, ears that looked too big, and a little belly forming above his belt. His smile displayed charming dimples in the roughened skin on his face. His face lit up whenever he saw Bertha.

He told Bertha he would soon plow a few acres around the shacks to give them a firebreak. "Prairie grass fires erupt out here easy as pie . . . Well, a'course pie ain't so easy, I s'pose you know better'n me," he said. "A train throws a spark, a settler don't get a fire out, a drunk man tosses a smoke, the lightning strikes. With this Dakota wind, a flare starts and soon there's miles of flames with smoke t'ick as tar."

Bertha would learn from Ole that he'd come to Dakota from Wisconsin two years earlier after a girlfriend jilted him. He supported her when her father died and she coped with her mother's hysteria. He even stood by her while she flaunted her wares, especially her large breasts, and flirted with other men as Ole watched. Now he had a homestead, had broken seventy-five or more acres, and had wheat growing. If only the weather permitted, he'd have a good crop in the fall. He'd never heard from that girl Eleanor since he left, and though he'd attempted to put together a letter for her, he'd never finished it.

"Miss my mother, my brothers and sisters, but I hope my younger brother Daniel will come to Dakota to homestead. He's helping my older brother farm, but says his heart is in the West with me. Hopes to file a claim of his own once he turns twenty-one," he told Bertha.

Later, Bertha would tell Tillie, "That Ole, even though I hardly pay him any attention, and he's not handsome to look at, he's nice to be around. Seems to want to talk with me." She turned her face downward and then raised her eyes to see Tillie, while her mouth gave a shy smile. "He actually seems interested in me, rather than always wanting to tell of his own accomplishments like Lars always did. He looks right into my eyes with his deep-set hazel ones."

Tillie shook her head just a little and smiled inwardly.

"I sure do miss Lars though, the way he danced and his easy way with words so I never needed to search for topics to talk about. Loved his almost black, thick hair that I'd run my fingers through." She shook her head sideways. Her shoulders moved forward as she turned her head downward. Then she looked up at Tillie. "Sometimes I feel so happy and excited to be a young woman with life and love ahead to discover, but sometimes I just feel so confused, like I don't know my own mind."

Tillie nodded to her. "I think we all have these confusing thoughts."

Silky Black Gelding

The cool nights grew warmer as June ebbed. But near the end of the month, an unlikely cold spell hit for a couple of days. "I'm afraid our little garden plants could freeze tonight," Bertha declared one evening. "I'm covering some with a sheet, even if it means more washing."

In the morning, she was relieved to see no frost developing as the sun arose. She told Tillie she had stayed awake much of the night worrying about the garden. "Bet our neighbors worried about their tender grains."

The garden survived with not a blemish on the young potatoes, beans, carrots, and beets; a cloud cover that developed overnight prevented frost. Two weeks later Tillie received a letter from home. Her mother told of a frost that hit the Watson area on June 29, damaging tomatoes badly and nipping the leaves of many plants. Tillie realized the cold spell that had hit Kincaid earlier must have moved on to southwestern Minnesota. She wished that air could carry her back home as easily as it carried the weather. The letter also reminded her of the luscious tang of tomatoes and the piquant aroma that arose when they were cooking. She knew the season was too short to grow them at the estate, and would miss them.

As summer progressed, Bertha suggested it was time to put up their lean-tos for coal. So she and Tillie dug holes for two-by-fours left over from shack construction that would serve as footings and support for Bertha's lean-to. After planting the posts, they began nailing poor-quality boards onto the two sides and roof. With the unusually quiet air that day, it was likely the pounding resonated in the ears of most of their neighbors.

The day ended with another celebratory vinegary wine tonic for each of the women, along with bone-aching tiredness. Bertha joked that homestead life might just make them into floozies.

"That'd take some doing," claimed Tillie, while the small amount she imbibed brought an easiness of spirit she was not accustomed to.

She and Bertha had judged some of the men for having whiskey in their pockets at community gatherings, a practice certainly not acceptable at home. "You'd never know this was a dry state!" Bertha had exclaimed.

Tillie shook her head. "I don't know. Does seem to be a different attitude about drink out here, even though it's illegal. But most of the men seem to enjoy a few swallows, or maybe a little more, but do no harm. Maybe different customs are understandable, even of benefit so far from home and normal civilization."

"Suppose with all this grueling work, a little drink-induced relaxation must be healthy," said Bertha. "We even imbibe some out here." Her eyes brightened as she raised her eyebrows. "Feels good!"

Both women giggled a little. "Sometimes I tell you to lighten up, Tillie, but maybe I need to lighten up myself."

Silent reflection ensued as deepening shadows heralded darkness.

Before yawns sent her inside to bed, Tillie declared, "What we need now is a horse. Maybe a buggy in time, but first we need a good horse."

So during the next week she asked her neighbors how they might find a suitable horse. Hans knew of an upcoming horse auction in Bowbells on July 15, so Tillie and Bertha made plans to travel there with him and Helen.

In the meantime, Bertha asked Ole to pick up fence posts and wire at Kincaid General Store. "Don't like having to pay for fence posts," she lamented to Tillie a little later. "Back at home, the trees would have provided ample material."

Tillie agreed. "Didn't appreciate the trees as much as we should have."

Once Ole delivered the supplies, the girls started fencing off a pasture for their hoped-for horse.

Bertha wiped her brow once they had planted the last post. "Damn tough work," she said as she sat down in the grass. She looked at Tillie. "Yes, I know *damn* is a swear word, but I think I've a right to sound like a man after all this work."

Tillie smiled and sat down next to her. "Darn right, well . . . damn right."

Bertha giggled.

———

It was a hot, sunny day, their bonnets hardly keeping the sun off their flushed faces as the bidding began. They had their sights on a twelve-hundred-pound silky black gelding, fifteen hands high. He seemed to be a gentle horse, yet strong enough to hold both women for short distances at least. Bertha already had a name for him—Samuel, or Sam—and Tillie thought it a good name.

Since the girls had never bid at an auction, Hans made the calls for them. Bertha fidgeted with her handbag. Her brow showed worry lines. Tillie was nervous, too, since their cash was running low, but she hid her emotion better. They hoped the forty dollars Bertha contributed and the forty dollars Tillie picked up from her account at the recently opened Bickford and Bond Bank would be more than sufficient.

Hans made the first bid at forty-five dollars. Others joined in. The bidding continued. Hans called out, "Fifty-nine."

A man with a straw hat yelled, "Sixty-one!"

"Sixty-two."

"Sixty-three!"

"Sixty-four," shouted Hans.

"Sixty-five!"

Finally, the auctioneer pounded out, "Going, going, gone at sixty-nine dollars, a steal for this beauty, to this man with the red suspenders," and pointed at Hans. Tillie let out a whoop of joy as she and Bertha headed to claim Sam. After a visit to Hamilton and Corey where they purchased a good saddle, as well as a harness they'd need sooner or later, Tillie mounted Sam, a sturdy and docile horse, and followed Hans, Helen, and Bertha back to the B&T Estate.

A little later, Hans dropped off some oats to add to Sam's grass diet.

"Thank you, Hans. Bertha and I would be lost here without your help."

"Aw, we all help each other out," he said.

Days later, the friends finished construction on Tillie's lean-to, which they made bigger than Bertha's. Sam could use it for shelter from a summer storm or winter blizzard until the following summer, when they planned to build a stable or shed of some sort. The lean-to was an eight-by-five-foot space, six feet high with a slight slope. Just outside the door on the south side of the shack, it would get the least snow. Rather than leaving the whole front open, as they had on Bertha's smaller lean-to, they covered half of the opening with roughhewn boards to give Sam some protection from storms.

The lean-to complete, Bertha plopped on the warm ground, almost cocooning in the grass. "Uff da, I'm tired!"

Tillie plopped near her. She lay there staring at the cloud formations, just wisps of white floating in the heavens. They looked as if she could easily nudge a twig through them, sending one part drifting away from the other.

"Have you the energy to make an angel here in the grass?" asked Bertha.

"Just enough, I think," Tillie responded and slowly began stretching her arms and legs.

"A couple of angels now grace the estate," laughed Bertha. "Keep away the evil spirits, they will."

When their energy returned, they picked prairie roses. They'd use the hips for winter tea to help keep them healthy. Black-eyed Susans bloomed bright yellow in the dull grasses. Tiny harebells yielded delicate blue flowers, mostly hidden in the grass. Spikes of blue vervain rose above the prairie. Tillie and Bertha gathered some of the flowering tops. Winnie had once told them a tea from vervain could help restore tired muscles, heal sprains, and make a good tonic for women who worked too hard. "Guess that's all of us," Tillie had responded.

Walking back to their shacks, Bertha said, "Do you smell that? That's yarrow. Love that scent—spicy, sweet, heady—hard to describe, but something potent."

A couple of days later, the sky painted itself a menacing yellowish-green, so both women retreated to Tillie's shack as the churning clouds took on a look of black smoke. The wind blew so fierce it knocked down all of Tillie's photos, rattled the door so hard she thought it would come loose. "It's wailing louder'n a banshee!" Tillie exclaimed. The timbers moved as if a gigantic wolf were huffing and puffing.

Bertha kept shaking her head. "I hope our shacks don't blow away. I'm about ready to pee my pants."

When the wind finally died down and the rain diminished, the friends looked outside to see the prairie grasses flattened all around them. Some of the tar paper had torn off as the wind and rain lashed at their shelters, so the two needed to repair it.

Cutting hay for Sam's winter feed summoned the women as soon as the grasses dried from the storm. Both had used scythes at home, although their work was restricted to areas that were hard to reach with the new hay mowers most farmers in Minnesota had by the end of the century.

The job in front of them seemed daunting, but they plowed on with their scythes day after day. Two weeks later, they raked the hay from the windrows into haycocks.

That task completed, Tillie saw the need to construct a root cellar, in part to store potatoes, carrots, onions, and turnips, but also to serve as a storm shelter. "After that last storm, we need a better place to protect us," Tillie declared.

Bertha agreed that they should dig a cellar, but said she had baking to do. With Bertha inside, Tillie grabbed her shovel and began digging, creating a bit of a cavern not far from her shack. Near noon, Bertha finished baking and went to find Tillie for lunch. She found her soaking wet in the midday sun, dirt plastering her arms and caking her face with rivulets of sweat running down her cheeks. "*Vat* are you doing?"

"What do you think? We've got to make us a root cellar."

"I'd say you could use some help, sure, and I think we should get a bit of advice from Hans and Henry, or Ole too."

"You're probably right," admitted Tillie, leaning on her shovel and knowing she had not an ounce of energy left. Her newly formed muscles quivered from exhaustion.

A few days later, Ole, having recruited Halvor and Herman, arrived at the estate and completed the cellar which the girls had hollowed out following Ole's instructions. It was on the same hill, if one could call it that, on which Tillie's shack stood. They lined the cellar with wooden boards and rocks and, where it was not built into the little rise, framed it up to support a small roof, which they covered with sod. An undersized door allowed entrance into the small space and the women had to bend forward inside. "We likely won't be able to use it during the verst of the vinter, if what I am told by you fellows of vinters is right, but it should keep our potatoes and carrots from going bad," laughed Tillie, enjoying using brogue. "And give us some shelter from summer storms."

The men dug a latrine as well, covering it with a one-holer bench. They used some of the leftover lumber from the cellar to construct the frame for the outhouse. The women would nail on the knotholed lumber to cover it a day or two later.

Before they left, the men insisted upon coming back to help the girls build a good haystack. "You girls are damn good at most everything and sure can get it started, but you'll need help pitching hay as it gets higher," Ole said. "I'll check on yer progress. Don't you go hurtin' yerselves pitchin' hay," he added with his thumbs tucked under his suspenders and a stern look on his face.

"Thanks. All of you are so kind and helpful. I'm awful grateful to get the help," Bertha said with a demure smile. Tillie thanked them too, for all their work and with relief that she wouldn't have to follow her memory of watching her papa and brother build a good stack that could withstand the weather.

"Finally, we'll have some privacy when doing our duties. Men can do it so much easier." Tillie grinned. "Was especially hard when I had my monthlies."

"High grasses of summer helped, sure. Couldn't anyone see our private parts when we hunkered down. But we all know that straight-ahead stare we have when we're emptying our bowels. Out here on the flat prairie, can see a long way."

"Don't have to worry 'bout that anymore."

Gathering of Mothers

When Tillie and Bertha spent their first night on their staked land, just thirteen neighboring shacks formed the community. As the summer heat increased, the community held two more gatherings for shack raisings, along with two barn raisings. On the flat treeless prairie, many of the shacks were visible from Tillie and Bertha's land even though some were about two miles away.

Tillie and Bertha received information from the Department of Public Instruction approving their plan to teach. The government of North Dakota had wisely set aside 640 acres as school land in each township. The site in Meadows Township abutted the eastern border of the B&T Estate. However, since no school was yet built, the teachers would use their own shacks for schooling, at least for the first year.

As Tillie and Bertha's first summer on the North Dakota plain receded, they gathered the women who had children and made plans. Bertha would teach the six younger children in her shack; Tillie would teach the older ones in her own. A couple of mothers volunteered to donate a few appropriate books. Tillie said she would write to her family requesting specific books, along with her lesson plans from earlier instruction. Bertha would ask her family to do the same. The Department of Public Instruction would provide two dollars and eighty-five cents per month for each child to cover the teachers' pay as well as needed supplies, such as slates and chalk.

At the meeting, the women decided school would start in mid-September after the wheat harvest, then continue until the spring snow melted and children were needed to help with planting and other chores. The teachers also encouraged the mothers to talk to their husbands about putting up a school building the following summer.

The gathering of mothers served another function. They drank coffee, ate a little lunch together, chatted, arranged for shared chores, and laughed and cried about their trials on the desolate land. Some felt free to complain about their husbands, as well. Herman went to the Blind Pig too often, according to Millie. Frank could be a bit harsh in disciplining the children; "But only when he's had too much to drink," said Ellen in a soft voice while her face exhibited an empty look, or so Tillie thought. Nels, his wife said, let her do much of the hard work while he sat outside the Pig and shared jokes with other men. By this time, Tillie and Bertha understood that the "Pig" was a speakeasy of sorts—a Dakota version—a shack where the men would supposedly pay to see a blind pig and get some bootlegged liquor free. Such places had cropped up all over Dakota since the state was declared dry.

In spite of these complaints, most of the women seemed to enjoy their newly found community. All of them seemed to be strong, not given to minor complaints. Each of them had endured travails they might not have thought themselves capable of surviving a few years earlier.

Winnie told of burying their seven-year-old child while on the way to Dakota in the wagon. "I'd learned from my mother and grandmother how to heal the sick and tend to mothers in childbirth. Yet I couldn't save my Sylvia," she said stoically.

"Whatever happened?" asked Bertha, her hand covering her open mouth.

"She fell ill with scarlet fever, probably was just getting it when we left. Likely, my sister's girl had it and we saw her just before leaving. Sally survived, but Sylvia? I didn't have so many herbs with me. T'was harder to care for her as we traveled on. Slipped away one night, my arm around her." Some tears formed in Winnie's eyes as she said this, but she didn't cry. Many of the other women let drops roll down their cheeks.

Belle had learned about Sylvia's death soon after coming to Dakota. "Winnie's tough and she helps us all out when we need her, better'n a doctor, she is," she stated. "Understands the misery we feel at times."

"We all do our share. All have hardships of one kind or another. But it's a damn good life out here in spite of it all," declared Winnie.

———

Tillie and Bertha put up preserves from their small garden, and dug some of their potatoes and carrots. "Look at the size of these tubers," gloated Bertha, glorying in their harvest. "Never saw such big ones at home."

"And a dozen or more in almost every hill," added Tillie, as delighted as Bertha.

They purchased supplies of coal, kerosene, oatmeal, butter, wheat flour, yeast cakes, molasses, salt, and sugar, hoping it might last through the winter when trips to the general store might be more difficult. They each constructed a tiny cellar in their shacks under the floor beneath a trapdoor. In it they could keep eggs, buttermilk, and meat cool, but hopefully not frozen.

Initially, they had planned to dig a well on one of their sites, but with the little lake nearby, they had decided to manage without one, at least for the first year. They told themselves and each other that hauling water was good exercise. Each had purchased a large barrel to collect rainwater from the occasional rains, and they planned to use snow in the winter, assuming it would snow enough, which they heard it usually did. "Hardly need to worry 'bout getting plenty of snow, y'know," Ole had told Bertha. "Though there was a winter with almost no snow some years back, I heard tell."

Now, though, the friends agreed they'd need to put in a well the following year. Carrying water for Sam's thirst, along with everything else, surely built their muscles that didn't need more building, but just as surely drained their energy and dampened enthusiasm about their adventure.

After a good rain, the women cut one-by-two-foot pieces of sod to lay in stacks around the perimeter of their shacks for winter insulation, a much more difficult task than they had imagined, as was true for many of the chores on the Dakota plains. "Don't think we have the time or energy to get up a stable," lamented Bertha. "I reckon Sam'll need to manage bad weather in your lean-to. Poor guy. Ole offered to help build a shed, but the men are getting busy with the harvest. I wouldn't think of asking him."

"I bet we can manage to get one up ourselves next year, but I feel badly, too, that Sam won't have good shelter."

The women had routine chores to do as well. They used their cook kettles and washboards to wash their laundry, swept dust from the incessant dry wind out of their homes, cooked simple meals, and managed the homesickness.

That last task was the hardest. "Even though you are such a dear friend and our neighbors are so helpful and kindly, I've never felt more alone," Tillie confided to Bertha one evening. "I long for the day-to-day care and love I felt from Mama and Papa and for the naturalness of family help. Yet I want to be self-sufficient. Sometimes I have such mixed-up feelings."

Bertha, too, said she felt more loneliness than ever. "It's the separation from family, from church, from lifelong friends. Yet I've never felt as connected to anything or anybody as I feel in this community. It's an odd thing. Some nights I wallow in the loneliness, or maybe it's homesickness, hardly thinking I can go on another day, then get up in the morning to a sense of purpose, glad for the chores, glad for the gatherings. I've never slept in a place all alone, so sometimes I'm even glad for the mice and their incessant chewing at night."

"But you are never alone with me here in the next shack, Bertha," said Tillie, reaching out to touch her friend's hand. She paused. "Yet I understand how a mouse can be such a bother, but kind of a friend too. Just hope I don't get any rats." With that, the morose mood left and the friends burst out laughing.

The wild sounds at night—the mournful wailing and yapping of the coyotes, the hooting of a great horned owl, and, especially, the howling of wolves—intruded upon Tillie's dreams at times. In one such dream, she stared down a ferocious wolf; in another, she was running from a bobcat when she awakened.

Daytime brought snake fear. Tillie understood there were a few rattlers in the area, though very few, and the hiss of the hognose snake sometimes made her run. Even though she knew hognose snakes were harmless, she hadn't yet learned to distinguish their hiss from the initial sound of a rattler. Bertha would giggle a little when she noticed Tillie running from a hognose snake.

Almost every evening, Bertha and Tillie enjoyed a simple meal together at one of their shacks, each of which had enough homey touches—photos, dishes, crocks, rugs, and so forth—to be called "home," though of course nothing like what they still called home in Minnesota. It was only when one or both of them were too exhausted to do anything other than grab a piece of flatbrød and a bit of cheese that they abandoned their shared meal.

At sunset, they often sat out of doors and watched as a jackrabbit darted by or a pair of red fox trotted past. On rare occasions, one of them spotted a mule deer and sometimes a porcupine or a skunk. They heard from older homesteaders that buffalo used to roam the area by the thousands, but now not a one dotted the distant prairie and their deep grunts were absent from the chanting of the land. Sometimes the girl homesteaders would hear the call of the bobolink or see a golden eagle soaring on a thermal. They learned to identify the chirps and calls of a northern flicker, the pipit, grasshopper sparrows, and ground squirrels. Bertha, especially, loved to watch ground squirrels. "They look so adorable when they sit up and hold their front paws up like hands. Like they are giving a little speech," she said. "Hate to kill the little things, even though they eat the carrots and peas and most anything else they can find."

Sometimes one or both of them sat outside as evening descended and the prairie became still. "I love the silence," said Tillie. "Seems to call forth wisdom I didn't know I possessed. Can't even describe it, just a sense of the connection of everything, like a spider web that responds when a mosquito touches it."

While the women rarely experienced boredom, they eagerly anticipated community gatherings. Birthday or anniversary celebrations, as well as shack raisings, broke up the tedium of chores and relieved some of the lonesomeness. Preparation for school created a welcome diversion, as well.

———

That evening Tillie wrote a letter home.

Dear Mama and Papa,

I miss you so much. The nights get especially lonely out here, and just a bit fearful, though mostly imagined fears.

Bertha and I have been preparing for school to start sometime in September after the community harvest and fall work. It has been a good outlet for my intellect, which I have sadly neglected while I've been exhausted from physical work. Thank you so much for sending schoolbooks and others, which will be put to good use. I haven't even had much time to read the Bible, but I try to get to a few verses before my eyes fall closed from tiredness as I prepare to sleep. The coming winter should provide more reading time.

We've gathered some of our potatoes and carrots and have most of them in the root cellar. We canned some of them, knowing that it will be hard to pry open the door of the cellar after heavy snows come. Our neighbors tell us the winds and snowstorms can be really fierce, even worse than in Minnesota. We've had coal delivered, but we have also been gathering cow chips from the neighbors, who encourage us to do so. We use the cow chips now for cooking and perhaps will have some left over for winter heat.

We were so grateful when the mason jars and zinc covers arrived at Kincaid General Store. Most all of the women gathered there and we portioned out the jars, so each of us got some.

I have much enjoyed the companionship of other women here. Some are a bit coarse, but still very nice and seemingly good Christians. Some have had pretty tough lives with men who drink too much and expect too much of the women's more fragile emotions. Even so, the emotions of the women are truly strong, just sometimes injured by their husbands' demands.

We have been having a kind of church service at one of the shacks. In bad weather, we all crowd together indoors so we can barely move, but in nice weather we sing and pray out of doors, which is quite pleasant. Our neighbor Orlo Larson planned to go into ministry many years back, but it apparently didn't suit him. He leads the service and gives a very short sermon. Sometimes other community men say some words, as well. The men are talking about putting up a small church next year. Perhaps they will build a school within a year or two as well.

I have put my rifle to good use on jackrabbits, which make tasty stew, though not as good as the cottontail stew we had at home. I've even shot a few ground squirrels. Not much to them, of course, and they have a strong flavor, so I use them in stew with plenty of onions. We've had some venison from a mule deer a neighbor shot. Not many neighbors have beef cattle or pigs ready for butchering yet, so beef and pork are in short supply, but neighbors have been generous with butter, milk for buttermilk and cheese, and eggs, as well. We'd like to shoot a deer ourselves this fall and salt some of it, but we've only spotted two or three all summer. Of course, if we got one, we'd share some of it with the neighbors who have been so good to us.

It has been a pleasant summer, warm and humid many days, but almost always perspiration from our labors floats away on a breeze or a wind.

Greet all of the family and neighbors. Tell Peter I think of him often. And send greeting to Bertha's family when you see them. It was so good of Jergen to visit just before we left, so if you happen to see him, tell him I think of him occasionally and hope he is doing well.

Med kjaerlighet,
Tillie

In truth, Tillie thought of Jergen quite a lot, thought of him especially on the chilly nights when a quilt was not quite as much warmth as she wanted. Even after reading her Bible and saying her prayers, she allowed herself the luxury of imagining the warmth of Jergen's body, not having any actual idea of how it would feel.

During supper one evening Bertha commented, "I'm wondering if we might not think about getting a buggy now. What do you think, Tillie?"

"Yes, yes, we need a buggy. Kept wanting to delay it until we can get a shed built, but . . . well, maybe both the buggy and Sam will need to manage a winter in the snow."

"Well, Ole says he found a buggy might suit us when he was in Bowbells a few days ago, a nice little two-seater, used a'course.

Would cost us twenty-five dollars, though Ole says he bets he could get it for a bit less. Do you think we should get it?"

"Well . . . sure," said Tillie. She was smiling inwardly, trying not to let it show. She could tell that Bertha was becoming more than a little sweet on Ole.

They arranged for Ole to pick up the buggy and deliver it to the "girls." Tillie had begun to dislike it when people called her a girl, believing she was demonstrating that she was more grown up, a woman, a teacher, not a girl. She didn't like to be called a lady either. She thought the word suggested a refined woman in a fancy dress. Certainly not her with her calloused and often dirty hands and nails, hair always falling out of her bun, and plain skirt and blouse.

Harvest Celebration

As the August heat waned, prairie grasses dulled and heads of swollen wheat kernels dried and bounced, flowed, and dipped in the wind. Harvest time came, when the community collaborated in full measure. The men formed two teams for reaping. They used the reaper jointly owned by Hans and Henry along with the one that Knut Aakre purchased just that summer. The women worked together for stacking and shocking and, especially, the provision of food for the harvest crew. This year, without grain to harvest, Tillie and Bertha contributed primarily by making brown cheese and dried beef sandwiches, cookies, and cakes. Sometimes they brought out baked potatoes, along with butter. When the men worked close by, Tillie and Bertha brought the crew hot coffee for morning break, noon luncheon, and an afternoon little lunch.

After the wheat dried sufficiently, the men used Nels Iverson's threshing machine to thresh all of the golden grain, with the women and children providing sustenance and assistance. After it was fired with coal, that machine frightened cows and pigs and likely any of the wild animals as it belched and screeched and hissed the day long, the sounds echoing throughout the community.

Then came time for the harvest celebration.

Tillie and Bertha busied themselves preparing dishes for the gathering. The men had decided to hold the get-together on the site where they'd agreed they would build a little church the following year, on Orlo Larson's land. It was just over half a mile from Tillie's and Bertha's shacks, an easy walk in nice weather.

The two new homesteaders had more time available to cook and bake than the married women who often worked alongside their husbands to get the harvest in, as well as to prepare food for the harvest crew. So Tillie decided she and Bertha should provide deliciousness to the celebration.

Since they had too much to carry for a walk, Bertha harnessed Sam and she and Tillie loaded the newly purchased buggy with oatmeal bread, pies, a gingerbread cake, and ginger snaps, along with sage-grouse hash, which they wrapped in towels to keep warm. "We can show off our new buggy," Bertha said. Though she didn't say so out loud, Tillie wanted to do just that, so proud to be demonstrating she and Bertha could manage homestead life.

As Tillie and Bertha arrived, they saw that many neighbors had already gathered. Hans and Henry, with Helen and Belle, were there. So were Helga and Nels, along with Millie and Herman, and Winnie and Willie. Anna and Olga walked in shortly after Tillie and Bertha, each carrying a dish to share. Girls were jumping rope. Some of the boys and men were playing mumblety-peg, throwing a pocketknife and trying to have it stick into the ground near their feet.

A new couple, Luther and Tina Dahl, joined the gathering, followed by the new bachelor, Ernest Saue, whom the women had not met but had heard about. The Dahls came from Iowa and Ernest had just come from between Hancock and Morris, Minnesota, not so far from Tillie's and Bertha's homes. Everyone greeted the newcomers warmly, happy for additions to the community. Tillie smiled warmly at Ernest, who introduced himself as Ernie. "What a welcome sight to see someone from near home," said Tillie, noticing he looked smart, dressed in clean, dark pants into which he'd neatly tucked his almost-white shirt. "Bertha and I came from near Watson just this past spring."

"Well, I'll be," he said. "I'd heard that a couple of girls had set out for Dakota last spring. Never expected them to make it, much less meet them, but here you are and lookin' good, I'd say." At that, a sheepish grin crossed his face that displayed full cheeks, a wide nose, and warm chocolate eyes with some fullness beneath them so they narrowed when he smiled.

"Well, we can catch up on some news from home after I get things going with the grub," said Tillie. "Can't keep hungry folk waitin'."

As Bertha was arranging a table with pies, she heard the familiar "Hallo."

Turning around, she saw Ole beaming at her. "Looks like you done made some darn good pie."

"Well, these aren't all mine, a'course. I made the gooseberry and the custard." She smiled demurely. "You be sure and get a piece, Ole," she said.

"Custard's my favorite. I'll be first in line if I can help it."

"Well, I better get the pie cut," said Bertha, turning toward the table. "See you later."

"Sure 'nuf."

As Tillie helped set out food, she talked to Anna, who was complaining about men as usual. "Men! Think they work so damn hard on harvest. Never even recognize what all the womenfolk do. Don't even have our own wheat yet, just the flax, but Olga and I worked right along with the men, stackin' straw and such. Brought out dinners and lunches for da men, then spent evenings cookin' and bakin' some more. Course you know 'bout that."

"So true, so true," Tillie said politely, then excused herself. She arranged dishes on one of the other tables. It was then that she saw Ellen and Frank coming, along with their three children. She looked up and called a greeting to them, "Hello! Welcome. So very good to see you, Frank and Ellen, and I can already see that your children are growing. Shooting up, as they say."

"Oh yeah," said Ellen. "Grow up so fast, and course Sven helps with the chores and Brunhild is learning to get in the eggs and weed the garden."

"Of course, good to see them growing up, and proud you might be," said Tillie. "I hope to have children someday myself, but that will be a while off."

Frank gave the kind of lecherous smirk that suggested to Tillie he thought making babies was all women were good for, but she smiled demurely at him. "Marriage and children will need to wait while I prove up on my claim," she added, looking directly at him.

Frank looked away, though his eyes narrowed and he didn't erase the smirk.

"Well, I'll talk with you folks more once I get the food set out," said Tillie.

The older children got a baseball game going while the younger ones played tag. Tillie remembered that just a few months ago, she knew none of them, and now . . . well, she knew most of them at least a little, except for Sven, who always seemed so solemn, rarely making eye contact with anyone. While watching the game, she yelled particularly loudly when Sven hit a home run. "Great going, Sven, great going!" She hoped to find a few minutes to talk to him later and encourage him to come to school.

Everyone gathered around the tables when Orlo called *vaer sá god*. He said a short prayer: "Thanks be to you, God our father, for the land so ripe for planting your seeds and harvesting your grain.

Thank you for this gathering and this food. We'll soon be putting up a church to worship you in. Amen."

"Amen," said most of those gathered.

Everyone filled their plates, heaping big mounds of stew, ladles of hot dish, along with bread and plenty of butter and jam. Some had seconds, followed by pie and cookies or bars, with most of the men and older children and even some of the women gobbling the desserts as if they hadn't already eaten a big meal. Occasional burps could be heard. Most parents reminded their young ones to say, "Excuse me please," which often came out simply as "S'cuse."

While the women were cleaning up, Tillie sidled in next to Ellen. "I haven't yet had a chance to talk to Sven, but I'm sure hoping he's planning to come to school."

"Well, I'm not sure," said Ellen softly. She was thin and perhaps just taller than Tillie, but she stood with her shoulders hunched forward rather than holding herself erect, so she didn't appear tall.

"Well, I'd be delighted to have him in my class and, of course, I'd understand when he might need to help with chores, so please let him know I'd so welcome having him."

As Ellen leaned over to scrape off a dish into the bowl for dogs, Tillie thought she saw a purple bruise on her chest. She couldn't be sure and didn't know if she should ask Ellen if she had hurt herself. She decided to say nothing, but did comment about the bulge that was beginning to show somewhat lower. "I think I see you might have another child coming along. Am I right?"

"Ummhmm," said Ellen, not meeting Tillie's eyes.

"Well, how wonderful, a new baby will be coming to the community."

"Ummhmm. I don't know, though, it's sure hard enough to manage three children, without another mouth to feed."

"Of course, of course. I can't imagine how it would be. But please let me help in any way I can. I love children and also know it's easier to, um, accommodate them, when they go home to someone else at night. I've not had any practice with any of my own like you have, of course, but I'll be happy to help."

"Sure, and t'ank you."

A little later, Tillie noticed that Frank's words were rather slow, his gait awkward. Something seemed amiss with the family. She also wondered about the practice of drinking, especially becoming near-drunk, on ground that was to become a church. It seemed a desecration, but she kept her judgment to herself.

Then it was time for square-dancing to start. Knut took up his accordion and Hans his harmonica, the music and camaraderie creating an oasis of glee on the stark prairie. Willie did the calling. Soon the skirts started twirling and legs started bouncing. As partners passed from one to the other, Bertha danced with Ole, then was off to another partner.

When square-dancing stopped, Hans and Knut started playing slower tunes and married couples found themselves in each other's arms, doing two-steps and waltzes. Ole approached Bertha. "You might dance?" he asked.

Smiling, Bertha said, "Yes, of course." When they began dancing, he leaned toward her and, as she leaned in to him, his left arm encircled her and pulled her to him. It was the first time since Lars that she'd been held tightly by a man, and a wide grin emerged on her face.

Halvor was dancing with Olga, leaving Tillie and Anna along with Ernest.

"I don't dance so good," said Ernest to Tillie, "but if you'll not mind if I step on toes a time or two, I'll swing you 'round."

"Why not? I don't dance so well myself."

Tillie enjoyed the dancing and heard a bit of news from near home. Her family had brought their wheat to be milled at the Morris City Mills, so Tillie had occasionally visited the city. Ernie told about a new steel bridge that had just been built across the Pomme de Terre River and a new brick high school had been built just a year or two back.

"So good it is to hear about happenings from home, Ernest. One gets quite ravenous for such news out here."

"For sure. Already I'm starved for such news. But call me Ernie. And, do tell, how did you two girls happen to come to this place?"

"Well, we were both teachers. Life was good, but I guess both of us hungered for some adventure. I'd always dreamed of coming to the West. It was a sort of a beckoning that tugged at me from time to time, almost like the land itself was calling. Bertha and I started dreaming, then started planning, took the train, and here we are." She smiled at him, hesitated a moment, then went on. "I miss my mama and papa especially. My brother too. But the community here is so helpful and, I don't know, there's something about doing all my own work—laboring until I can barely walk back to the shack—that satisfies me. The solitude too, the times when I'm alone with the grass and the creatures and a cloudless sky . . . I feel full."

Ernie gazed at her with a slight smile. "Like you, I come from a farming family. Left my mother and father and two brothers to come west for some of that fullness you talk about. Older sis died in childbirth not long ago, leaving a baby that her man and my folks care for. Made things a little glum, though the little guy brought some cheer. Didn't want to take over the home place. Can't even tell you why. Don't mind hard work and guess the adventure of homesteading tugged at me. Seemed like I'd always dreamed of comin' west."

"Like me. I dreamed of comin' in a wagon, but came by train." She smiled at him and his grin grew wide. "Hope to hear more of your story another time." With a nod, Tillie moved on.

As the evening drew to a close, the women gathered their dishes while the men hauled away the makeshift tables. Bertha and Tillie again attached the buggy to Sam and drove away, waving fond farewells.

On the way home, Tillie said, "I t'ink you're a bit sweet on Ole and he sure is on you."

"Oh. . . " Bertha shook her head. "Don't know 'bout dat."

"I haven't heard you talk like that since we went to normal school, where they drilled it out of us."

"Oh, I know, but I don't like to embarrass him, so I try to sound a bit like he does, I guess. And then I forget myself."

"Anyway, it sure was fun. Lots of good eats too. Kind of reminded me of home. Ernest—he tells me to call him Ernie— seems like a nice man, but I felt sorry for Anna when he asked me to dance, left her all alone."

"Well, I kind of think Anna doesn't have too much interest in men. She's probably made that pretty clear. I like her forthrightness, though."

"Me too," said Tillie.

"I heard some wondering about whether Anna and Olga are really sisters, so unlike they are in looks," said Bertha.

"Oh, people talk a lot. Somehow can't get away from a little gossip."

Sam trotted on and the women savored the last moments of light on the wide plain, the grasses moving gently in the breeze, the nearly full moon rising in the east, the air light and still warm from the glow of the sun that set not much earlier.

"We've been lucky," said Bertha as the women neared home. "No prairie fires so far. Course it's usually late fall or early spring when fire strikes. Ole said the average rainfall here is fourteen or fifteen inches, 'bout half of what it was back home, y'know. Good for fires. Good he plowed the firebreaks."

"Let's hope for some rain before fall turns to winter, but as you said, we've been lucky. First summer out here has been even better than I hoped," Tillie responded, smiling to herself at the frequency with which Bertha mentioned Ole. "Getting to know neighbors, feeling a part of the community. Yet we've done so much with our own hands. Think it built character, as John the locator predicted."

"Hope so. May need a lot of character to get through the winter."

Bertha secured Sam in his pasture, and while they walked back to their shacks, Tillie said rather quietly, "I thought I might have seen a bruise on Ellen's chest. Didn't say anything to her about it. Probably just injured herself somehow, but Frank seems to drink more than the other men. Kind of made me wonder. Oh, and then I noticed she's in a family way. Didn't seem too thrilled about it. I wonder what women do when their time comes."

"There's not a doctor except for Doc Henry in Bowbells and people say he's rather rough and without much care—well that's what I heard from Ole—but Winnie's good to help. Better'n a doctor, as they say. Especially for women things."

Schooling in Shacks

Both teachers set up their shacks to accommodate the school-aged children. The mothers of the younger children made rag rugs for students to sit upon, so each morning each pupil would find his or her rug. At the end of the day, they would pile the rugs in a corner. A couple of the fathers made benches for the older students, there being no room for desks.

Tillie's family sent McGuffey Readers. Slates and chalk for students' use came to the post office from the Department of Public Instruction. Tillie, with Bertha's help, constructed two blackboards of sorts, using large pieces of lumber, each about two-by-three feet, which they painted with egg white and then heavily sprinkled with ash from charred potato skins.

When most of the families had completed the bulk of their fall work, school began on Monday, September 24. The children in Tillie's class arrived, four walking. Only Erik rode his horse, carrying his younger brother Lars, who would attend Bertha's class. Since no real school bell was available, Tillie used a handheld bell, which one of the mothers donated, to call school to order. After a warm welcome and a Bible verse reading, she led her students in singing the first verse of "Columbia, the Gem of the Ocean," which Erik and Elizabeth seemed to know in part. Then, even though she could easily see who was there, she called out attendance, noting that Sven was not there. But she had five students, plenty for her little shack, with Susan and Elizabeth looking especially bright and eager and Peter remaining quiet. He didn't seem agitated, just distant, like he'd rather be helping with chores or doing something with the men.

In her own shack, Bertha excitedly faced her seven students. The day started with a Bible verse she had chosen, a short one from Matthew: "*You are the light of the world.*"

She explained that Jesus was telling them to let their talents and abilities shine in the world and that education would help them do that. Then she led the students in singing "My Country 'Tis of Thee," which none of the pupils knew well, but would learn in time.

Tillie would teach the students in her class reading and spelling, grammar, penmanship, declamation, arithmetic, and geography. She would also lead them in song and music lessons. Bertha would try to teach her students reading, spelling, grammar, and arithmetic. She hoped that learning a song, such as "Rally 'Round the Flag," would add to the students' knowledge and patriotism. Recess would give them time to use their energy and learn new games such as Ring around the Rosie and Come with Me, and perhaps Button, Button and Musical Chairs in inclement weather.

The teachers got together at Tillie's for a simple meal of boiled potatoes and salt pork after the first day of school. "I can't believe that most of the children don't even know any Bible verses," said Bertha. "You'd think they'd at least know 'The Lord Is My Shepherd.'"

"Don't be too hard on them, Bertha. Most of these families are just trying to survive out here, let alone teach the Bible to their children. We'll take what we get and try to teach them a few manners at least. Most of my students didn't know 'Columbia, the Gem of the Ocean,' but they've had little schooling."

A moment later she added, "I missed Sven, who I hoped would come, and Peter acted like he'd rather be cutting hay, but the day went pretty well. Feels good to be doing something that used to be routine, even though I feel more exhausted than I remember feeling after a day of teaching at home."

Bertha exclaimed, "I feel more tired than after a day spent in hard labor! Must be because I worry that I'm not teaching the right sort of things out here." She headed home to the haystack early.

As evening darkened, Tillie's thoughts darkened too. *What am I doing out here? Can this be the work I'm called upon to do?* She didn't let her doubts enter during the day, but night was different. Coyotes wailed and the wind blew, rattling her shack. Winter was coming. She wondered how she would manage the solitude on those dark, cold nights and how she would fare trying to keep the shack warm enough not only for her students, but for her own sake. She wondered if her own values were pertinent to her students, since it was likely most of what they remembered of their lives was in this community, a place where survival was much more important than good manners.

The next morning Bertha frowned as she voiced her own doubts to Tillie. "How will I ever teach these children, who need practical skills more than Bible readings, when I don't even know if I can survive the coming winter? I feel less confident today than I did yesterday."

"Well, we just have to do what we can to teach whatever might help them manage their lives, hoping we teach ourselves in the process."

Still, each class started with a patriotic song and a short Bible verse.

———

On Saturday, after that first week of school, Tillie mounted Sam, clucked to him, and rode to the home of Ellen and Frank, and of Sven, Brunhild, and Karl.

"Oh," said Ellen upon seeing Tillie. "Not often we get someone at the door." Then she displayed a slight smile. "Frank's gone just now. Want to come in to our very humble shack?" she asked while her smile disappeared.

"I'd love to," Tillie said upon entering. "All of us struggle to make our shacks our homes, don't we?" She took off her coat and hung it over some others on the peg by the door. "So good to see you, Ellen. I miss the companionship of women and of men, too, of course." She hadn't meant to say that last part and she blushed just a bit.

"Please sit down," Ellen said, rubbing her hands on her apron. "I'll boil up some coffee."

"Oh, you needn't bother. I'll just stay a few minutes. I see you're busy cooking or baking something." Tillie noticed Ellen's red eyes, but said nothing.

"Gettin' ready to bake up some bread. Had to use up the compressed yeast I bought 'fore it went bad. Used a piece to get my own started again. Sorry it's so hot in here. Just started the stove. Almost hate to use it when it's warm out. That's why Frank's gone, I guess." She formed the bread into three loaves for the second rising.

"We made our own yeast back home, but it seems more trouble than I've had time for this summer."

"Always busy out here. First year's the worst." Ellen wiped her hands on her apron again. "Brunhild is so enjoying Miss Harstad's teaching. Looks forward to going to school every day." She sat down and motioned for Tillie to do the same.

Tillie sat down. "Bertha—well, Miss Harstad—is a good teacher and so kind with the children. She so enjoys having Brunhild in class. That's part of why I'm here, school that is. I was so looking forward to Sven being in my class. Is he too busy with chores still?"

"Oh, yeah, he has chores." Ellen looked down at the table where the two women sat. "Course I'd like him to get some schooling but Frank, he don't t'ink dat's so important."

"I see. Well, perhaps I can talk to Frank sometime and see if there's anything I can do to help."

"Oh, I don't t'ink dat would be of much help, though I t'ank you for the offer. Frank, he's pretty set in his ways, you know, like all men are . . . I guess." Again, she looked at the table.

It was the *I guess* that made Tillie wonder. "Well, yes, men can be rather bullheaded sometimes, of course. Still, perhaps he might listen to my thoughts about why reading and arithmetic can help even in farming chores. Of course, I know the practical things that men do are so very important to learn, especially here in Dakota, and I'm sure Sven is learning them from Frank, but still . . ."

Ellen was frowning just a bit and Tillie didn't know what else to say. "Well, you'll tell Sven and Frank that I sure would like to have Sven in my class, won't you?"

"Oh, of course," she said, nodding her head slightly.

"And how are you doing out here with the three children, another one on the way, and the family to feed all the time and winter just around the corner? I see you've put up lots of preserves. Course you've survived a couple winters here already, something I don't quite know how I'll manage. I'm sure you could teach me a thing or two, or a lot more."

"Oh, I don't t'ink I could teach you nutin'. Ya just hang on and hope for the best, y'know."

"Well, sometime when you have a little extra time, if that ever happens, please come call on me, with the children of course, and we can talk a bit more. I'd love to hear your stories of winter and how you manage with the children and all. I have no idea what it would take to have children out here. You're a very brave woman."

"Oh, not so very brave," Ellen muttered, shaking her head, again avoiding Tillie's eyes.

"Well, please just say the word and I'll come and help with the children or anything else." Not wanting to intrude any longer and make a pest of herself, and not really having more she could think of to say, Tillie added, "Must be getting along, still have some carrots that need digging." She took her coat from the peg and nodded to Ellen with a smile. "Thank you for inviting me in, and listening to me."

Ellen nodded her head a couple of times.

The following Monday, Tillie was quiet as she placed bread on the table, along with milk gravy to ladle on bread for supper. She wondered how to share her concern for Ellen with Bertha. She looked at Bertha, who sat with her chin resting on her hand while she looked out the window.

After sitting down, saying grace, and beginning to eat, Tillie said, "I was wondering how Brunhild is doing in your class."

"Oh, she has such a bright face when she comes to school. She does her best. I'm not sure just how bright she is, though, and she seems so anxious to please that it almost frightens me. She's always apologizing for one thing or another."

"Hmmm . . . I sensed something not quite right again when I visited Ellen. Like she's . . . I don't know . . . almost scared of Frank or something. Thought she might have been crying 'fore I came. And, like I said, I thought I saw a bruise on her chest at the harvest gathering when she bent over. Maybe was just a shadow.

Perhaps when you see her at church or some place, you'll tell her how polite and well behaved her girl is. Seems like she could use encouragement."

"I'll do that, and I'll give a little extra attention to little Brunhild, such a dear." A short time later, she added, "Sometimes I feel inept as a teacher out here. Doesn't seem it should be so hard to put some learning into just a few young minds, but it's not so easy. Book learning's important, I know, but I also know that these children need a lot of practical learning I can't give them.

"I'm trying to adjust, too, and it does seem harder. Keep trying to figure out what's important to teach and what's not. At home, I just followed the basic things we were taught to cover. Here? I keep trying to think of ways to make the book learning relate to skills they'll need out here, but I hardly know what those skills might be."

"Well, I suppose readin', writin', and arithmetic will stand them in as good stead out here as at home.

"Got some spelling tests to correct, so let's get the dishes done up and I'll go back to my place, correct the tests, get ready for tomorrow's lessons, and get to bed early."

Columbus Day arrived on a sunny, but cool and blustery, day. The two teachers gathered their students together out of doors. They had arranged for the Department of Public Instruction to send a United States flag with its forty-five stars, which they hoisted with a rope pulley on a tall pole Ernie had provided. Tillie pointed out that North Dakota was the thirty-ninth state added to the Union, so was the thirty-ninth star. The teachers taught the students the Pledge of Allegiance, which was only several years old. Then they told the students to salute the flag and recite the pledge with them:

I pledge allegiance to my Flag and the Republic for which it stands, one nation, indivisible, with liberty and justice for all.

Snowstorm

The first blizzard came in late November. A couple of times earlier, snow had fallen gently like cottonwood seed, but this storm came in earnest. Skies darkened as if the sun were dying. Light snow began falling fast.

School was in session. Bertha came running to Tillie's in the late morning. Together they decided to send the students home immediately, warning them to go straight there and not come back to school until the wind and snow stopped and it was safe.

Just before the students left, Knut Aakre and Henry Berge rode up on their horses. Tillie hiked Peter onto Knut's horse and Elizabeth climbed up behind him. Henry pulled little Hildegaard up onto his horse and off they rode, her pigtails flying. The two families lived farthest from the B&T Estate, more than a mile, while the other children lived closer. Tillie made sure the children in the same families or those who lived in the same direction were together and sent them off. "Now skedaddle! Do not dawdle," she yelled, even louder than when using her teacher voice.

After the children left, Tillie scurried to get potatoes, carrots, and onions from the cellar while Bertha secured Sam in the lean-to away from the northwest wind that was starting to howl like a coyote. Each woman gathered coal and brought it inside. The little lake was frozen over, so snow was the only water source. Tillie and Bertha each scraped some of the little snow that lay on the ground into their buckets and brought them inside.

By midafternoon, heavy snow blanketed the land and piled on roofs. The fierce wind whipped the new snow, creating a veil of white. Tillie opened Bertha's door. "You best come over to my place. We don't want to ride out this storm alone."

"I'll get my quilt, add some coal, stoke the fire, and be there shortly."

Tillie retrieved the scoop shovel from the coal shed and brought it inside, fearing it might get lost in the snow and expecting to need it once the blizzard subsided.

"Well, let's bake us up some bread," said Tillie after they were settled. "Might as well have something to do while the storm roars."

Dinner that evening was bean soup and freshly baked brown bread. "Dear Lord," said Bertha, "do keep us safe in this storm and I hope you've watched over all the children, making sure they got home safely and their families are safe. And thank you for this warmth and soup and bread that you have provided. Amen."

"And thank you, Lord, for our neighbors. Knowing they are close by gives me courage," added Tillie.

As evening progressed, the wind grew stronger, battering the shack like a sledgehammer so that at times Tillie and Bertha had to shout to hear each other. "I surely hope all the children made it home. No one could survive out there now," Bertha yelled.

"I'm sure they did," Tillie shouted back, although she fretted about them in her own mind.

"I keep thinking about all the creatures and wonder how they manage such a storm."

"I suppose some don't," replied Tillie pensively.

Before they snuggled under the quilts leaving most of their clothing on, Tillie added more coal to the stove, then closed the damper most of the way. Looking outside, she could see nothing as snow pummeled the window.

Warm and cozy, Tillie snuggled against the warm being next to her. She felt protected by the heat emanating from the other body. Cuddled and comfortable, she slept on. Gently stirring, she slowly became aware of the aroma around her, dank and musky. Unusual. Something moved very gently next to her, against her back. A deep breath? Warmth emanated from the breath, the body next to her, the arm surrounding her. As she became more aware, she realized the arm holding her was not covered with skin. Slowly, her awareness grew. Dark, of course. So dank. Something heavy covered her chest. She moved her hand to feel it. Fur. It was warm and cozy. She fell back asleep.

Awakening, she felt chilled. She arose and stoked the fire, then added more coal, inhaling its acrid odor as she did. Gradually, she remembered her dream. *How strange. I felt such comfort from a bear. Perhaps with Bertha here I just felt less alone than usual.* She returned to bed, pulled the quilt almost over her head and tucked it all around her. Soon she slumbered again.

Long before the light of morning, the two women stirred. Getting out from her quilt, Bertha exclaimed, "My, it's cold!" She lit the kerosene lantern. Crystals of snow covered the blue walls, giving off a sheen in the light of the lantern. "My goodness, we'll need to brush snow off the walls!" Snow or frost even lay thinly on top of the quilt. "The shack doesn't keep *all* the snow out," she added, "but I can't remember being quite so grateful for shelter."

Tillie relit the fire in the stove. "Uff da. I think we'll need all of the coal and those cow chips as well before this winter is over."

"That's what Ole said, sure 'nuf." She began sweeping snow crystals off the blue walls.

With the fire blazing, Tillie moved a rug and opened the trap-door in her floor where she stored a wooden box. She retrieved eggs she'd covered in salt, eggs still left from fall when neighbors' chickens had been prolific in their offerings. She scrambled them and put bread in the oven to warm.

The hot eggs and warm bread, along with steamy black coffee, warmed their innards while the stove's radiance brought color to their skin and lubricated their joints. The blackness that had covered the window began to diminish, but snow kept out most of the light. Crystals covered the sill a quarter-inch deep in places. The wind still blew, but with less ferocity than during the night. "Do you suppose there's a drift high enough to cover the window?" asked Bertha.

"We'll know as soon as we try to open the door," laughed Tillie. "Best get out there to water Sam and see he has some hay. We'll be able to write home about our first real snowstorm on the Dakota prairie."

"At least we can say we survived. At least I think we'll be able to say so."

Breakfast over, the last drop of coffee gone, the women laced up their boots and donned their coats, hats, and woolen mittens. Tillie tried to open the door. It didn't budge. "I think the door is frozen shut. As strong as I've become, I can't open it. Get a knife and run it through the crack while I pull."

Bertha used the knife and Tillie pulled on the knob. When the door finally gave way, snow tumbled into the shack revealing a flat plain with snow swirling and twirling and whirling on the white landscape. Tillie grabbed her shovel and Bertha followed her into the snow. "Don't you go farther than where you can see me and the shack," admonished Tillie.

"Yeah, yeah, Miss Melbakken."

Tillie dug through the snow to get another bucket of coal and to check on Sam, who stood motionless. After seeing his eyelids almost frosted shut, she rubbed his mane, tenderly brushed the snow away from his eyes and nose, pulled off her mitten and held her hand by his eyes to warm them. She hugged him tightly, perhaps to feel the companionship of another creature on this sea of snow. She went inside, fetched some water, and found oats for his treat after managing the storm.

The sun filtered hazily through swirls of snow. "Have you ever seen anything quite this pristine and beautiful?" ventured Bertha, gazing out across the plain stretching forever toward the horizon. No animal tracks yet marked a trail in the ocean of white. Bertha's shack was just visible, almost appearing to be an apparition. Bertha stood motionless, simply gazing into the landscape.

Tillie looked up from her shoveling and noticed Bertha staring into forever and decided to let her stare. The scene was beautiful, though frightening. Exciting in a way that mingled thrill with fear. Awesome and intimidating. She returned to her shoveling and freed the door so it could fully open.

When Bertha stopping staring, she trekked back to Tillie. "Don't think I better venture to my shack yet, but I worry about my canned produce freezing. Fire must be out over there. Don't see smoke rising."

"Yeah. We best get back to my shack. I'll share my canned goods with you if needed."

Both women spent several hours in the shack, first wiping up the dampness from the crystals that had melted off the walls and other surfaces, then preparing a light lunch, and finally preparing lessons for school when it would resume. Tillie stoked the fire periodically.

By midafternoon, the sun shone, spreading shimmering sparkles across the snow. Only a light breeze blew. Nonetheless, snow kept dancing and swirling like a dervish across the white prairie.

Bertha said she'd been worrying about her canning all afternoon, so before dusk darkened the landscape, the women made a path to Bertha's and freed her door. Her shack was cold, but nothing seemed frozen, not frozen solid anyway. Bertha kept her coat on until her fire roared.

Tillie again dug out an area in front of the lean-to and caressed Sam, who still stood unmoving, eyelids again crusted with snow. She warmed the frost away with her open hands, feeling thankful for having Sam, thankful for his strength and endurance, his ability to trudge through snow when she could not. "I'm sorry we didn't have a better place to protect you, Sam. Next year we will," she promised. She brought hay and more oats for him to munch, gave him fresh water from melted snow, and again hugged him tightly. She felt grateful for his warmth, which she sensed even through her thick coat.

———————

The storm had not been as severe as many others on the prairie, not nearly as intense as one that would strike in February, but the snow limited gatherings. Rarely did anyone venture out at night. School resumed three days after the storm. Practicing for the Christmas play and sing-along took precedence over other lessons.

Bertha and Tillie spent time together in one of their shacks after school to support each other's teaching efforts and talk about the students while they prepared an evening meal. "Little Gunner's a smart little thing, already knowing all of his letters and numbers. Then there's his brother, Nels. Struggles so to learn the alphabet, never able to tell *b* from *d* or *h* from *n*."

Tillie nodded. "Most of these children don't get so much encouragement from home, so we need lots of patience, I reckon."

"Little Brunhild is coming along pretty well with her learning. She concentrates hard and tries to learn her letters and all. Seems so afraid of making mistakes, though, as if she will be punished. She works hard, but seems fragile, like a porcelain doll."

"I keep thinking about her mother. She hasn't come to Orlo's for a bit of church just lately. Keep wondering how she's doing with the baby coming soon. Does Brunhild say anything?"

Bertha shook her head. "Not a word."

After dinner, each woman retreated to her own shack most nights, though when the temperature plummeted and the wind blew especially hard, they stayed together for the warmth and company. Bedtime was always early, since the candle stock was diminishing and kerosene was in short supply.

In the fall, the community women had gathered at Henry and Belle's after butchering the steers. They melted down fat from the beef, then boiled it to make tallow, which hardened on top of the water as it cooled. Helen brought a deep pot for this. Using string, they dipped one end and then the other in the tallow and continued to dip as the tallow cooled on the string, making two taper candles, each nearly an inch thick and about seven inches long.

Although Bertha and Tillie had purchased string for the group, they didn't take many candles at the end of the day since they hadn't had anything to do with feeding the cattle or butchering them. But the candle-making day had been another good one for the women of the plain, passing stories along, sharing recipes, complaining about the men. Hans's wife, though, never complained; nor did Ellen say much about Frank, whether from lack of complaint or from fear, Tillie wasn't sure. She suggested to

Bertha that maybe Ellen thought she'd said too much when she'd mentioned Frank's rough discipline of the children after he had too much to drink.

Since that day, each time Tillie lit one of those candles, she remembered the warm companionship of the neighboring women with deep fondness.

Christmas, 1900

It was nearly Christmas when Bertha saw Orlo riding up on his horse and went out to greet him. He handed her a letter that he'd picked up at the general store. She looked at the envelope and her eyes widened while a smile spread across her face. She hadn't received a letter from Lars since she'd come to Dakota. Now, here it was. She wanted to rip it open right in front of Orlo and bathe in Lars's words. Instead, with a thin smile she asked, "Do you want to come in to warm up over a cup of coffee and a tiny bit of lunch?"

"I could use some warming up," he admitted.

When Bertha opened the door to the shack, she noticed that she'd hung her undergarments on a line by the stove. She averted her eyes. "Sit down there at the table," she said, and motioned to the side facing away from the stove. She put coffee on to boil and sat down at the table. "How's your family back home? Did you get a letter too?"

"Naw. Haven't heard just recently. Likely means things are okay."

"No news, generally good news," she responded. "Pick up any news at the general store?"

"Eleanor, she say Doc was called over to the Swedes. Man got blood poisoning from accidentally shootin' himself in the leg."

"Too bad. Probably not too much Doc can do."

"Give him laudanum, I guess. Let him die in as much peace as can be found. Hope he's got some religion."

"Sure, sure, likely have some kind of a minister over there. Do you know?"

"Never heard."

Orlo was soft-spoken. He had an angular face and only rarely did the corners of his mouth turn upward. He didn't have an angry look—more a pensive one. He was a man of few words and many silent moments passed as the two sipped coffee and ate rusks sprinkled with sugar and cinnamon. Bertha's foot gently tapped under the table. "What brought you out here to Dakota?" she ventured.

"Just thought I'd make a new start," he said, "after I left seminary."

"Was there any particular reason you left?"

He sighed. A long awkward pause ensued as Orlo nodded his head while looking into the room, not at Bertha. "I guess I didn't have enough words in me," he said finally. "They thought I'd make a poor preacher. Were probably right."

"Well, we're happy to have you here and you do right well filling in as our preacher."

"Well, maybe . . ."

Bertha asked how he'd managed his first winter. "Well," he said, "most of it went okay, but I had me just one Jersey cow and I'd thrown up a poor shed for her before the snows came. When a blizzard hit, late January I think it was, couldn't even get outta the shack for over a day. Found the Jersey bawlin' and brimmin' with milk standing in a foot of snow. The roof of the shed had collapsed. Lucky didn't kill her, I guess."

They each sipped coffee quietly. Bertha glanced at the letter sitting on the table. "Yeah," Orlo said, "I better be gettin' along." With that, he stood and thanked her for the coffee.

"Well, thank you for bringing the letter and for the company," she said graciously.

As soon as he'd closed the door, Bertha tore open the envelope, finding a short single page.

Dear Bertha,

I struggle on in the heat of the Philippines, where I've been assigned to protect our country's interest since the war is over and we have possession of the islands. Imagine you're out on the plains of Dakota. I hope to be relieved of duty soon. I received your letter. Nice to hear from someone from home. I'm doing fine, though of course the conditions here are awful and I miss home. They tell me it takes nearly a month to get a letter there, more sometimes, so maybe this will reach you by Christmas or the New Year. 1901. Just think of it.

Best regards,
Lars

She sat down at the table, sat there looking at the letter, the words like one might write to a mother or sister—or even simply an acquaintance. She had confided to Tillie not long ago that perhaps Lars did miss her, probably was just in a place where he couldn't send a letter. The letter made it clear to her that her hope had been for naught.

She sat there, staring at nothing, while the shadows her lantern created hanging in the sunlit window moved along the wall; then she got up, paced, paced more, back and forth across the small room.

After a time, she went over to Tillie's. "Well, I heard from Lars; his letter's about as romantic as some cow dung." She burst into tears.

"Oh my, oh my, Bertha. There, there. Men can be so unfeeling. Maybe he just doesn't know how to tell you he cares."

"Oh, I doubt that!" she said after a sob subsided. "I think I've known it was over, just was hoping it wasn't. When I saw Lars's handwriting, I could barely manage to sit pleasantly with Orlo, wanting so to look at the letter . . . Orlo's such a nice man, but he's hard to talk with, seems wounded or something." She wiped away the tears that kept spilling. "I don't even know how I feel or what I should feel. Could be a blessing, I suppose," she said quietly after sniffing her nose. "Maybe we just weren't right for each other and I can start to think a little more about Ole and less about him."

"I'm so sorry you're feeling hurt. Wish I could offer some comfort. I think of Jergen some, too, even though we've not even gone courting, and I imagine he doesn't think about me. It's the forlornness out here in this desolate land that makes us want some caring, some loving."

"Well, I've got to get myself together. Best go out and shovel some coal or do somethin'," Bertha said. She took her coat off the peg by the door and put it on.

"Best stay for some coffee and somethin' to eat."

"Best go out and work," said Bertha in staccato.

On Christmas Eve, just as daylight was dying, the small Norwegian community gathered at Kincaid General Store, the biggest building around with a stove. "Strange to use a store for a church," said Tillie on the way there. It was a cold four-mile ride on Willie and Winnie's sleigh, even with blankets wrapped around them. The brilliant stars speckled the heavens, some nodding on and off, others shining steadily.

Tillie and Bertha arrived to calls of "*God Jul.*" Candles, perhaps as many as thirty, cast flickering light within the warm store, creating ethereal shadowy images on the walls.

The group sang carols, prayed for a good winter without serious blizzards (which they all knew was maybe more than God would deliver), and honored the birth of the Christ child with some words from Orlo, the few words seeming to Tillie not quite enough for the occasion.

Then they drank coffee and ate *sandbakkels* and spritz cookies. Eleanor and Knut, who owned the store, had received a shipment of pickled herring just before Christmas. They opened enough packages to share some herring with all the gatherers. The robust aroma was enough to send some of them into ecstasy. "This is even better than lefse and rommegrøt," said Ole with a jolly laugh. Everyone seemed to agree as they savored the morsels of tasty fish.

"Now all we need is a little *akvavit* to go with the herring. Really remind us of home," chortled Herman.

"Don't have that, but I got me some hard cider," said Nels. Most of the men, and a few women, took a pull or two on the bottle.

After Ole had his swallows of cider, he walked over to Tillie and Bertha with a smile as big as a clown's. He winked at Bertha as he drew close. "You two might even enjoy a sip," he said.

"No t'anks. Think the bottle is about drained now, anyway," said Bertha with a grin. The three chatted amicably and wished each other a God Jul.

Neighbors shared laughter, letters from home, and of course, more God Jul wishes, then readied for the journey home. As they started out, light of a nearly full moon set in a sparkling sky bathed them with a sense of the holy.

On Christmas Day, the friends gathered at Bertha's for Christmas dinner: a roasted grouse, potatoes, carrots, lefse they had made together, and custard pie. Tillie gave Bertha an apron she had sewed, which she had embroidered with "Dakota 1900." Tillie received a flannel lap quilt from Bertha, a quilt that would feel good to snuggle in while sitting at the table correcting school papers or reading by kerosene lantern.

1901 Dawns

New Year's Eve 1900

Ole showed up at the B&T Estate midafternoon, bringing with him a bottle of cider he'd purchased at Blinker's Grocery in Bowbells in the fall. "It's gone a little hard, so it may spread a bit of *hurrorop og gaity*," he said, laughing. Bertha pounded on her window to alert Tillie. Getting no response, she leaned out her door and yelled for her.

Tillie, hearing the shouting, poked her head out the door, saw Bertha's beckoning finger, put on her coat and mittens, and hurried over to the shack where the festive camaraderie of friends warmed her even more than the cow-chip fire did. Bertha brought out flatbrød to share and took down her crystal cordial glasses brought from home. She had only three left of the four, one having broken in her trunk on the passage to Dakota.

Bertha spread the table with her best cloth and placed flatbrød and butter on it. Ole poured the cider and made the toast, "To such good and beautiful girl homesteaders, unlike any pair I could imagine out here on this blessed and forsaken prairie. Skål!"

"Skål!" responded both women, raising their glasses. "And to good friends."

"To such good friends," responded Ole, coloring just a bit as he so readily did.

The three reminisced about events and developments of the previous century. They made it a game. "Ole, you go first," said Bertha.

"The Civil War," said Ole without a moment's hesitation.

Something in the way he said it and his solemn face caused Bertha to respond, "And were some of your folks involved in the war?"

He hesitated a moment or two. "My pa. Came hobbling back from the war, never really recovered. Shot hisself, he did, just a few years later. War can do awful t'ings to a man, y'know."

"Oh, Ole, I'm so sorry," said Bertha softly, reaching out to touch his arm.

"Vell, it was years back a'course, so I don't think about it so much no more."

"But, still, what a sad thing, and how old were you, den?"

"Oh, I was just a babe in Ma's arms when he went. Don't think I'd recognize him if he could walk right up to me. It was mostly Ma's sadness that made things so gloomy, y'know, so I tried to cheer her best I could."

"I'm sure you did."

"Vell, your turn now," said Ole, putting a fake smile on his face.

"Well, the steam locomotive was developed and the transcontinental railroad was completed. Then Tillie and I got here because the Soo Line put in tracks all the way to Portal," declared Bertha with a grin.

"Here, here! And skål to that," said Ole with a twinkle back in his eyes, and they each raised their glasses and took another swallow.

"The telegraph," said Tillie. "That added to our willingness to dare this adventure."

"Don't think I would have dared leave Minnesota if I hadn't known I could get in touch with folks back home," said Bertha. "And now it's your turn again, Ole."

"Vell, that guy Benz overseas made somethin' called a motor buggy or somethin'. Runs itself, don't burn coal for steam, don't need no horses."

"And the typewriter," said Tillie.

"The sewing machine."

"Vell, I don't know so much as you ladies. But how about the t'reshing machine run by steam, not horses. Darn good to get rid of some of the grueling work of t'reshing."

"Yes, yes of course," said Bertha.

"I've heard of something called a gramophone for listening to music or a sermon after it was said," declared Tillie.

"And there's some sort of a piano that plays itself," put in Bertha.

"The hay mower," said Ole. "Got to get me one soon, maybe this comin' summer. With cows gettin' ready to calve toward spring, gonna get to be too much work to cut hay by hand, and then I can help you girls out with the hayin'."

"That'd sure be nice, Ole," said Tillie. "And now, let's see. There's that newfangled thing called . . . umm . . . the telephone, I think, with wires strung in Minneapolis so people not even in the same house can hear each other talk. Putting them in even some smaller towns now, I heard," said Tillie.

"Heard 'bout that just before I left home," said Ole. "Heard the first one used old sewing machine parts to connect the wires to the different places."

"Really?" asked Bertha.

"It's what was said. But I suppose it's my turn. Well, that Edison guy made a light that glows from wires or somethin'."

"Imagine that. Well, let me think," said Bertha. "How about the friction match?"

"That's been a big help with cooking, for sure," replied Tillie. "Though I heard or read that something in it causes problems for people who make the matches or if a child eats off the end. England uses something different in them now, I think."

"White phosphorus, I t'ink," said Ole. "That's the bad stuff. Causes jaw problems and sometimes worse. Yet would hate to be without 'em."

"Get used to newfangled things, then can't seem to live without them," laughed Bertha. "And you sure know a lot about things."

With that, they turned their thoughts to the future, with the new year coming in just a few hours. Their imaginations saw electric lamps even out in Dakota and steam-driven machines that could plant wheat.

"Might even be a flying machine with wings like birds," said Bertha with her eyes twinkling.

"Might just take us up to da moon," said Ole with a grin. All three of them laughed at that.

"You stay with us for supper, Ole," declared Bertha. "I have soup going already."

"Vell, that'd sure be nice."

Earlier in the day, Bertha had put rabbit meat she'd salted last fall into a pot with water, hoping the toughness of the rabbit would diminish with the vinegar she'd added. Now, she took a can of carrots from the shelf. She smelled them and looked for any sign of spoilage before adding them to the pot along with chunks of potato, chopped salted side pork, and dried onion. The friends reminisced about the past year while the alluring aroma of soup filled the shack.

Before supper, Bertha put together flour, an egg, buttermilk, and baking powder for dumplings and floated them on top of the soup.

"This is quite the community," said Tillie. "All of us a bit lonely for home. Makes us more willing to help each other out. Good variety of people too. From Anna who is coarse as hell," she laughed, "to Orlo, quite a serious man."

"Orlo's a good man. Been though a lot. Hard workin' and thoughtful he is," said Ole. "Course most everyone out here is hard workin'. Have to be."

"What do you think about Frank?" asked Tillie.

"Vell, seems to get the work done. Drinks more than I like to see. Has a bit of a temper. Don't want to cross the guy. Most of us don't get too close."

"I kind of worry about his wife."

"Yeah, ya never know. Best just to keep out of their affairs, I s'pect."

After supper, some of that gaiety Ole had suggested erupted in singing "Auld Lang Syne" and the women discovered that Ole had a grand voice. They kept him going and joined in—"Camptown Races," "Old Folks at Home," and "Billy Boy." When Ole started in on "Jeanie with the Light Brown Hair," the women stopped their singing and listened, Bertha with her mouth hanging open. Finishing, he said rather softly, "Course I dream of a gal with dark brown hair named Berta, too." Then he flashed an embarrassed smile.

Both women clapped. "Your voice," said Bertha. "So deep and melodious. How did you learn to sing so well?"

"Was my ma," said Ole. "Had her a lovely voice."

"Well, your mother taught you well," said Tillie. "You've a beautiful voice."

Bertha put out *søtsuppe* to finish the meal and they all savored the fruity taste of the holiday dish. After that, the evening seemed to draw to a close and Ole, having good sense of such things, put on his coat and went out into the frigid night after a brief kiss on the cheek and semi-hug to Bertha and a headshake to Tillie.

"He sure is a nice man," said Tillie as soon as he was out the door.

"Yeah, seems to be a good man, a very good man," said Bertha with eyes that looked dreamy to Tillie. "Made for a special New Year's Eve to have him stop by, sure did."

———

The cold that penetrated through coats as easily as July sun penetrated through blouses, the brutal winds that could make the cold pierce to the bones like a dagger, and the long nights of January often felt like a never-ending nightmare. Yet the few January days that were sunny and windless brought Tillie and Bertha some hope for an ending. The schoolchildren seemed to manage the cold better than the teachers. They ate whatever they brought in their lunch pails: usually liverwurst or hard cheese sandwiches, a hard-boiled egg with a butter sandwich, or at times a potato Tillie baked for them. Then they wanted to play Pump-Pump-Pull-Away and Fox and Geese out in the snow even when the weather was bitterly cold.

Lying awake, shivering and not wanting to get out from under the quilt to throw more coal on the fire, Tillie wondered at the naïve hopefulness that had driven her to Dakota.

Once, when the women had gathered following a church service, Helen and Belle told stories of what they called "Dakota lunacy." Not a few women, and some men, had succumbed to it.

"A few ended up in the insane asylum in Jamestown," Belle had declared.

"One woman wandered out into a blizzard with no coat," Helen said. "They found her body in the spring. One woman became mad during January after having her baby and threw the baby out into the snow."

"And I heard about a man who picked up his rifle, shot his horse, then shot himself," added Belle.

The "old-time" homesteaders, those who had been in Dakota two or three years, encouraged the newcomers to get help from the other women if the long winter turned their thoughts upside down. "Got to rely on each other to help. Otherwise any of us could go mad," Winnie added.

"Can't imagine getting mad enough to throw out your own baby," Tillie said with her eyebrows pinched together.

"No, you seem way too strong for that," Winnie said. "But, still, you might have some strange thoughts in the middle of a cold winter night. Always good to share our fears so they don't take hold of us."

Thinking about these happenings on a moonless night when the only sound to be heard was the distant howling of coyotes or wolves, Tillie could imagine a woman getting deranged enough to walk out into the night and let the cold penetrate into her tissues and her bones. While she knew she'd never do such a thing, the idea no longer seemed so bizarre.

But morning would come, and unless the weather looked dangerous, school responsibilities called and she would clean ashes out of the stove, put on her fur coat, dump the ashes where she thought the garden might be resting under the snow, then bring in more coal for the stove along with buckets of snow to melt. The eagerness of most of the students would cheer her and she'd forget her thoughts of the previous night.

Blizzard

Finally, January turned to February and on February 11, the girl homesteaders, as they were regularly called even now—though some called them the teachers, Miss Melbakken and Miss Harstad—could see that snow was about to begin falling, the dark skies having that foreboding look that suggested a humdinger of a blizzard was coming.

They sent the children home in late morning, again with severe warnings not to dillydally. Again, Tillie and Bertha decided to stay in Tillie's shack for each other's company, as well as the warmth under the quilt when crystals of snow might again float onto their bed. Then they each tended to their own chores in preparation: bringing in extra coal, bringing Sam to the lean-to and giving him a fresh drink of water along with plenty of hay, and putting snow in a pot on the stove to melt for cooking and washing up. Bertha warmed her shack well, then closed down the damper to keep the fire going as long as possible. She wrapped a red woolen scarf around her neck, put on her seal coat and mittens, took the quilt from her bed, and went to Tillie's.

By midafternoon, snow was falling heavily and the wind churned it up like feathers in front of a fan, sending it scurrying this way and that across the flat plain. Bertha couldn't even see her shack—in fact, could see nothing outside except the snow whipping around as if a tornado drove it. But she'd forgotten her needlework, so she decided to venture into the blizzard to retrieve it before the snow piled higher. With a piece of twine wrapped around her finger connected to the post by Tillie's door, she slowly made her way to her shack, letting out the twine as she went, frightened the whole time that the twine would break, or she'd drop it, and get lost in the endless white.

Reaching her door, she kept the twine on her finger until she got inside, then firmly attached it to a peg by her door. While there, she added more coal to the fire, got it blazing hot, then again closed down the flames. She got her needlework and, again twisting the twine around her finger, stepped out into the furious storm. Finally, when just a few feet in front of Tillie's shack, she saw the outline of the dwelling and let out a sigh.

While listening to the wind tear at the shack, making it tremble, the women prepared a supper of potato soup with plenty of onion, along with fresh biscuits. After eating, they each tried to read by candlelight, then went to bed early.

Each of them awakened periodically through the night to hear the sound of the wind continuing its howling and moaning.

By early morning, with snow still driving across the plain and wind pounding on the shack sounding like the incessant clanging of a locomotive, Bertha suggested that it might do to bring Sam into the shack.

"Oh goodness, Bertha. Who knows how he'll react to comin' in. He might knock everything down or kick a wall in and he'll stink for sure."

"I know, Tillie, but I hate to think of him out there."

"I do, too, of course."

"Could we just try it?"

"Well . . ." Tillie paused to think it over. Eventually, she nodded her head. "I suppose. Just help me put away anything that he could break."

It took both of them to open the door. Then Tillie braved the storm, having to feel her way to Sam just a few feet away. She led him to the door. Entering, she stomped her high-topped boots on the rug in front of the door to loosen the snow, then slowly guided him into the shack. Sam stood looking around wild-eyed. He thumped his tail against the wall while stomping his hoofs. After a short time, he recovered his usual placid demeanor. Snow melting off him pooled on the floor. Tillie bolted the door against the snow, being careful to stay clear of Sam's backside.

The storm raged the whole day while Tillie and Bertha tried to keep the fire going. The women spent the day doing handiwork. Tillie knitted mittens while Bertha worked on a small piece of hardanger. They were sometimes able to make small talk and laugh a little, but more often lapsed into a solemn quietness and tried to manage the barn-like stench of Sam.

Before dusk, Tillie again faced the storm and let Sam out into the lean-to, hoping that with the smell of manure on the straw, he'd relieve himself out there.

Before the sky blackened, and with the fierce wind continuing to pound at the shack, she went out again and led him back indoors and bolted the door against the stormy night. He accepted coming in with less distress than earlier.

"I think he appreciates the shelter," said Bertha with a smile.

"Hope he appreciates it enough to keep his droppings inside of him." Tillie frowned, but then gave a slight grin.

Eventually, both of the women climbed into bed. "Hope we can get through the night without nightmares."

"Might be better'n lying awake all night worrying about Sam."

Soon their breathing deepened into sleep. Sometime later, both of them bolted from sleep when they heard a pop, then a rumble like a clap of thunder.

The stink of Sam's gassy eruption quickly filled the shack. "Oh, goodness, Tillie. What a stink. Hope he limits it to passing wind. Chamber pot's almost overflowing already. It's not big enough for *that*."

"Let's hope he doesn't splatter everything with pee now." Tillie sighed, lay down, pulled the quilts up to almost cover her head, closed her eyes, and hoped for sleep.

Eventually, they both fell asleep again. Bertha woke up screaming once, having dreamed of falling into icy water and Tillie screamed in response, then comforted her friend as best she could.

Sam nickered. "It's okay, Sam," Bertha said laughingly. "I'm not deranged. Just had me a bad dream."

In the morning, drifts of snow obliterated the window, almost covering the shack. The friends were slowly prying open the door when they heard the splatter on the floor. "Oh my gosh! We've got to get him out of here," Tillie yelled as the door gave way. She pushed away the snow in front of it, and hurriedly cleared out space in the lean-to for Sam, then pulled him out of the shack.

"You start shoveling to your shack, Bertha. I gotta clean up some in there," she said while motioning with her head. "Might never get that smell out." She retreated to the shack to start scrubbing while Bertha began shoveling a path toward her place.

She went back to Tillie's once to warm her toes and fingers. Tillie was still scrubbing, but although the reek of Sam lingered on curtains, quilt, and clothes, the horrible stench of him was gone. "I'm sorry, Tillie, for suggesting he come in. Do you want some help?"

"It's okay. Think I got most of the smell out. I'll sprinkle soda on it. You go on with your shoveling."

Eventually Bertha made it to her shack. While she warmed the place, she heated water for hot chocolate. She'd picked up some cocoa powder at the general store just a week earlier. When it was ready, she went to Tillie's and told her to come over.

"My, does the sweet odor of chocolate smell good after managing Sam's stench," Tillie said, chuckling as she removed her coat.

"Glad to see you're laughing. Feared you might be mad at me for wanting to bring Sam in."

"Better to laugh about it than cry or holler. Besides, I'm glad we brought him in."

"Vell," said Bertha after pouring the steamy chocolate, "ve survived another blizzard, ve did."

"Sure 'nuf, sure 'nuf," laughed Tillie, savoring the hot, creamy drink. "Now we've only some four years to go. Ve'll have to have a celebration in the spring when the first year is up, assuming we survive that long."

"Oh, but we must survive."

Not everyone survived that storm.

The next afternoon, Ole put on snowshoes to go check on the girls. Smoke drifted out the chimney of both shacks as he rode toward them and slowed his pace, which diminished the huffing that had caused frost to form on his unshaven whiskers.

Bertha invited him into her shack without summoning Tillie, even though she had been taught that it was unwise, that a chaperone was necessary to provide suitable decorum when a courting man and woman were alone in a house. And here she was, a teacher, expected to be upright. But different rules seemed to apply on the plains of Dakota.

As soon as Ole got his coat off, he put out his arms and wrapped her close. She held him to her just as tightly and her breathing deepened to sounding almost like sighs.

"I'm so, so glad you're safe in the shack. I vorried for ya," Ole said, still holding her to him.

Bertha boiled coffee and brought out flatbrød. Though eggs were in short supply, she even added an egg to the coffee.

"I guess Tillie must be okay too," Ole ventured.

"Oh, yeah, we rode it out together, along with Sam. Brought him into the shack, Tillie's shack, for his safety. His warmth too. He stunk so that I could barely sleep even when I wasn't near scared to death. Then he piddled on the floor just before we got him outside."

Ole raised his eyebrows, then after a moment suggested, "Well, guess it weren't a bad idea, stink or no stink, ya got to take care of the animals. But yer lucky he didn't put a hoof through your floor that's not so awful strong." His face displayed the dimples within his reddened cheeks.

"I never even thought of that." Bertha grinned sheepishly.

"Not everyone vas so lucky as you. Ve heard this morning that Ellen is in pretty tough shape, having lost the baby during the storm, I reckon. Prob'ly too cold for the poor little thing. No one was there to help and I'm sure Frank wasn't much use."

At that news, Bertha put her head in her hands. A few tears trickled out.

Seeing her reaction, the determination showing on her stern face, Ole admonished, "Now don't you go trying to get there. Vait a day at least till the snow settles a bit more. It's still blowin' out there. Makes it hard to see. And there's nuthin' for you to do now."

She shook her head up and down.

"That's not the vorst of it. Ernie Saue stopped by just before I came here to tell a story he heard after riding out the storm in

Bowbells. Seems a mother came on her horse to pick up her little girl from the school outside Bowbells and got lost in the blizzard's wrath tryin' to get home. The woman's husband found 'em this mornin'. They'd almost made it back home. He saw the horse standing. No one on the mare. Found his wife lying next her. The woman was gone but the child, cuddled against her ma, still breathing. They sent for Doc Henry."

"Oh my, oh my, oh my! We sent our pupils home quite a long while before the snow started coming down hard, but I still fretted about them in the night, worried that they might not have gone straight home even though we admonished them to get there as fast as their feet would carry them."

"Vell, the children 'round here seem to have good sense of t'ings. Dey might do foolish t'ings sometimes, but not when a storm's comin' in."

"I hope they went right home, sure. And how did you manage the storm den?" asked Bertha again falling into brogue.

"Oh, I hunkered down. Brought the dog inside a'course. Even slept vit the guy. Animals done seem varmer than a person." As usual, color rose on his neck with those words.

Bertha laughed a bit then and the couple chitchatted while they finished their coffee and flatbrød. "Well, I better get somethin' done," said Bertha. "Got lessons to prepare and such."

"I best skedaddle. Haven't even checked on the cows and horse yet, but I got dem in the barn before the storm hit."

"Vell, Ole, t'ank you so much for coming. I 'preciate it and feel . . . well, it was nice that you were concerned."

He stood up then, opened his arms and hugged her hard again, this time planting a little kiss on her mouth.

As soon as Ole and his horse were out of sight, Bertha piled on her warmest clothes, and looking like an elephant without a trunk, hustled over to Tillie's. She told Tillie the news and together they decided they couldn't wait to get to Ellen. They rode double on sturdy Sam who slowly but steadily plodded through snow, though the way was difficult to discern in the forever white landscape. They soon saw smoke rising from a shack and hoped it was Ellen and Frank's.

Approaching, they recognized the shack. After tying Sam to a post, they made their way to the door and knocked. Sven answered, showing alarm as he opened the door.

"Oh we do hate to trouble you, Sven, but we heard your mother might be unwell. May we come in?" asked Tillie. Brunhild recognized Bertha, even with her heavy coat and scarf all covered with snow. Her face brightened as she ran to Bertha and patted her soft, smooth coat.

Once inside, Bertha and Tillie could see Ellen lying on the bed covered with quilts. Frank was nowhere around. After removing her outer clothes, Tillie approached Ellen, Bertha following. Ellen opened her eyes and looked vacantly at the two neighbors. "We came to see if we could be of any help," said Tillie. Getting just a nod, Tillie felt Ellen's forehead. "Sweaty," she said, looking at Bertha.

"Don't imagine she's been cleaned up?" Bertha looked at Brunhild, who shook her head.

"I didn't know vat to do." Brunhild looked at the floor.

"Of course, you didn't, dear child. We'll take care of her," said Bertha.

Sven put on his coat and left the shack. "Be in the barn."

Tillie heated water on the stove, found some cloths, and, after encouraging the children to read something or find a game to play, together the women removed the blood-stained sheets and washed Ellen's bottom parts, finding the afterbirth still in the bed. Tillie wrapped that in a cloth thinking she would dispose of it on the way home, perhaps leaving a gift for the coyotes or wolves. She laid clean cloths under Ellen. Neither she nor Bertha had attended a birth before and didn't know just what to do, but they had of course cared for sick ones in the family. "Is there anyone we should try to find?" asked Bertha.

Ellen just shook her head. Neither Tillie nor Bertha had asked about the baby yet. Tillie kept wondering what had happened to it but didn't dare ask.

Bertha asked Brunhild if she had eaten anything. Brunhild shook her head, so Bertha found a kettle and cooked oatmeal.

When Tillie left her own shack, she'd grabbed some salted side pork from the box under her trapdoor, along with frozen grouse broth she retrieved from the box in her lean-to. She put them in a kettle with water to heat. Seeing a jar of carrots on Ellen's shelf, she opened it, smelled it, and added the carrots to the broth. She found flatbrød and lard and set the table for the two youngsters and saved some for Sven. She prepared a small bowl of broth for Ellen, brought it to her, propped her up, and fed her with a spoon. Ellen barely opened her mouth. Soon thereafter, she fell asleep.

When Sven came in, Tillie asked him where his father was. "I dunno, prob'ly went to the Pig. Took the dead one with him," he offered with his usual sullen expression.

"Did he go for a doctor or Winnie, who helps with babies and all?"

"I dunno."

The two women stayed on. Bertha had asked Tillie if perhaps she shouldn't try to go find Winnie, but Tillie thought it best for both of them to stay until Frank returned at least. They tried to engage Brunhild and Karl in a game of I'm Thinking of Something in This Room. Brunhild responded, but little Karl just sat looking at his mor.

In late afternoon, Winnie burst in. "Oh goodness," she said, "I just got the news a bit ago and came as fast as I could."

Ellen was awake now and smiled wanly.

"I'm so sorry about the baby," said Winnie, taking Ellen's hand. "Let's see what's needed now."

"We cleaned her up as well as we could. The afterbirth was there in the bed. She's had just a bit of broth."

"Good, good. Let me look at the afterbirth, make sure it all came out." Tillie unwrapped the bloody cloth and showed it to Winnie who then looked under the quilt. "Looks like there's some more bleeding. Been a lot. I'll see what I can do. Brought a mixture of yarrow and wild geranium for that. Sven, boil me up some water to clean her with and to make some tea." With that, she set about the work she'd learned as a child from watching her mother and grandmother.

Sven left for the barn again.

After getting a few words out of Ellen, Winnie told the women that the cord had likely been wrapped around the infant's neck when it was born. Tillie shook her head sadly while Bertha looked at Ellen, who had a penetrating sorrow written on her pale, stoic face.

What was wrong with Ellen? Winnie wasn't sure. Perhaps childbirth fever; perhaps not all of the afterbirth had come through, though Winnie said it looked like it was all out. Ellen was clammy, but didn't feel too warm. She looked as if all color had leached from her face, so it seemed likely the heavy bleeding had made her weak. Maybe she was just heartbroken. "When I'm sure the bleeding is under control, I'll give her some herbs to help the blood. I think she'll make it okay."

After a little while, Winnie said, "It was so good of you two to come. The wind's still blowin' some out there and dark is settling in. You ought to get along home. I told Willie I'd spend the night here with Ellen, or even longer if needed. And I'll send Sven for you if I need help."

The two slowly put on their wraps, hesitant to leave, yet knowing Ellen was in good hands. "Bye, Brunhild. I'll see you in school when the weather gets better. Help your mor best as you can," said Bertha. Brunhild hugged at Bertha's legs, seeming reluctant to let go.

"Thanks for helping, Sven. We appreciate it. And, thanks so much for coming, Winnie. You're so good to help in these things. Hope all goes well. And do send Sven to get us if we can be of use," volunteered Tillie.

Ellen survived and gradually recovered her strength as the winter dragged on. A breeze gave hope for a spring thaw a couple of times; then the weather plunged back into frigid frightfulness. Tillie and Bertha continued lessons for the children most days, but had given up hope of instilling much of the learning they had been prepared to teach. While letters and numbers were important for all to learn, the priority was what it took to survive on the Dakota plains, so the students sometimes taught the teachers as much as the teachers taught the students. The women were sure, though, that having the children gather was important, even if not a lot of book learning occurred.

Pasqueflowers Bloom

Looking long across the land, one could sense a vague greenness emanating from the plain. Within her, Tillie noticed a fluttering, as if she were a young robin about to take flight, not that robins were anywhere to be seen. But creatures of the plains and a few birds were about. A jackrabbit, starting to lose its winter whiteness, bounded near the shack and pronghorn appeared in the distance.

During the past winter, Tillie had occasionally spotted a gray wolf motionless against an even darker gray sky, watching the shacks as if a sentry. On cold windless nights, the eerie howling of wolves sounded beautiful, yet frightening. On warmer days, she'd glimpsed coyotes in small packs, checking for mice or carrion, coyotes that regularly attempted to raid chicken coops on neighboring property. On occasion she'd heard the ghostly hooting of a great horned owl.

Now, although she couldn't see them, Tillie heard bobolinks, chipping and chirping and singing their ecstatic bubbly songs as if life itself depended upon their spring voices, so Tillie knew they had returned from their winter sojourn in the south. It was a Sunday, a day to give thanks and she and Bertha would soon head for the church gathering. "It's a good day," Tillie said to the bobolinks, to the land, and to the almost cloudless blue sky.

Huddled together in Orlo's shack, the Norwegian Lutherans congratulated each other for surviving the Dakota winter, some for their fourth year. Nels and Helga Iverson, along with Knut and Eleanor Aakre, would be completing five years the following spring and could claim the land as their own. Nels said he and Helga were considering returning to Iowa once they proved up on their stake. Knut said he was sure to tarry on in Dakota. "Like the grasses of the plains, my roots have grown too deep in the Dakota soil to leave. And our children know Dakota as their home," he said.

During the short service, the singing was stronger than usual, previously having been subdued by winter hardships. Song flowed easily with the anticipation of green and abundance or at least whatever the plains' rains would produce.

———

With spring progressing, the trilling of redwing blackbirds was deafening, especially when huge flocks stopped at the little lake. Most would continue north for the summer. Jackrabbits and ground squirrels, along with pronghorn, appeared to be flourishing and the girl homesteaders did as well. *My strength has increased*, thought Tillie. *Guess God is by my side after all.*

The pasqueflowers were the first wild flowers to bloom, sending shivers of excitement up Tillie's back at first sighting. Their delicate petals painted with the palest purple suggested that tender and sensitive life could flourish even in a harsh and unforgiving land. The early morning cooing of mourning doves, now home from their winter holiday, brought a sense of peace to Tillie.

School lessons continued daily until mid-April. By then spring chores demanded that even young children help at home, so the teachers held school only three days a week until it finished in early May. While the men plowed the soil and prepared for planting, the women and children broke up gardens and tended the hens and chicks, cooked, baked, and gave their shacks a good cleaning, leaving their handiwork behind until an occasional rainy afternoon. Some of the women, as well as older children, were busy in the fields along with the men, and those with Jersey cows milked them, separated milk from cream, and made butter. Some had started onion and cabbage seeds in their windows as the sun cast its warmth. Soon the onions would be ready for planting outdoors.

Tillie and Bertha, too, attended to spring chores. They made a larger garden, dug up the soil from the previous year's, and weeded away grasses that encroached, the prairie trying to reclaim itself. A week after Easter they planted potato seed set aside from fall harvest. The previous day Tillie had cut potatoes into several pieces, each having at least one eye, while Bertha measured out rows for planting and dug trenches about five inches deep. They let the pieces dry overnight to help keep them from rotting in the soil in the unlikely event that heavy rains came.

A few lingering drifts of dirty snow still scattered the countryside on the sunny day when they set the potato seed in the cool, almost cold, soil. Some warned it was too early to plant in Dakota, but Tillie knew that potatoes were hardy plants and could tolerate spring freezes, especially with some straw covering them. They were hardy like she recognized she and Bertha had become. Too, she could barely wait to see green potato leaves emerge from the soil.

Their chicks arrived from Minnesota, along with rhubarb roots, a welcome sign of home. Bertha planted rhubarb while Tillie set up the chicks in the coop. She called them *chirping angels* and took control of managing them while Bertha spent more time in the garden. Bertha came running to Tillie when she saw the first green potato leaves emerge from the soil. "The potatoes! We'll have potatoes! Several are poking through."

Spring energized Tillie, brightened her thoughts, and exhausted her body, but it was a healthy exhaustion, causing her to tumble into bed at twilight and wake refreshed the next morning.

The romance between Bertha and Ole was beginning to blossom along with the pasqueflowers, opening just a delicate petal at a time and then closing again.

Ole seemed patient and respectful of Bertha's reticence. He was older than she, nearly thirty, and although he'd had the fling with Eleanor back home and had called on another woman a few times, nothing had come of it. Bertha was the first woman in Dakota who sparked his attention. Of course, there had been few to look at. Although he held Bertha's hand, and occasionally gave her a bear hug, he hadn't tried to kiss her, apart from the touch to her lips after the February blizzard. Not yet.

Tillie watched her friend, recognizing that Bertha was beginning to fall in love, although Bertha denied such a feeling when Tillie suggested it.

———

On the fifth of May, the community assembled just after dawn climbed into the cloudless sky. Ole had spread word that sharp-tailed grouse had gathered for their annual mating dances. The males gathered on a little hill near Ole's to fluff their feathers and fan their tails in pursuit of mates, similar to prairie chickens. They would stomp their feet, rattle their feathers, and dance, sometimes dancing around and around. The males produced unearthly hoots, punctuated with quacks, while their stomping created a chatter. The children delighted in the hilarity of it. The few questions they asked about what it meant received replies such as, "Oh, they are just having fun in celebration of spring," though of course almost all the children had seen mating in farm animals and even guessed what their folks did under the covers in their one-room homes, and in time, figured it out for themselves, or with the idea planted by a sibling or schoolmate.

Some pasqueflowers still bloomed in little mounds. Most within the mound were gone for the season, but a few still had buds about to open with their heads bent over looking like a little gosling. The palest of purple petals on most had fallen off, their golden stamens lost, leaving only their plumed seed head of lavender threads. Although more prairie flowers would follow, Tillie thought none's beauty could surpass the delicate pasqueflower.

Winnie showed Tillie and Bertha where a breadroot was just breaking through. "It's often called a prairie turnip," she said. "When the top starts drying down in July, pull it up. Cut it up and use it in a stew for soup, or just cook it in butter. Good nourishment. Can even chew it raw. Helps with stomach and bowel problems. And that's penstemon there," she said pointing. "That'll be bloomin' soon you'll see, good for toothaches, y'know. In time the coneflower will bloom. That's something, that plant, the root is good for almost all that ails a being."

"You are a wealth of knowledge, Winnie. Good to know all the plants we can use."

"Nature provides for us when our gardens don't. Provides for the animals, too, of course. There are plants to help see a pregnancy through and even plants to end one; plants to help with gout—that's the nettle—and plants to heal most anything that troubles a soul or a body."

In mid-May, after planting their own wheat, Hans and Henry showed up to break sod at the estate using a sulky plow pulled by a team of oxen. With Tillie's and Bertha's assistance removing rocks, the thirty acres took a week to plow. They'd been lucky that no rain fell until just after they completed the job. They planted flax as the warmth of May deepened.

Tillie lay awake the night after the planting. *Only four more years to go. Can I manage it? It's not the hard work; it's the homesickness and worrisome weather and wondering what could go wrong next.* There were aspects of life in Dakota she loved: the gatherings, especially gatherings of women for sewing projects, or baking, or canning, or getting ready for a community celebration. She cherished the exhilaration she felt after completing a job with her own hands, like putting up the chicken coop. She appreciated the community spirit of helpfulness, with each member adding a skill to the patchwork quilt of the Norwegian neighborhood.

But she missed her family, the times spent sitting quietly doing needlework with her mother, the *julebukking* fun at Christmastime, the Sunday gatherings of cousins, aunts, and uncles. Although the gaiety and energy of the young homesteaders could bring such joy, she also missed the quiet wisdom of older people, with nary a person over forty anywhere nearby. The struggles, storms, even fear of failing in her endeavor—all these things wandered through her mind at night when she wasn't distracted by chores of one sort or another.

Ernie had been acting rather shy toward her, stumbling over his words, even though she'd noticed he chatted easily with others. Tillie wondered if he was starting to pay her special attention, as Ole clearly was to Bertha. But she dismissed the possibility for herself. She didn't plan to end up falling in love and living out her life on these wide plains. Besides, she still had a dim hope of finding Jergen in want of her when she returned, even though she knew she had no good reason to believe he would wait until then to find a wife or that he even thought of her as anything more than a friendly acquaintance.

Ernie seemed like a nice enough man, even a gentleman of sorts—a country one, certainly not a city one. It seemed rare in Dakota to find a man even resembling a gentleman, though Tillie wasn't at all sure what a gentleman was. But, although she admired Ernie, it was thoughts of Jergen that caused a tingly feeling to emerge. Jergen was genial with those around him without being overly friendly. He shared his ideas forcefully, though seemed careful not to show disrespect for other men. He projected a deep intellect, of that she was sure. Perhaps it was especially that quality that drew her thoughts to him.

———

Building a shed and corral for Sam would be the first major task of the summer. Following a community shack raising for Jorgen and Marta Hegg, who'd just arrived, Tillie and Bertha mentioned their plans to Ernie and Ole. "Well, we can sure 'nuf put it up for you girls." Ole dug his thumbs under his suspenders, as was his wont when he wanted to make a point. Ernie nodded his head.

"We plan to do it ourselves," Tillie asserted. "Or at least try. Besides," she said to Ernie, "you've got plenty to do on your own place with a barn to put up and all."

"Well, we'll cut up the sod for ya at least. Too hard a job without a plow. It'll take darn near an acre of sod. Not even a couple'a men would do it themselves. I'll help Ernie with his barn when that's needed. So will others." Ole looked firm.

"Well, I suppose that sure would help," Bertha softly acknowledged, smiling at Ole. Even Tillie nodded her agreement.

With some guidance, primarily from Ernie, who was the better builder, they developed plans for construction of a twelve-by-eighteen structure with sod walls, a slanted roof, covered with tar paper and then a layer of sod. A large swinging wooden door would open to a corral with a gate that could accommodate a buggy, along with Sam of course.

Tillie and Bertha rode in their buggy to Bowbells and purchased supplies at McClellen's—posts, cheap lumber for roofing and the door, tar paper, nails, and such—and arranged for delivery. While there, Bertha went to Kruger's Dry Goods, where she purchased calico for a new skirt.

First, the men framed the building for roof support. The women watched while Ole hitched his oxen to a grasshopper plow that he borrowed from Orlo, then cut sod, starting at the site where the shed would stand. The pieces measured a good five inches thick, a foot wide, and two feet long. With the women's help, Ernie piled them on a wagon to move them near the construction site.

The women insisted upon working alone to lay the walls. Sod side down, the walls were two feet thick. They laid the first row the full thickness of the wall; on top of it they laid sod bricks at a ninety-degree angle to the row below it and continued to alternate the direction of the bricks. They got the first few feet of the walls up without help, working until the last stream of sunlight had left the land. Their arms and backs ached, and no strength remained. "Never have I been so tired," admitted Tillie. "Hardly know if I can make it into bed. Might just sleep on the grass."

By the next morning, Tillie and Bertha were back at the task when Ole and Ernie arrived. With the walls growing higher, the women readily accepted their help, the men marveling at what the women had done the previous day.

While Ole labored in his short-sleeved shirt, his arm muscles bulged and gave off a sheen. Dirt and sweat formed streaks of black on his neck. Occasionally he uttered a "damn" or a "hell" as drops fell from his forehead; then he apologized for his words. While Ernie complained some of the heat, he confined his outbursts to "Jeez!" and "Golly man!" Tillie and Bertha worked alongside the men and kept their grumbling to "uff da" or "namen." In addition to the heat, the air was still and, with the recent rain, mosquitoes had hatched. So swarms and more swarms of mosquitoes added to the misery that day. "When we need a breeze, it stays still; when we don't want wind, it blows," Bertha muttered.

Tillie fetched water from a pail she kept in a deep hole in the ground and the four friends sat down on the wagon. They drank noisily, but otherwise remained quiet. After a short time, the cool water eased their thirst and refreshed their tired limbs so they could resume their toil.

When they finished the walls, both women admitted they could use the men's help with the roof as well, and Ole and Ernie agreed to return the next day to try to finish the task.

Refreshed the next morning, though with tired muscles, the friends worked together to put on the roof. The men laid rough wood sheathing on the two-by-four rafters with braces on the low end to keep the sod in place. Then the women laid tar paper over the wood while Ole and Ernie cut sod for the roof and hauled it to the shed. Ole cut the bricks just three inches thick to lessen not only the difficulty of hoisting the sod to the roof, but to lighten the load on the roof.

The next morning, Ole and Ernie found Tillie and Bertha already at work, having managed to get a few pieces of sod laid. For the rest of the morning, the four worked together to hoist the sod to the roof and then lay it on the tar paper, "sunny-side up," as Ole joked.

When the structure was finally complete, with only the corral to build, both women expressed deep thanks for the assistance.

"This taxed my body more than any other grueling task I've done," admitted Bertha. "We both know we wouldn't have managed it without the help." All four had dirty faces and arms, sopping-wet shirts or blouses, and undergarments soaked with sweat.

"Let's go for a swim," suggested Ole.

"All of us?" asked Tillie.

"Sure, why not?" Ernie was laughing.

"You men go first," said Tillie.

"I might just join the men," said Bertha. "Can't look any more ridiculous than I must look now. Come along, Tillie."

Tillie, too modest and inhibited to consider the idea, said, "I'll go get you all some towels," and went to the shack.

The trio walked to the little lake. The men stripped down to their sweaty drawers and Bertha to her bloomers and shift. All of them acted a little embarrassed, especially Bertha who crossed her arms over her chest. Her eyes focused on the deeply tanned *V* extending downward from Ole's neck; then she looked away. His arms were brown as toast against his white body. His eyes fell upon the curve of Bertha's hips and the fullness of her bosom, then he looked away, but quickly returned his gaze to her. But the cool water of the lake called and they all plunged in laughing and splashing, regaining energy drained away by sweat and the grungy work of moving sod.

When Bertha saw Tillie back with the towels, she edged toward shore. Covering her chest with her arms, she walked out of the lake and surrounded herself with the towel Tillie handed her.

"Thanks, Tillie." Bertha didn't look Tillie directly in her eyes, as if she knew Tillie disapproved of what she'd done, but when she turned away, her mouth drew itself into a huge smile and she let out a titter.

The men followed Bertha out of the lake, wrapped themselves with a towel, dried off the best they could, and pulled their sweaty overalls over their wet drawers.

"Boy, did that feel good," said Ernie. "We'll get out of here now so Tillie can jump in."

"We'll fix you two men a scrumptious dinner on Sunday," declared Bertha. "We couldn't have done it without you. Well, Tillie might think we could have, but it might have killed us," she said grinning at Tillie, then winking at Ole.

"I must agree. We wouldn't have succeeded in getting up the shed without you two. Tusen takk, tusen takk."

When the men left, Tillie removed most of her clothes and plunged into the lake. Turning back after several strokes, she called out, "It's the best swim I've ever had." The cool, fresh water dissipated her exhaustion and irritation.

After putting on fresh clothes, the two women, one at each side, led Sam into his new home. "Now you've a place to keep you warm enough in the winter and cool in the summer," said Tillie. "No more winter storms for you to endure out of doors or when we might need to manage your stench and pee."

"And we might join you to escape the heat of July and August, 'specially when the shack is a sweltering oven," added Bertha.

The other major event of the summer was putting in the well. Tillie and Bertha had considered doing it themselves, but they agreed that was not wise. Their neighbors, especially Ole, strongly advised against it, his thumbs under his suspenders. So, they decided hiring help was worth the cost.

First, the dowser from Portal arrived with his witching stick. As he began his work, he held the forked stick, one side of the fork in each hand, with the end on the stick pointing upward. He walked back and forth and, soon enough, the butt end of the stick turned downwards. "Here's a sure spot," he said, standing just east of Bertha's shack.

Well diggers arrived the middle of the following week. Using picks and shovels, they dug down until the hole was too deep to dig from the top. One of the men climbed in while the other hitched a horse to a pulley with an attached bucket that was connected at the apex to a tripod over the well hole. They lowered the bucket, filled it with dirt, and then the horse went around and around in a circle to raise the bucket.

As the men labored, passing twenty feet, then passing twenty-five feet, Bertha and Tillie watched with anxiety showing in the crease lines on their foreheads. "Either the dowser was wrong or that ad that said water could be found at twenty feet was telling a tale," lamented Bertha.

Between twenty-eight and twenty-nine feet, water seeped in and everyone cheered. "The witch was right," Bertha giggled as she twirled around.

The well diggers kept up their work until they could go no deeper, then climbed out with their clothes soaking wet to build the wooden cribbing to support the walls of the well. After supporting the walls with the cribbing, they used rocks to add support at the well's base.

Tillie and Bertha would need to wait days until the dirt settled before bringing up their first good bucket of water, but what a joy it was. "Life just got simpler!" Tillie licked her lips after a sip of fresh water.

———

On a sunny afternoon in early summer, Tillie rode over to see Ellen, ostensibly to bring a couple books for the children, as well as to ask whether Sven might be interested in coming to school in the fall. Her real reason was to check on Ellen, which she had also done a couple of times after the death of the baby.

Ellen was alone, working in the garden, with Brunhild and Karl playing tag a distance away. Sven and Frank were nowhere about. Ellen wiped the sweat from her face, rubbed her hands on her faded calico apron, and pushed her limp hair away from her forehead.

"Got the stove going already, gonna cook up chicken stew for supper," said Ellen. "Easy 'nuf to boil up some coffee. It'll be hot in there, but please come in?"

"If it's no trouble. For nice of you to ask."

Ellen washed up her hands in the wash basin and put water in the blue enamel pot. With small eyes that looked to be a color between hazel and gray, she looked hollow, as if soulless. Tillie wondered if her eyes would be capable of brightening at a coneflower opening its pinkish petals or even the birth of a child.

The two women chitchatted about the weather, what was growing in the garden, and other innocuous things while the aroma of the fresh brew filled the shack. Ellen poured two cups, placed them on the table and put graham crackers she'd made on a chipped plate. Tillie noticed that it was a pretty plate, decorated around the edges with tiny blue flowers, perhaps harebells. "What a beautiful plate!"

"First belonged to my *bestemor* in Norway. Mor gave it to me just before she passed," said Ellen with something that looked like pride on her usually expressionless face.

Ellen sat down, took a sip of coffee, then blurted out, "He done it to me again and now I got me another child on the way. Barely recovered strength from the last one."

Tillie reached out and took her hand. "Oh my, oh my, oh my. Please let me and the other women help you get through it this time. We'll of course help with anything if you will but let us."

Ellen nodded, but said nothing as many moments elapsed. "I'd want the help, but he doesn't let me ask for any," she said softly, looking down.

"Well, he can't stop me from checking in on you."

"No, he can't stop you, but . . ."

"But?"

"Well, he gets so furious if ever I let anyone in. Good he's gone now and I don't t'ink he'll be back anytime soon; likely at the Pig again."

"And what does he do when he's upset?" Tillie asked in a voice just above a whisper.

"Oh, I don't . . ." And again she trailed off. "Maybe best we talk at church or someplace."

And thus the conversation went with no further enlightenment, though Tillie tried to better understand. While there were men she'd known who swatted their children too hard, hitting them with a belt or big stick of some sort, and men who yelled obscenities at their wives when something went wrong, she had no experience dealing with a man who would actually injure his wife, although she'd heard of such things.

"Well," said Tillie, "I'll get all the mothers of the schoolchildren together regularly. That'll give us opportunity to talk and maybe to help a little or at least to know when your time is coming close."

Ellen nodded again, thanked Tillie for the visit and for the books for the children. "Brunhild can make out the words better'n me now. We're learning together to read English words."

"Like you, most of the women here are learning to read English along with their young ones."

On the way home, Tillie felt deeply distressed. She knew that Ellen was having trouble at home, yet she wondered if there was anything she could do without raising Frank's ire and maybe causing more problems for Ellen.

She committed herself, though, to finding some way to make sure Ellen was cared for when her time came, even if she were unable to help her in other ways.

Pestilence

The latter part of July brought warm mornings and hot afternoons that didn't cool until twilight when the sky deepened to grave purple in the east while the smoky indigo sky in the west displayed a glowing golden arch.

August dawned with dry heat. The grass was prickly, the fields thirsty, the soil blistered. Garden vegetables wilted in the heat of the earth. Tillie was giving Sam water when she heard a tremendous whirring sound, a sound as unfamiliar as might have been an automobile. Not knowing what to make of the sound, she ran to Bertha's and summoned her to listen.

Looking in the direction of the racket, they saw the darkened sky. Soon something that sounded like hail began hitting the ground and the shack. "Grasshoppers!" yelled Bertha as the creatures descended, swarms and more swarms of them, hopping and jumping as if they had the St. Vitus dance, the beating of their wings whirring like a tornadic fan, tyrannical as a blizzard.

Both women ran into Bertha's shack, pummeled on their way. They spent the rest of the day and evening in dread, not daring to venture out of doors.

Once they landed, the pests ate spring wheat, oats, barley, and flax. They depleted gardens of much of their produce. They poisoned wells in sites where the homesteaders hadn't been home to cover them or hadn't heard of what to do if grasshoppers came. They made a greasy mess on the roofs of buildings and on the ground. Some got inside shacks and women and children, and even a few men, screamed when hit in the face. Some men built bonfires to help kill them or send them off, then feared for starting a prairie fire.

Tillie remembered her father telling stories of the ruined crops and desolation of the homesteaders of his era and now feared for herself and her neighbors. While none of these Kincaid homesteaders remembered the locust plagues of the 1870s, they'd heard tell of those calamities and feared total destruction when the invasion began. But, the following afternoon the clouds of insects moved on, and while they left what looked like devastation in their path, in truth the damage was not nearly as devastating as initially feared.

Tillie had so loved looking at her field of beautiful flax, the flowers blooming a brilliant blue in the sunlight while most of the fields were golden with wheat. When she ventured out, she first checked the flax field and saw broken stems and grasshoppers, some dead, some alive. Amidst the damage, most of the stems held onto their blue blossoms and Tillie grew hopeful that the flax had not received too much damage.

For her part, Bertha checked the garden, much of it appearing badly damaged, but with root crops underground and already grown plump, most of the harvest would be fine. The pullets paraded around the yard grabbing mouthfuls of the beasts and Bertha suggested to Tillie that maybe chickens were the answer to the plague. "Thousands of chickens would eat the nasty critters." Sam, who ordinarily appeared unfazed by storms and other natural events, looked anxious, his eyes darting while his tail swished away at the critters jumping near him. Occasionally, he stomped a hoof.

Tillie moved around in a haze for the rest of the day. She cleaned away what she could of the grasshoppers, but her normally optimistic spirit that enjoyed nothing more than hard work was as wilted as the leaves of squash in the garden. She accomplished little. Too tired and desolate to clean all the pests out of her shack that evening, she brushed the dead ones off her bed and tumbled in.

She awoke early when one of the insects hit her in the face. That morning she and Bertha cleared the grasshoppers out of their shacks, some dead, some quite alive, and some just twitching. They washed curtains stained with grasshopper exudate. As well as they could, they cleaned the insects away from paths where they usually walked since the hoppers squished underfoot when stepped upon.

Men worked in the fields, examining the loss, plowing under some areas that the critters had especially damaged. "At least the dead ones'll make good fertilizer," Ole would later tell Bertha with a smirk.

It was just after most of the grasshoppers left that the community men put finishing touches on the church, steeple and all. The steeple bell called worshippers to the first service, the deep chime sounding throughout the community on the unusually still morning. The only sounds on the air were the cooing mourning doves, along with pings made by the remaining grasshoppers jumping in the deep grasses. "Wonder if they are mourning hopper damage or raising their voices in praise at their leaving," said Tillie with a smile.

Walking into the pristine yet rustic abode of their God, the homesteaders expressed admiration to each other for the simple yet sacred beauty of their church. Yet the blight surrounding them seemed to diminish their reverence and most appeared pensive. While no one said it out loud, Tillie wondered if others, like herself, questioned whether God appreciated their work, appreciated the hardships they'd endured, appreciated them enough to send some relief from the dry heat.

Misgivings aside, the Norwegian worship service was beautiful and the prayers were especially earnest. The worshippers prayed for rain, prayed that the grasshoppers hadn't done too much damage, prayed for managing the coming winter with smaller stores of wheat, oats, winter vegetables, and preserves. They sang "The Little Brown Church," along with "Abide with Me," most singing as if their lungs were bullhorns. The service gave Tillie hope that God would indeed hear their prayers.

After the service, they had a potluck picnic on the makeshift tables outside the church. They had built a large campfire before the service began and women took turns tending the fire and preparing food, which was abundant, even if the homesteaders worried that it might run out before spring. Early potatoes, warm and delectable in their fresh and wholesome taste adorned with newly churned butter. Young carrots floating in cheese sauce, snap beans with a touch of vinegar and honey. Crisply baked dark bread, venison roast, and plenty of chicken with milk gravy.

Anna and Olga had collected grasshoppers and fried them alive in butter. Most of the homesteaders gave them a try and found them quite tasty. "Maybe we ought to start raising these critters for food," suggested Henry with a loud chortle, his long beard bopping up and down.

After the main meal, the women removed dish towels that covered pies, bars, and cookies, and put out fresh coffee, along with milk for the children.

"Which pie did you make?" Ole asked Bertha.

"The rhubarb. And Tillie made the custard."

"Ah," he said, "pie plant's my favorite."

"Thought you said custard was your favorite," she said with an impish grin.

He displayed a sheepish smile. "Well, any pie you bake up is my favorite."

Children played tag and ran races with burlap sacks on their feet. Some of the men joined them. There were songs and poem readings. The day ended with a tribute to the community of hardy Norwegians and finally with the hymn "Holy, Holy, Holy," sung just as the sun was setting and casting streamers into the western sky.

On the way back to their shacks, Bertha admitted to Tillie that her mind was muddled, her trust in God weakened. "We need rain so desperately. How can he allow this to happen when we've just built this house of worship for him? Doesn't he pay any attention to us? Who or what is God, anyway?"

"Perhaps God was just waiting for the completion of the church and was testing our fortitude."

"Perhaps. But sometimes it's hard to have faith," Bertha commented quietly. After reflecting for a time, she added, "Perhaps God is something like life itself—life finding expression in many forms. We humans sometimes forget we are just a part of creation. I suppose even grasshoppers have some purpose ordained by God."

Tillie nodded her head and admitted she had her own wonderings about who or what God was and whether he noticed their struggles.

The next morning clouds formed above the western horizon and moved closer. All the homesteaders watched the sky, looking for the clouds to thicken and darken. But by early afternoon, the skies lightened. Like all the other times, the homesteaders sucked in their disappointment.

Toward dusk on Friday of that week, the sky again darkened. Soon thunder bumpers climbed to the heavens, and thunder began booming in the west, along with lightning and then rain. Tillie, alone in her shack, heard the first few droplets as they hit her roof, then the pitter-patter of drops, and finally she saw rain gushing from the roof and hitting the parched land so hard it pinged.

She opened the door, felt the lovely texture of droplets hitting her face, tasted their sweetness on her tongue. She inhaled the aroma of wetness that brought forth the scent of rich soil and a feeling of cleanliness. Her face exhibited a broad smile when she finally closed the door. Already the front of her blouse and skirt were dripping wet. She blotted away some of the wetness and wiped away some drops that glistened on her table and moistened photos of family that hung on the walls. After lighting the kerosene lantern, barely able to contain her glee, she began singing as she prepared a simple supper.

When she lay down in bed that night, she said to the walls, to God, to the community, and to herself, "This indeed has been a magnificent day." Although she'd learned that God was omnipotent and that prayer could bring God's intervention, she often wondered whether life wasn't too complicated for that notion. She thought that perhaps prayer didn't cause God to effect some change, but rather that prayer altered her own beliefs and actions. Yet today, with the rain coming so soon after the first service in the new church, she believed in God's glorious work in bringing it.

The Kincaid area received nearly two inches. Everyone celebrated in their own homes, some men even dancing around naked outside their shacks as was said to be one way to give thanks, or maybe that was just drink talking. In spite of the rain, the homesteaders became watchful for prairie fires that might have started from a lightning strike and would move swiftly over the still thick but parched grasses, the hoppers seeming to have had little taste for it.

———

Women of the Norwegian community organized a Ladies Aid and elected Helen as president. Helen was a stocky woman with long braids, which she wound around the back and top of her head. She had a commanding presence, but her tough exterior gave way to a warm and thoughtful demeanor. She was the kind of woman who would befriend anyone needing help and might also stand up to a bully.

After a Bible verse and prayer, the women sewed items needed in the community: aprons, children's clothing, lap quilts, and curtains. While sewing, the river of stories flowed, good news and bad. Tillie saw it as another opportunity to offer support to Ellen, who attended the first meeting. "I see the baby is beginning to round your tummy," she commented genially. "How have you been feeling?"

"I'm doin' okay, growing rounder as you say. Morning sickness gone now, t'ank goodness."

"I'm sure. Morning sickness must be quite awful. Can I come and help with some of the fall chores, digging potatoes and such?" asked Tillie. "You ought not strain yourself too much now."

"Oh, I manage okay. Brunhild helps some now."

"And Frank? Does he help you manage things now?"

"I guess. Some." She looked to the side. "Course, he's got his own work."

"Yes, of course. Well, like I've said, Winnie and I and maybe some of the other mothers will check in with you. Maybe come a time or two a week as the winter comes on. We so want things to go well with you and the little one."

Ellen did not respond to that, except with a slight nod of her head. After a bit more chitchat about the rug Ellen was working on, other women came over and changed the conversation.

The greater community around Kincaid was growing. Danes had organized their shacks near each other, as had the Swedes, and of course the Norwegians. But the men of all heritages, and sometimes the women, got acquainted in town, a town that was growing. Two of the Danes put up a grain elevator that summer so that wheat could be stored, then sold at better prices. They predicted their customers would get up to seventy-five cents a bushel for the best grade.

Tillie and Bertha enjoyed visits into town and hearing the local gossip while examining goods at Kincaid General Store. "What have you heard about Sig?" Eleanor asked one of the Swedes at the counter.

"He done lost his mind, they say. Was acting like the spirits took hold of him, yellin' and shoutin' 'bout who knows what," the Swede said. "Doc slowed him down a bit with somethin', but they say life out here just got to him. May need to give up their homestead, his wife do say."

Sig was a Swede, a big, burly guy with a reddened complexion and large, almost glassy-looking eyes. Tillie and Bertha had met him and his wife at the general store last fall and seen him a time or two since.

"I guess some just can't take the desperation that sometimes settles in out here," said Bertha to Tillie. "Understandable enough, I guess. Sure hope I can keep on managing."

"Oh, sure 'nuf you will," said Tillie. "We've done the hardest part. They say the first year's the worst." But, even as she said this, she wondered if her own strength could bear almost four more years. At times, nothing seemed better than the community spirit that had formed and the physical work that strengthened her body and her spirit; other times, her homesickness and hunger for the amenities of home, especially a good bath, and longing for her family were almost more than she could bear.

Harvest Time

Time again came to cut hay for Sam, which was mostly slough grass, western wheatgrass, and blue grama. The women used scythes, then let the grass dry. The aroma of newly cut hay lay heavy on the air, earthy and vibrant with a hint of spice. "You know," said Bertha, "I bet men like this scent as much as we do, maybe more. We ought to bottle it."

"Great idea, assuming we can figure out how to make the smell last." Tillie was laughing.

Each evening, after a day of cutting hay and raking it into windrows, both women were too exhausted to make any cooked supper, so they simply nibbled on dry bread and cheese and sometimes some dried beef. Yet the next morning, after a hearty breakfast of eggs and kitchen toast, they hefted their scythes and continued swinging them back and forth, back and forth, as the grass fell. When finally done with scything, they raked the windrows into haycocks, then let it continue to dry.

Ole had insisted that he would help when it came time to rake the haycocks together and form a haystack. And he did. Both women felt deep gratitude for his help, not only for his muscle power throwing the hay up high, but for his skill in building a sturdy stack.

Through the heat of August, the friends spent days in the rhythm of chores: harvesting carrots, beans, beets, and turnips; canning carrots and beans; making beet pickles and sauerkraut; stocking their root cellar; and cleaning their stove pipes. They awaited the beginning of school, not with the nervous energy and anxiety of the previous year, but with confidence they gained by surviving for over a year in one of the harshest climates on the populated earth. With that self-assurance, Tillie embedded herself in preparation for school, with Bertha doing much the same, although her romance with Ole consumed some of her time.

School would again take place in the two shacks. Although the teachers had hoped to have a school building by September, the community men decided there wasn't time—the harvest was upon them—but promised to build a school the next summer.

When the wheat was ready, the men formed two teams to reap it. Most wore their overalls. Then women and older children helped with stacking. When the stacks were dry enough, threshing began. It was the busiest time in the community. When the early settlers had come to Dakota, they used a walk-behind plow to break a number of acres, then simply broadcast their seed. They harvested with a sickle and flailed the wheat to separate the chaff, a process that might take the whole winter. But agriculture had developed better tools as the nineteenth century drew to a close and some of the homesteaders had enough cash to buy the new equipment.

The year before Tillie and Bertha came to Dakota, Nels Iverson had bought the first steam-powered threshing machine in the community. He planned to recover much of the cost and make a little money by charging each farmer a small amount each time he used the machine. So now, all the community members were involved in harvesting as the machine traveled from farm to farm, with the men working in unison, saying little, just sensing the timing of the work in tune with the clanking and hissing of the machine.

The women baked and cooked for the crew and did what they could to help.

During breaks in the work, the camaraderie of the men was apparent as they joked and told tall tales while the women shared their worries and fears along with such joys as digging up a potato hill that revealed a dozen plump tubers or digging carrots nearly a foot long. Tillie always found comfort and inspiration during these gatherings, from hearing about hard times and struggles as much as from listening to the happiness that could come from hearing a bird chirp or seeing a bush with elderberries plump and ripe for picking.

After threshing, the women joined the men to bag the wheat. They would save some of the wheat for spring planting, keep some at home for hand milling and for sprouting to add a little freshness to winter meals, and deliver the rest to the elevator. From there, the wheat would eventually be shipped to a mill in Minneapolis.

After wheat threshing, it was time for flax harvest, and Tillie and Bertha eagerly awaited learning what their land produced. As the men threshed the flax, the women bagged it and when they finished, Hans estimated there were over two hundred bushels, half of which belonged to Tillie and Bertha. "Not a bad harvest," said Hans, "given the hoppers ate some of it. Should bring a dollar eight a bushel."

With the harvest complete, the community celebrated. Accordion and harmonica came out. Jorgen Hegg added his mandolin to the harmony and dancing began. Many of the women wore newly sewn bright calico skirts and, with the promenades, do-si-dos, and allemande lefts, skirts twirled merrily like toy tops, creating the most festive sight the women homesteaders, as they called themselves, had yet seen in Dakota. After square-dancing, waltzes started, with couples pairing up. Ole asked Bertha to dance, of course. Ernie, looking splendid in his red-and-black suspenders over a mostly clean white shirt, came over to Tillie. "Don't suppose you would dance with me," he said, looking at the ground.

"Oh I think I just might," she replied, and so it began.

———

When school started, there were a few more students: Karl, Ellen and Frank's little boy; Gustav, Millie and Herman's little one; and Thor, Willie and Winnie's boy. Then those new to the community: Rena, ten, and Herbert, eight, the children of newcomers Jorgen and Marta Hegg; and Sharon, nine, daughter of Earl and Josie Hovde. The students fit into the two shacks, if a little more tightly than the previous year.

A few of the initial families to settle in the community had their first decent harvest of berries by 1901. When the women were new to Dakota, they had talked of missing the fruits and berries of home and reminisced about plums, purple and succulent; crunchy apples, snapping with sweet tartness; and strawberries, swimming in their sweetness. Pioneers in the area had told the first home-steaders that fruit trees might grow, but would not bear much, if any, fruit. The only native bushes in the area skirted the small lake, so most homesteaders had none on their plots. To satisfy their cravings, the women had planted chokecherry bushes, elderberries, black currants, and sand cherries, along with raspberries, then tried to give them water enough to bear fruit.

On a Saturday, so school was not in session, Eleanor and Winnie invited all the women to gather at Eleanor's to share their berry harvests. The younger children came along and most played outside, making up games.

Tillie and Bertha brought sugar, along with buffalo berries they had gathered from the shrubs by the lake. Tillie noticed that after the first frost, the berries' mouth-puckering tartness had diminished, giving way to a slight sweetness. Winnie told her they would make excellent jelly and a meat sauce similar to catsup. "The Indians used them for medicine. I'm quite sure they are good for healthiness, though I've not used them enough to understand just what they do. But be careful. Eating too many will give you the trots," Winnie added with a wink.

"With enough sugar," said Eleanor, the stocky shopkeeper with eyes so bright they exposed an inner light, "all these berries make excellent jams and pies."

———

Helen and Belle brought raspberries, the only berries sweet enough to enjoy eating fresh, and all of the women got a taste before they turned some of the berries into pies, others into preserves.

"Oh, how this reminds me of home." Bertha closed her eyes and puckered her lips before swallowing, then licked her lips clean. "The most delicious thing I've had in a long while."

The women made jams and syrup, ladling hot wax on top of small drinking glasses or jars to seal them. They pressed those berries that were well past prime into juice. With sugar to sweeten and ferment the sharp and bitter liquid, it would serve as a Christmas cordial.

The afternoon ended with coffee and a thin slice of pie for each of the women and, for some, a slice to bring home for a hungry husband, unless children found it first.

"My, this pie must be the best I ever tasted." Tillie savored the taste, eating as slowly as she could manage. "Surely all of our produce fills us up. Can hardly beat the taste of new potatoes or carrots with a bit of butter. But this pie beats anything."

"Wait till the winter doldrums when the cordial will be ready," said Winnie, with a twinkle in her eyes and some berry juice on her chin. "We'll share it at Christmas or the New Year. Can make a roaring blizzard seem like God's gentle grace." All the women laughed at that.

The only sad part of the day for Tillie was Ellen's absence. "Too bad Ellen couldn't join us," she said to Bertha on the way home.

"You worry 'bout her a lot, don't you?"

"I'm quite sure she and her family suffer from Frank. He must take out his anger on them, maybe especially on Ellen. I don't know what to do."

"Maybe not much to do, at least not now. Try to offer our support when we can."

"I guess," responded Tillie. "Just wish she would come to more of the gatherings. Could at least let her know we care."

Fall was beautiful that year. Many sunny days, with a short day or two of much needed rain mixed in to bring hopes of a good planting season in 1902. While the harvest had not been plentiful, it had been "decent" as most of the farmers said, given the grasshopper damage.

As the cool days of October waned, Bertha received a letter from her sister, Hilda, that told of family and community news and hinted that Hilda might have a beau. She had added near the end:

I happened to run into Lars, home from the fighting now. He looked rather thin. Without him asking, I told him

some of your news. We had just a short conversation. Have
you received some letters from him?

A day later Bertha told Tillie about the letter. "I've had no letters, of course, or I would've told you. That episode of my life is over." After a few moment's pause, she added, "Y'know, I could become a spinster if I don't start thinking of marriage soon."

"Thinking of Ole?" asked Tillie, guessing the answer.

"Oh, I suppose," she said diffidently. "Seems steady and dependable, considerate of my wishes. Don't feel as much exhilaration as I did with Lars, but maybe my feelings are more genuine, not just girlish infatuation." After a few moments, she added, "But this is not home. I can't think of leaving home forever."

One late evening as the last remnant of sunlight gave way, she and Ole walked to the little lake, arm in arm. A full moon cast light for the walk. As they approached the lake, the moon could be seen reflecting in the water, quivering gently. "What a beautiful sight!" she exclaimed. At that, Ole drew her to him. Holding her with reverence, he moved his mouth to her lips. She quivered like the reflected moon as the kiss deepened and became passionate.

After the kiss, they stood hand in hand, gazing at the rippling moon. Neither spoke for quite some time. Eventually, Ole turned to her and asked, "Was it okay?"

"Ole, it was a kiss that made me feel I was a gift to you as you are to me."

At that, he drew her close again with another kiss that penetrated each of their lonely souls. In time, as the moon moved higher, they walked back through the deep rippling grass, its tips glistening in the light of the moon.

Bertha didn't immediately tell Tillie about that first passionate kiss. But anyone paying close attention would see she was smiling to herself quite often the following days.

———

School brought relief from the usual chores. The teachers knew that in teaching the youngsters they provided something for the community that others were less able to give and felt proud of their contribution. "This year," said Bertha after school that day, "most of my pupils seem eager to learn to read, write, and do simple arithmetic like that they might need to figure out how much fencing to buy or how much fabric for new curtains might cost. Last fall, it seemed hard to even get their attention. Better this year."

"Seems that way to me, too, though Peter doesn't seem quite as keen as the others. Some of mine even seem enthusiastic about geography and astronomy. Perhaps some of them long for escape from this rough existence."

"Maybe we just helped them get accustomed to schooling last year. Now they're ready."

"Y'know what, Bertha? Maybe we adjusted ourselves to this life like we accustomed our pupils to studies. I almost look forward to winter this year. Last year, I dreaded it."

"Well I don't know if I quite look forward to it, but at least I'm not so scared of its comin' as I was."

While cooking up a pot of soup one late afternoon when the first dusting of snow arrived, Tillie noticed the gentle flakes of snow and sensed almost an intoxication. She thought that watching snowflakes float in the breeze and tenderly settle on the land while aromas floated in the air from a pot of soup simmering on the stove was at least as pleasing as feeling drops of rain splash against her skin after a long dry spell. Watching a snowstorm descend, although always concerning, was also thrilling. And seeing a winter full moon with a halo surrounding it felt sacred.

It was comforting to know more about survival, more about what to do in a blizzard, more about how to keep the shack reasonably warm, skills she had lacked at the beginning of the previous winter. Too, she felt comfort in knowing that Ernie Saue would help however he could, as he had told her, and she knew Bertha's Ole would do the same. She and Ernie weren't courting, exactly, just finding time to be with each other at community gatherings and talking in private when they could. Although Tillie had not given in to romantic thoughts about him, she did appreciate knowing he cared for her in a way that no one else in Dakota did.

Joy and Despair

As December was about to wreak its icy fury upon the land, Tillie met with Winnie and Helen to arrange a look-in upon Ellen. The next morning a solemn Tillie mounted Sam, dreading the task she'd agreed to do. She rode to Frank and Ellen's. As she approached, she saw Frank looking out the window. She knocked and waited a bit for a response.

Sven opened the door. "Oh, how good to see all of you. I hope you don't mind my intrusion," Tillie said upon entering the home without waiting for an invitation.

Everyone stared at her. "Do forgive me for coming without being asked." She swallowed. "All of us are so glad to have another baby coming in the community, so Winnie and Helen and I have decided that one of us will check with Ellen often now. Of course Ellen has not asked for a thing and of course we do this for the other women when their time is coming." She'd added that last part for Frank's sake.

She found it hard to find enough spit in her mouth to continue talking, but went on. "Frank, I'm sure you see that Winnie is so good to help with these things, so please ride for her as soon as your wife's labor begins," she stated. "If a blizzard threatens, Winnie said she will simply come and check with Ellen. She'll stay, of course, if the baby is about to come."

Tillie told Sven too, that he must try to get help for his mother if the baby was coming. She didn't ask what the couple thought of her plan. She presented it as a simple fact of life. And, although Frank looked glum, he didn't shoo Tillie out of the place. He didn't tell her that her plan was impossible. He said nothing.

Having said her piece, she wished the family much happiness, again asked pardon for intruding, and set off for home.

Once on sturdy Sam, Tillie felt her breaths relaxing and her taut muscles letting go. She guessed that no one had spoken to Frank with such firmness for a long time. Surely not a woman. He hadn't quite known what to do when she made a bold declaration. She believed she could tolerate Frank's ire, but she feared he could take out his anger on Ellen and maybe the children. *Probably even Sven fears his father, either for himself or for his mother's sake. I wonder if this plan is wise. Perhaps it could do more harm than good. Yet certainly I have some responsibility to try to help, don't I? I can't imagine tolerating such a situation as Ellen does, yet I suppose it could be different if someone were hurting me. I simply can't imagine. I hope I've done the right thing.*

Tillie went to Bertha's as soon as she corralled Sam. When she told Bertha how the visit went, and she acknowledged her fears, Bertha replied, "Tillie, I couldn't have done what you did; you did right. I admire your courage. Wish I had more pluck. Perhaps I should have gone with you."

"Oh, you've plenty of pluck, just in different ways. Besides, Winnie offered to come, but we feared two of us might be too much for Frank to tolerate, thought it best I go alone."

Bertha's unwavering support eased some of Tillie's anxiety.

Bertha, for her part, checked with Brunhild each school day, asking how her mother was getting along and whether she thought the baby was coming soon. Winnie and Helen took turns calling on Ellen on Monday, Wednesday, and Friday mornings. Winnie always checked to see that Ellen was taking raspberry leaf tea regularly now, a tea that Winnie said would strengthen the womb for the hard work of birthing.

Tillie checked in with Ellen on Saturday afternoons. Frank usually had left for town by then. The one time when Frank was home, he left the shack when Tillie arrived, not even nodding to her greeting. That time, Ellen didn't smile or greet Tillie when she arrived and waited until Frank left to give a slight smile. But usually she smiled pleasantly when Tillie arrived. She didn't say much, but answered Tillie's questions with nods and brief explanations. She never sounded snappy and always gave a brief, "Thank you," and a small smile and nodded her head a few times when Tillie was about to leave. Tillie mentioned this to Winnie, who agreed with her that Ellen seemed to appreciate their care and concern, even though she was rather short of words or animation.

By mid-December snow had fallen twice, blanketing the wide prairie with several inches. Yet the ferocious winds so typical of Dakota didn't accompany the snow. The holidays were coming. The children had practiced the Christmas pageant at church and had already presented the school program with Christmas songs, as well as a spelling bee with words related to Christmas or perfection. Susan, daughter of Herman and Millie, won the spelling bee by spelling *quintessential*. Her face sparkled when she was declared the winner and her red cheeks added to her blossoming beauty.

The three women began checking in on Ellen almost every day since Winnie could tell the baby would come soon. On the morning of December 24, Helen went to check on Ellen and found her in labor. Frank was not home, so Helen told Sven he must go get Winnie. He got up, put on his coat and boots, and left, leaving Helen to hope he'd do as asked.

Obediently, Sven rode to Winnie's and gave her the news. Winnie gathered a few things she might need and first rode down the path to Millie's. When Millie answered the knock, Winnie stood outside. "Millie, I'm going to Ellen's. Hard to know how long it'll take. Will you check in with Willie and Thor and maybe help Willie out with some food if I can't be here for Christmas dinner?"

"Of course. They can come over here. Can celebrate Christmas together. Gonna have goose for dinner. And I'll make sure Santa finds his way in, though I suppose Willie will take care of it."

When Winnie arrived at Ellen's, Helen left to join her family for Christmas. She stopped at Tillie's on her way home to let her know what was happening. Tillie left her Christmas baking, pocketed the crocheted booties she'd made, told Bertha about the impending birth, mounted Sam, and rode for Ellen's shack.

Winnie was there making preparations and comforting Ellen. Tillie assumed the task of occupying Brunhild and Karl. Sven came and went, tending to outside chores or simply trying to stay out of the way.

It was after deep dark had fallen on Christmas Eve. The Christmas pageant was taking place at the church. Ellen had been struggling for hours, sweat pouring from her face with deep guttural cries coming forth from time to time. Winnie gave her castor oil to help the labor along. Frank had not returned and Ellen said he had known she was laboring and didn't want to be around to hear her cries.

It was clear to Tillie that Winnie was concerned, though Winnie kept reassuring Ellen that things would turn out fine. Whenever Ellen's spine-chilling cry came forth, Tillie worried that her own face revealed her fear.

Tillie held Ellen's hand, rubbed the sweat off her brow, and followed Winnie's direction for when to encourage Ellen not to push and when to push, push, push. At times Tillie helped Ellen sit up so she could push more effectively, then helped her lie back to rest. She found it both fascinating and terrible to watch and wondered whether birthing a baby was always this difficult.

Winnie made Sven keep hot water ready and washed up her hands periodically between Ellen's contractions.

After Ellen's endurance was so spent that Tillie thought she likely could not take another minute of pain, Winnie said in a strong voice, "It's coming. The rump and legs are coming first. Breech. Keep pushing, Ellen. Keep pushing. Push, push, push. Hard. Hard."

When the bloody baby's lower parts came through the birth canal just far enough for her to see it looked to be a boy and then stopped coming, Winnie slipped her hand and lower arm into the birth canal. She deftly rotated the tiny body, first to one side, then another, while telling Ellen what she was doing. Through her own cries and anguish, Ellen likely heard nothing. "Be ready to take the baby from me when it comes," Winnie calmly said to Tillie.

Nervously, Tillie waited for a time that seemed longer than it likely was. With Winnie's help, the baby's shoulders and head finally found a way to push through, perhaps during the singing of the final carols at the church service. Winnie caught the slippery infant, and carefully handed him to Tillie. "Now rub him hard all over, as much as you can. I must attend Ellen. She tore a lot. Lots of bleeding."

While Tillie rubbed as vigorously as she dared, a small cry came forth. She was sure she'd never heard as breathtaking a sound as his cry when it came from his tiny limp form.

Winnie took over care of the infant then, cleaned him off, checked him all over, and then cut the cord with a sharp scissors that she had cleaned in a flame.

"It's a healthy boy," Winnie softly said to Ellen, laying him next to her. "His head is a bit misshapen from his journey, but it will right itself. Merry, Merry Christmas."

Ellen began silently weeping. When Tillie put the baby on Ellen's chest, letting her look upon his face, Ellen said so softly that Tillie could barely hear. "I'll call him Kincaid to t'ank you and the women here for his life." Whispering, she added, "Haven't even told Frank what the child would be called, if a boy."

The children, even Sven, gathered round to look at the crying infant. Then Sven retreated to the barn.

When the afterbirth came, Winnie did what she could to stem Ellen's bleeding. She and Tillie removed the bloody cloths and washed Ellen, and put clean pads of cloth between her legs, pads that Winnie had brought along. Tillie noticed the odor of the blood, like earth drenched in coal drippings, sour and yet blooming with life itself.

Tillie put the booties on Kincaid's tiny feet, all the while marveling at the wonder of this child being born on Christmas Eve. She felt expansive, as if she weren't a single being, but rather part of the whole of life. Gratitude filled her, along with awe at life's mystery. The candle glowing in the window displayed a luminescent halo as if proclaiming the beauty of it. Tillie also hoped against hope that this event would help heal the broken family.

After a bit, Winnie encouraged Tillie to go home and celebrate the good news with Bertha while she would stay until she was sure the bleeding was under control, the infant had nursed for his drink of first milk, and Ellen was okay. "I'll put some sugar on where she tore down there once the bleeding slows down," she said. "Should help her heal."

Reluctant to leave, Tillie exclaimed, "Winnie, you are a font of knowledge and talents. I so admire your skill. Whatever would we do without you!"

"We share our gifts in our own ways. We've you to thank for making sure I was here to help."

"Well, yes, I suppose, yet . . ." she trailed off.

Before she left, she cuddled the little children to her and told them that Santa had provided the best gift of all this Christmas—a tiny brother. She'd noticed stockings hung by the stove and wished she'd thought to bring along some little gifts or at least a few pennies. Just before she opened the door, she again looked at the bed. Enraptured, she gazed at the sight of Kincaid flailing his arms and whimpering while Ellen helped him find her breast.

Tillie again mounted Sam and set off for home. On the short ride her feelings alternated between exhilaration and concern. She worried about the safety of the woman, weak from childbirth, with her husband not around to help. She decided to bring Christmas dinner to the family the next day.

Arriving at the B&T Estate, she stopped at Bertha's to give her the news. "I'm so weary, Bertha, yet way too excited to think of sleep. Please come over after just a bit to share some Christmas with me." She led Sam into his shed, then entered her cozy shack finding that Bertha had kept her fire going. The two friends shared handmade gifts with each other and talked into the wee hours of Christmas Day.

———

In February, another Dakota blizzard hit the Kincaid area. Luckily, it had started on a Saturday, so the children were not in school. Most of the Kincaid homesteaders were at home, but some were caught in town—at the Pig—when it began. Hans and Henry decided to spend the night at the "hotel," really just a storage room at the general store, hoping their families wouldn't worry too much.

Frank, along with Earl Hovde who had come to the community the previous summer, decided to head for home, though the others warned them not to take the chance.

The blizzard raged until Sunday afternoon when Hans and Henry, after checking in at their homes and warming themselves, rode together to check on the two other men. First, they went to Earl's home and found that he hadn't returned. His wife Josie and their daughter Sharon were frantic. Josie let out a piercing howl when Hans told her that Earl had left the Pig in the late afternoon, intent upon getting home. Hans got a search party going while Henry went to check on Frank.

Frank had not returned either. Although Ellen let out a small whimper, she appeared stoic. Sven joined the search, which went on into the early evening when they had to call it off. Hans again checked in with Josie and found that Earl had still not returned. Helen had come to stay with Josie, whose eyes were red and sunken. Sharon, too, had been crying. She sat next to Josie, holding her mother's arm and rubbing it up and down from time to time. Josie spoke little. She thanked Helen and Hans for their efforts and said she'd like to be alone with Sharon. With tears wetting her cheeks, Helen put her arm around Josie and then put on her coat and said she'd call the next day.

Henry accompanied Sven home. Their eyes widened when they saw Frank's horse tied to the post by the door. Inside, they found Frank cuddled under quilts near the fire. He said he'd spent the night in an abandoned shed a couple miles out of Kincaid. He had mild frostbite on his fingers and toes, he thought, but otherwise he was okay.

On Monday morning, Earl's horse Jerry returned home empty. While the search went on for a couple of days, they would not find Earl's body until the spring thaw.

For days, even weeks, after Earl disappeared, Josie walked around and around in the tiny house, saying nothing, doing nothing much of the time. Sometimes she cooked a simple meal and cleaned up the dishes; other times she just sat in a chair gazing at the window. One could imagine she hoped to conjure Earl's image coming toward the house. "I don't have a whit of an idea what to do," she told Tillie. "Should Sharon and I return to Wisconsin? When Earl talked about the possibility of going west for a better life, I eagerly agreed, happy to leave my deranged mother who was confined to an insane asylum after my father left and went somewhere west himself. Now I wonder if I'm becoming insane, wonder whether I can withstand the loneliness here in Dakota or anywhere."

Kneeling next to Josie and holding her hand, Tillie, with the softest of voice, said, "Josie, no doubt you'll feel such deep anguish, but you'll look at Sharon and know that she needs the tender love and care that only you can give her and somehow you'll find the strength to go to her and comfort her. She'll comfort you, too."

Josie looked at Tillie and nodded. She nodded several times.

The community did what they could to wrap their arms around the child and her mother. Tillie gave extra care and encouragement to Sharon at school and visited the home regularly, bringing dried beef hash, fresh bread, cinnamon jumble cookies, or tapioca pudding. Orlo Larson took a special interest in helping out, especially helping with the heavier chores.

A month later, when Tillie visited, she noticed that Josie had baked three loaves of bread and that occasional smiles had returned to her face, along with a quickness of step that had been absent. When she observed the tenderness displayed on Sharon's face as she looked at her mother, Tillie sensed that it was this child who was gradually bringing Josie some semblance of peace.

As winter ebbed toward spring, while Tillie still complained of the cold and the howling wind, a wind sometimes so penetrating she believed her organs were freezing, she also found beauty in the winter scenes and sounds. The hoarfrost created a crystalline painting outlining tall grasses protruding from their blanket of snow. It glistened on the twigs of bushes so they appeared soft as feathers. A great horned owl hooted, sending an eerie, riveting, shiver through the still air. Jack Frost painted exquisite designs on the window, and the dim glow of Bertha's window was a constant friend. And at times the deep darkness that stared into her eyes when Bertha's window was dark brought a sense of pensive reflection that she felt was good for her soul.

Tillie even found enchantment in the popping sounds of coal when she added it to the stove. Best of all was the radiant warmth that penetrated through skin and tissues and organs while she stood in front of that stove after feeding and watering Sam, bringing in snow to melt and coal to burn, or returning from church or other gatherings.

Almost without warning, another blizzard hit the area in mid-March and raged over two days. This time everyone in the community sought shelter as soon as a fierce wind began blowing, accompanied by blinding snow. Except for Elizabeth and Peter, whose father came to pick them up, Tillie and Bertha kept the children with them. They worried, though, that their parents would think the worst, even though the teachers had said they'd keep the children in their shacks if weather turned dangerous before there was a chance for the children to get home safely.

After school, Tillie kept the boys with her. The girls stayed with Bertha, who made potato soup and served bread with plenty of butter and jam. Then she helped the girls make boiled frosting and they licked their fingers after relishing graham crackers spread with the thick icing. In the evening they made rag dolls, the older girls helping the younger ones. Just before bed, they played Find the Thimble in the candlelight. Then the girls piled onto the bed and Bertha slept on rugs on the floor with a quilt wrapped snugly around her.

Tillie made jackrabbit stew and tapioca pudding for the boys. Together they drew animals, then read stories until most of them got sleepy. The little boys slept with Tillie on the bed while the older ones slept on the floor. In the morning, after eating oatmeal, the older boys shoveled a path to Bertha's and out to the shed. Then the younger ones went to Miss Harstad's shack for school and the older girls returned to Miss Melbakken's.

Many Dakotans would remember it as the worst blizzard that befell them during the early homestead years, a time when many homesteaders perished, along with some of their livestock. The Kincaid area, although hit hard, escaped the worst of the storm's wrath and no one in the community died, though a couple of them lost some cows and chickens. Arne and Emma thought they had lost their dog, but on a sunny day a week later, the limping dog returned home with frostbitten ears and a paw either frozen or injured in some fashion. "Can't remember such joy at seeing him limp toward the shack since I last gave birth!" exclaimed Emma at church that following Sunday. "Didn't even don a coat, just ran to him."

———

Finally, as March turned to April, spring arrived. With the melting of snow, the earth hinted of emerging green. The first pasqueflowers bloomed. The few bushes budded. Creatures scurried about the prairie while golden eagles soaring above watched their movements.

Migrating birds returned or stopped briefly on their journey north. To Tillie and Bertha and most other homesteaders, the birds seemed more abundant than in previous years. Perhaps they were following the settlers west.

In late April Bertha and Tillie visited Kincaid General Store to stock up on staples. After totaling up Bertha's purchases, Eleanor handed her a letter that had just arrived that morning.

"It's from my sister, Hilda," said Bertha to Eleanor. Not wanting to open the letter with customers waiting for service, Bertha suggested to Tillie they sit down outside the store.

Bertha used her forefinger to tear open the envelope.

Dear Bertha,

Grandpapa has taken quite ill. He is in some distress, especially with breathing. Doc Smith says he's not likely to live long, not more than a few months.

Bertha burst into tears, emitted "Oh, no, no!" and grabbed Tillie's hand.

This grandfather, along with his wife who had passed on a few years back, had raised Bertha and her siblings after their mother died in childbirth and their father abandoned their care. Although Bertha maintained cordial relations with her father, it was her grandfather she'd always turned to for solace, for advice, for love. Bertha read on:

I know he would so want to see you before he departs this world. Would you be able to make a trip home when school is over, to give him the joy he most longs for, apart from seeing Grandmama again?

The letter then turned to other news, that of Hilda's beau and tidbits of neighborhood gossip. Bertha stopped reading.

"Oh, Tillie," she said, "I must return home as soon as school is over."

Her intense crying had stopped, but tears still flowed.

"Of course, of course," said Tillie. "And if you want to leave sooner, I can manage all of the children for the couple weeks that are left. The older boys already often stay home to help out with planting."

Controlling her tears, Bertha replied, "I think I can stay. I hate to desert my pupils right at the end of the year. I can even stop the classes a couple days early, perhaps.

"Oh, Tillie," she said, looking into her friend's eyes, "Grandpapa has been so dear to me. He's been so hearty, I somehow had forgotten that he is growing so old. He's been my anchor in life when all else was lost. I hope I can ease his dying days by my visit."

"I'm sure you will."

She used a sheet of paper Eleanor provided to write a short note to Hilda. "I'll be home sometime in May," read her message. She also asked Eleanor if she could return some of the flour, eggs, and butter she had purchased. Eleanor said, "Of course, Bertha, I'll give you the refund for whatever you won't be able to use."

Alone on Her Homestead

With a deep sense of loneliness setting in, Tillie said farewell to Bertha at the train station, hoping her friend would return in late summer as promised. Tillie believed she wouldn't survive the solitude of a winter alone, so she would need to abandon her hope of proving up should Bertha not return at summer's end.

Ole had come to the station with Bertha as well. Their togetherness had grown into a deep fondness. Bertha didn't admit it was love to Tillie, but acknowledged that she had developed an appreciation of Ole that went beyond friendship. There had been warm and tender kisses, and a few passionate ones when each of their bodies trembled with desire.

"I'll miss so much this summer," said Bertha as she prepared to depart, "the community celebrations, shack and barn raisings, the satisfaction I've felt in completing chores, but most of all I shall miss both of you."

Ole's sadness was written on his face. One could see longing there, could imagine his worry that he might never again see the woman he had clearly come to love. His adoration was visible in his respectful actions, his searching for Bertha at community gatherings, the smile he'd broadcast as he greeted her, the dimples that lit his face.

As the train left the station, Tillie watched its steam drift across the spacious plains. She listened until she could no longer hear the *whoosh*, or the *chug*. She gazed until the train disappeared on the horizon. When she turned to look at Ole, she could feel his anguish. Slowly, the two walked back to his cart.

Spring chores fell to Tillie, of course, though by now such chores were routine. She easily fell into the rhythm of the tasks that needed attending: preparing the garden, planting, cleaning up detritus left around when the snow melted, repairing an area of the roof, cutting some of the grass around the shack with a scythe. She also needed to tend hens and chicks, especially ensuring the chicks were warm enough and had protection from foxes, skunks, and coyotes. If nothing else called, the garden weeds did. In the evenings, she embroidered flour sacks for dish towels and worked on a doily for a shelf, a doily she was decorating with hardanger. She sewed a blouse as a gift for Bertha upon her hoped-for return, and she read. All of these activities put a haze around her loneliness, but didn't erase it.

Before bed Tillie often spent some minutes sitting on her doorstep, listening to the sounds of the prairie, feeling darkness closing in. Climbing into bed sometimes brought a sense of gloom, but on the evenings after she had brought her wash in from the line, the aroma and tautness of the fresh sheets delighted her. Bright and crisp, the scent seemed made of a pure cleanliness rarely sensed on the plains of Dakota.

She'd received copies of *Pride and Prejudice* and *Little Women* as birthday gifts from her family, and she relished the reading time and escape from her own life that it offered during evenings when she was exhausted from work but not quite ready for the hay.

She also read the *Bowbells Tribune* whenever Ernie shared his copy, which he bought for two cents at Kincaid General Store. In it she looked forward to reading the weekly chapter of *Arnewood Mystery* by Maurice Hersey. It was a captivating story that took place in Australia. It revealed the family disputes and intrigues that developed after a discovery of gold on their land. She also found herself searching for news from near home, as when reading that a man from Graceville, Minnesota, had visited the area and a man named Albrecht from Montevideo had settled on land near Bowbells. She would make it a point to search out this Albrecht when she was able to get to Bowbells because the last name was familiar and he was from so near home.

She even read a story about a man who had tried to commit suicide by hanging. "Too much mother-in-law" was the reason the newspaper gave as the apparent cause for the hanging. They found the man before he died, so he would likely have to put up with his mother-in-law a while longer. The *Bowbells Tribune* reported a great deal of national and international news as well. *What a wonder it is*, she said to herself, *that such news can travel by telegraph lines and rails and find me here in this land so far removed from the capital of the United States, let alone those of Europe.*

Millie and Martha complained that they couldn't read much. If their husbands caught them reading the *Arnewood Mystery* or a novel passed among the women, they called them lazy. Yet Tillie encouraged her friends, saying it broadened their minds and improved their English.

But all was not work with the occasional times for reading. There were a couple of shack raisings that summer, the Fourth of July celebration, church gatherings, and Ladies Aid, of course. Tillie's friendship with Ernie, too, developed into a kind of courting, with him inviting her to go to barn dances and join him on private picnics, as well as for community gatherings. It was not a serious courtship yet, and Tillie was reluctant even to call it courting, but she found his company pleasant. Too, she looked forward to the break from routine he offered her, and his handiness was so helpful. He could recommend how to fix a hoe, the best way to repair a roof, or how to attach a small cupboard to the wall. He expressed willingness to help with any of the harder chores, and even those that weren't so hard. Haying was one of the harder chores, but Ole had bought a mower and she knew he and Ernie would help with that one.

Halvor, one of the first homesteaders, was found dead in his home that summer, already rotting in the heat. He was likely over thirty but not yet forty, hailing from Iowa. He was rather coarse and doleful, though always cordial, a man who had made few deep friendships in the community. Whether he suffered an attack of some sort or had simply given in to the loneliness, no one would ever know. There was no gunshot or other wound.

His neighbors built a simple box for a coffin. Managing the stench by withholding his breath, then walking away from the body for occasional breaths, Orlo Larson dressed the man for a quick closed-coffin funeral. He also sent word to Halvor's family in Iowa, finding information about their whereabouts among Halvor's papers. Except for Earl, whose body had been found in the spring after the snow melted, his death was the first among the Kincaid Norwegian homesteaders. Most everyone expressed their anguish at his death. Ernie confided in Tillie that he felt guilt and regret at not having offered more friendship. Although Tillie had danced with Halvor on occasion, she had barely known him, since he was a man who kept mostly to himself and his crops along with his dog Roger.

It was the dog that had led Hans, his neighbor, to investigate. Although Hans gave the dog some food, it wandered around the neighborhood for a few days after Hans found Halvor dead. Then

Ernie took it in, but didn't really want a dog, which he mentioned to Tillie. She couldn't bear to see the dog go without kindness, especially since she understood that Halvor had loved Roger as he would have a child, even slept with him, which was unheard of in those days, or at least generally denied.

So, Roger became Tillie's. He was a medium-sized mongrel, golden tan, and mellow as his color. Oh, he'd bark when someone rode up, he'd chase a jackrabbit and sometimes catch it, but his manner was mild and endearing. Tillie would grow to love him. She also figured he'd warm her frigid winter nights and be a companion to ease the loneliness. And he became such a companion. He also became Tillie's protector, alerting her to a wolf pack nearing the shack and to the sounds of anyone approaching on foot or horse. Roger even became a confidant, listening with ears perked and head cocked to Tillie's dreams, her fears, and stories of her family life at home in Minnesota. Tillie especially appreciated Roger for what seemed to her to be his empathic attending to her thoughts.

———

As summer progressed, Tillie canned beans and carrots, adding vinegar and boiling the jars for a few hours to hopefully keep them from spoiling. She fermented cabbage and pickled beets. Most exciting, that summer the men put in the foundation for the little schoolhouse, just a small structure, but enough for twenty students. They sought Tillie's ideas for the school's construction, and she felt the men who would build it respected her recommendations. Like the church, it would be a frame building, eighteen-by-twenty-four feet, with a hip roof.

Lumber was hard to come by and expensive in Dakota, but some community members donated funds. The Dakota Department of Public Instruction provided additional aid. Plans even included a little tower for the school bell, for which Tillie's family sent funds.

Now the students would be able to have roughhewn desks. After receiving a lesson from Ernie, who was a skilled carpenter, Tillie managed most of their construction herself. "Golly man," he said, "you work harder than men and do it better."

Of course, said Tillie to herself. *Most men just don't know that women are so competent, or refuse to believe it.* Tillie even said out loud, "Oh yes, women can do most everything a man can if the need comes along." Yet she still depended upon the men for much of the heavier work and some of the knowledge she surely didn't have.

"Golly man," he said again, shaking his head. "But you're not going to do the haying yourself. Ole will cut it with his new mower, and we'll help build the haystack."

"Thank you. I'll accept your help with gratitude. Know I couldn't manage the task alone." She smiled up at him and gave him a peck on the cheek.

A Saturday in early August was set for the school raising. It was with relish that Tillie baked bread and pies. By now, she'd become adept at regulating the temperature in her oven so it was rare that she burned bread, cookies, or pie, or left gooey places in the center of a gingerbread cake. She spruced herself up for the occasion, wearing her best blouse, white with lace trim on the collar, sleeves, and bodice. She pinned her watch to the left side of the front. Around her neck, she wore a lace scarf with her brooch in the center.

As the men constructed the frame for the building, Tillie led the community in a sing-along. They sang "Columbia, the Gem of the Ocean"; "Oh My Darling, Clementine"; "She'll Be Coming

'Round the Mountain"; and other songs. When that was over, the children got games going, playing Cat and Rat, Blind Man's Bluff, and Kick the Can. They organized gunnysack races, which were hilarious to watch. Ellen and baby Kincaid were there, along with Frank and the other children. Kincaid was seven months old and looked healthy. Ellen was cordial, as always, though her face was pensive and unreadable to Tillie, as usual.

Hours later, when the men finished framing up the building and constructing the latrine, Tillie and the other women laid out food. Most everyone gobbled down the dried meat and cheese slices, vegetable sticks, and breads, and especially enjoyed the Knox gelatin salads, since gelatin had just become a popular item at Kincaid General Store. They chowed down on pie and cake. A ceremony followed, led by Henry. He hadn't trimmed his shaggy beard and his hands were rough and dirty, Tillie noticed, but he wore a clean white shirt under his mostly clean overalls. After thanking the men for their work in building the school, he added, "And we should give a nod to the ladies too. They kept us from getting hungry out here while we worked and they quenched our thirst. And, course they brung food for the ceremony. But special thanks today go to Tillie and Bertha, the prods that got the building plan going, and they taught our young'uns in their shacks for two seasons. I remember when I first met those girls on the day they came to check out sites. Never knew what a gift they'd be to us."

Everyone clapped at that.

While so appreciating the ceremony and feeling pleasure in the recognition of Bertha and herself, the words and the day brought a pit of sadness to Tillie as well. *Living here alone without Bertha has brought me feelings of loneliness I never knew before. Her little sayings always make me smile. I so wish she could have been here today to witness this.*

That day, the men of the community elected a school board, made up of Henry Berge, Willie Hegstad, and Knut Aakre. Ernie had made a plaque to hang in the building to commemorate the first teachers in Meadows School. Tillie made a short speech thanking the community for their tireless efforts. "I only hope Bertha and I are sufficient for the task of educating the youngsters, many of whom have more practical knowledge than I do," she said in ending.

"Well," proclaimed Henry, who'd been selected as president of the board, "I can't imagine bein' better served than having two such gifted teachers here with us. Proud I am, indeed, to have had a hand in constructing the school."

———

While late summer chores took a great deal of time, the evenings often lingered long and lonely for Tillie. It was on those evenings that she had a hard time not thinking of Jergen—and of Ernie, as well—in a way she knew she should not do. Such thoughts created a sensation between her legs and a year or so earlier she had started rubbing herself there when she was in bed and the intensity of the reaction almost overwhelmed her. She had forbidden herself to do it ever again. *Goodness, I am a teacher. Certainly, this is something that is forbidden by God. I simply must not do it again. Certainly, Bertha would never do such a thing, nor the ladies in the community. What is wrong with me?*

Yet one evening that lonely summer when dusk was just spreading its deep shadows, she removed her bloomers and went outside with a blanket. She lay the blanket down in the deep grass, sat upon it, raised her skirt and did this forbidden thing again.

Why she had decided to do this thing out of doors she had no idea, had simply felt herself compelled.

When it was over, she shuddered and then quickly gathered the blanket and ran inside. *My Lord, did God see that? Did my grandparents in heaven see that? What if someone in the community had a spyglass and could have seen me?* She felt overcome with shame. And, at the same time, just the tiniest bit joyous, the recognition of which increased her shame.

Once inside, she took out her Bible, opened it to Leviticus, which she believed told of damnation for such acts against God, read several pages, then turned to the New Testament, to John. She hoped she would get a little comfort from Jesus's words, and she did, just a little. She also prayed fervently for forgiveness and again vowed never to repeat this act.

Many years would pass before a nurse would tell Tillie that similar actions in her son were quite natural and were common in girls as well. Even then, Tillie could barely believe that what the nurse said was true.

Terror

It was another dry year on the Dakota plain as Tillie waited for Bertha's return. She had already harvested all the beans and most of the beets. Many other vegetables were ready to harvest: onions, carrots, and rutabagas, along with some of the potatoes. She was busy preparing lessons for the coming year when Roger's incessant bark, almost a yelping, at the door caused her to jump up and rush to him. When she opened the door to a windy day, she smelled something. *Something like what?* she asked herself. *Something scorched?* Roger continued barking, looking west. Tillie noticed the sky in that direction—an ominous orange topped with deep gray swirling clouds. *What in the world?*

Then knowing the answer in the pit of her stomach, she dropped her book and stared for a moment until adrenaline found its way to her brain. She ran outside and, gathering up the chickens like a sheepdog protecting her sheep from approaching coyotes, herded the squawking creatures into the shack. There, they might have better protection than in the coop, which was between the two firebreaks Ole had plowed while the shack was inside both breaks. She grabbed a rope to leash Roger, if necessary, then dashed to the pasture to get Sam. Running with Roger beside her, she pulled at Sam's reins. As the fierce west wind drove the fire toward her, she headed to the little lake while yelling, "Run, run, run!"

She was already feeling the warmth and could see flames. She glanced behind her in utter terror, as she felt the leaping flames draw close, fed by the dry rolling grasses. Never had she witnessed such terrifying beauty. Never had she felt such horror. Sam almost bolted from her grasp, but she held on as she ran, as she ran, gasping, gasping.

Reaching the water, she drew Sam down, down into the water with her. Roger stayed by her side beginning to paddle.

The lake was just deep enough to allow her to submerge herself while standing. Tillie held Sam's head down just touching the water. Roger paddled near her as the flames began to tear toward them. With utter panic, she submerged her head. She grasped Sam's reins with every ounce of strength she had. Feeling Roger beside her, she waited. How long? She had no idea, but her breath gave out and she gasped at the surface, finding air, hot but not sizzling. Panic filled Sam's eyes, but he stayed with her, not trying to bolt. Roger, looking terrified as well, paddled next to her.

It passed over them.

Slowly, she raised her shoulders out of the water, still grasping Sam's reins. All around her the grass looked scorched, but not in flames. Tillie waited and watched the flames roar past some shacks and toward others. Minutes passed. She edged out of the lake, gingerly inching onto the partially blackened landscape. She pulled on Sam's reins and he followed. Roger bounded out of the water, but stayed by her side. The trio made their way toward the shack. Apparently Roger stepped on a coal, and he yelped, but he stayed near Tillie.

The shack still stood, as did Bertha's. Even the chicken coop remained whole, though it appeared scorched. Sam's shed was fine, given its sod construction. Indeed, Tillie wondered at herself why she hadn't thought to put the chickens there. *Maybe all of us should have just huddled in the shed.*

She let out a breath she seemed to have been holding for minutes. She corralled Sam, and caressed his mane. "Oh, Sam, we all survived. You are a wonderful horse." She noticed scorch marks on the fencing, then went to the shack. The grass directly around the shack was scorched in places, but much of it had escaped burning as the fire passed over so quickly. Arriving at the shack, Tillie saw that some of the tar paper looked wavy, but it still protected the place. She heard chickens squawking. As she opened the door, a couple flew past her, so she let them all out, where they huddled together on the unburned grass near the shack. Inside, the chickens had made a mess with their pooping. They'd torn the curtains. "It's a small price to pay for their survival and mine," Tillie said to the walls. "I'll clean up the mess and sew new curtains."

Tillie looked toward the school and saw that it lived. But, even before putting on dry clothes, she ran to the school to check on it. Roger stayed close to her side. The fire had blackened much of the grass outside the plowed firebreak, but the grass near the school was still golden. The wooden siding felt warm and had some black marks, but nothing felt burning hot. On her way home, she noticed a couple of sparks and stamped them out. She checked the haycocks, not yet formed into a stack. Most were scorched, but didn't appear to be smoldering. She spent the next hour looking for more sparks and stomping on the few she found.

Back by the shack, Tillie raised cool water from the well and took gulping swallows of the delicious liquid. She poured some into a bucket for Roger and brought some to Sam's corral, then went into her shack where she removed her sodden clothes and put on fresh ones. She sat for a while, then picked up a rag, added soap to water in a bucket, and began cleaning the mess.

Hours after the fire passed, Ernie rode up on Rex. Tillie saw his approach and walked out as he rode up. "Golly man, you're safe, t'ank da Lord!" he shouted as he dismounted. "T'ings okay here? I see Roger survived." Tillie told him what she'd done, then asked how he'd managed.

"Was in town when the fire came through, at the Pig. Building started on fire, but we men doused it with our drink along with buckets of water, and even our pee," he said with a sheepish grin. "General store still stands," he added. "Looks a little charred. My own place made it through the flames, but lost me some of my hens and chicks. Guess the coop got too hot. Didn't burn."

Tillie invited him in, apologizing for the chicken-made mess that she hadn't totally cleaned up. She fetched cool water from the well and placed cookies left over from the school celebration on a plate. The two sipped the refreshing water, both without many words. "I'm grateful for surviving; yet still filled with fear," Tillie said softly. "As I ran to the lake, I know I felt panic, but I was too terrified to think about anything other than getting there."

He nodded his head and looked into her eyes, easing her fears with his warm chocolate ones. "And this wasn't near as bad as some have been, I've heard," he said. "Most of us had done the haying. Probably helped."

Soon, Ernie said he must be going to check on others and help look for sparks, but before he left, he surrounded her with his arms and gave her a kiss that lingered many seconds, a kiss full of more longing than any previous ones. Tillie thought her heart must be quaking as she kissed him back. She felt so grateful for his concern at this frightening and lonely time.

Most of the shacks still stood without serious damage, but the shack of the new arrivals, Esther and Harold Sieverson, was badly burned, likely because they had not yet plowed a firebreak. But the community would pitch in and get it repaired in no time. Tillie offered them Bertha's shack as a temporary residence until then.

The fire had come earlier than most, which were more likely to start in the fall when the vegetation was brown or sometimes in spring before the grass greened. With more land around Kincaid turned to cropland, the fires tended to be thwarted in their rage more than in the decades prior, the broken land providing firebreaks. Even so, some crops were destroyed. For most of the homesteaders, a diminished harvest would be the worst legacy of the fire.

However, someone in the Danish community near Kincaid had been caught out in the open on his horse and neither horse nor man survived the burns. They found both in tremendous pain. They shot the horse. The man lived a few painful hours before succumbing.

Many had recognized the approaching flames much earlier than Tillie, who had been so intent on planning lessons that she hadn't noticed the scent of smoke on the air. A few in the Danish community, where the fire burned with more ferocity, suffered burned flesh from trying to corral animals and struggling to beat out the fire with wet towels or blankets. Some of their cattle had perished, though most survived, sheltered in barns or within firebreaks.

Bertha was due to return the following week and there wasn't time to send a letter telling her of the fire.

Tillie sewed new curtains with fabric she purchased at Kincaid General Store, then added a border of lace she'd brought from home. She bought a roll of tar paper and started repairing the damage on her shack. Harold Sieverson noticed her labor and joined her to finish, then helped her patch up Bertha's. "We're starting work on my shack tomorrow," he told her. "Should be able to be out of here in a couple'a days."

"Thanks so much for your help, Harold. Tusen takk, tusen takk. When you start in on your shack, I'll be sure to bring food for you men." After a moment, she added, "I was comforted by knowing you and Esther were so close after the scare we all had."

She finished the order for school supplies she could obtain from the Department of Public Instruction now that there was a school and a school board: slates for the students, a real blackboard with chalk and erasers, some reading primers for Bertha's younger students, and copies of the *Adventures of Huckleberry Finn* and *Robinson Crusoe* to read to the older students. The local community would buy a cast iron stove to place in a sandbox, which would catch the coals. Ernie offered to build a teacher's desk.

Now that there was a building, she and Bertha would share teaching tasks. They'd need to work out how to do it, perhaps with one presenting a lesson while one worked with the other students. Most schools, of course, had only one teacher, but the two friends had agreed to share both the instruction and the salary, which Tillie now knew would be thirty-eight dollars a month.

Now that Tillie and Bertha's first wheat harvest would be diminished due to the fire, income for the two women would be minimal and the teacher pay would surely help. Other residents had equal burdens, some with much more worry than Tillie and Bertha, who knew their families would help them financially if it became necessary.

The Return

When the train pulled into Portal, Tillie was so excited to see Bertha, and so hoping Bertha hadn't at the last minute changed her mind about coming back, that she tripped just outside the station. The little bouquet of wildflowers for Bertha went flying.

When Tillie saw her friend, tears rolled down her cheeks. She ran to her and tried to embrace her while Bertha struggled to free her hands of her handbag and the travel bag that Ole had made and given to her before she left for her journey.

Bertha looked hearty, though exhausted from the trip. While Henry gathered her luggage, Belle noticed Bertha looking around. "Suppose you might have wanted to see Ole here," Belle said rather matter-of-factly. Bertha moved her head up and down a few times, her eyes a little downcast, her mouth slightly open with an apprehensive look.

"Well, he wanted to come," put in Tillie, "wasn't sure he should, but sends his greetings. I told him I thought it would be fine to come, but he wasn't so sure."

"Oh," said Bertha, with her expression looking much softer than it had a moment before. "I suppose I gave him some reason to worry about Lars. Didn't know for certain it was over until I got home. Should've written Ole to tell him, but didn't know just how to say it."

The four stepped into Henry and Belle's newly purchased buggy, which Belle had insisted upon using to pick up Bertha.

While returning to the B&T Estate, everyone jabbered away. Bertha told of marriages, deaths, courtships, illnesses, and the like of people from home. Tillie relayed some of the news of Kincaid, especially about the grass fire, which Bertha had learned about from the conductor on the train. "Everything turned out fine, of course," said Tillie. "All our chickens survived and, of course, Sam and Roger. Pulled 'em into the lake with me."

Bertha let out a chuckle. "I can just see you doing that. Relieved to hear that everything's okay. I was full of worry after the conductor told me about the fire."

Henry told Bertha about the new school. "I'm even head of the school board. Never in my life did I think I'd have that sort of privilege."

Then, in the back of the buggy, where Helen and Hans couldn't hear them so well, Bertha said to Tillie in a soft voice, "Lars asked Christine Pederson to marry him, with a wedding planned for December." She didn't shed a tear. "I didn't even talk with him apart from passing the time of day. So, that's sure over." With a smile, she added, "I'm looking forward to seeing Ole and getting on with life here in Kincaid."

She told Tillie that her grandfather had hung on to living for nearly two months after she arrived. "Then, with me, Hilda, and Hans at his side, he gave a little groan and breathed no more. I mourn his loss so, yet his time had come. I'm grateful for being with him in his illness and holding his hand as he passed."

"I'm so glad you could be with him," said Tillie.

Bertha said the rest of her family was well, apart from a cousin who had died of diphtheria and an elderly uncle who had been kicked by a bull and died shortly thereafter.

Bertha had seen and talked with Jergen. "I told him that you thought of him often, and that brought a smile to his face."

"Oh, dear," replied Tillie with some color rising to her cheeks.

"He said he thought of you, as well. Don't think he's courting anyone and certainly isn't engaged to be married."

Tillie, who had held her breath while waiting for that news, let it out now, still not understanding why she so longed for him now when she hadn't until she left Minnesota. Most of Tillie's family was fine, Bertha said, though a cousin died after giving birth and a grandmother on Tillie's father's side, still living in Norway, had passed, the news reaching the family just a couple of days before Bertha left for Dakota.

When they arrived at the shack, with the grass on the estate still looking scorched in places, Bertha looked around, and said, "Oh, my."

As soon as Bertha put her luggage away, Tillie, with Roger by her side as usual, took Bertha to the school and she nearly wept at the simple beauty of it. "To think this will be *our* school," she said softly.

———

Life went on at the estate. On their own land, Bertha and Tillie helped the men harvest the wheat, what wheat there was, probably some over four hundred bushels. They had hoped for a great harvest, but the fire had reduced it. They finished canning, harvested root vegetables and some of the squash, managed the usual chores, and made plans for the start of school.

Hans and Helen hosted a barn dance to celebrate the end of the harvest. The community danced and sang and drank as if the harvest had been the most plentiful ever. Tillie talked some with Ellen as she made a point to do whenever convenient. Ellen looked tired and worn, but said everything was just fine. Tillie noticed that Josie had not come and assumed she still was grief-stricken over Earl's death and unable to face a celebration.

Ole and Bertha, now comfortable as a couple and growing closer since Bertha's return, danced almost every dance together after square-dancing was over. And Ernie asked Tillie to dance a two-step and a couple of waltzes. She leaned in close during the waltzes and he responded by holding her tightly and gently kissing her cheek. The two walked outside, hand in hand, looking at the crescent moon and stars, saying little at first.

Tillie pointed out the fuzzy Pleiades group of stars now visible in the September sky. "It's in the constellation Taurus, the horse."

"Golly man, you impress me so with your knowledge, Tillie. I'm pretty good at fixin' things, buildin' things, shootin' a deer or an antelope, but you? You shine way above me in book-learnin'."

"Well, I had to learn such things at normal school. They are interesting, of course, but out here it's the practical knowledge you have that is more important than book-learned facts. You seem to have learned a lot in school too. And you don't talk quite like so many of da Norvegians, y'know," she added, smiling up at him. He took her chin in his big, calloused hand, guided it toward his mouth, and kissed her with clear passion. When she drew back first, in a weak voice he asked, "Was that okay to do?" She nodded, looking up into his chocolate eyes. She didn't know just how she felt. His good looks, his easy way in conversing with most everybody, his everyday intelligence, and the kindness he displayed drew her in and she liked him, even liked him a lot, yet something in her still held back. *Maybe I'm just a stick-in-the-mud, as Bertha says, and intended for a spinster.*

The two walked back into the barn, danced the one last waltz, and then each turned for home.

Ernie turned back to her and called in a soft voice, "Tillie?"

"Yes?"

"I sure enjoyed being with yous tonight—oops I said 'yous'— and I hope I wasn't too forward."

"I enjoyed it, too. I enjoyed it very much." She smiled warmly and threw him a kiss.

———————

With the harvest over, school began full time. On the first Saturday after the school bell had begun ringing each weekday morning, the teachers held a celebration for the community with a picnic lunch social. The proceeds from the lunches would go for school supplies.

Each of the community women decorated a container with picnic goodies: sandwiches, cut vegetables, cakes, cookies, and the like. They were supposed to hide the containers so their husbands and other men wouldn't see them; most of the women covered them with an embroidered kitchen towel, then decorated them with a ribbon or two.

Henry Berge explained the rules: (1) Each man would bid on the container he wanted; (2) lunches made by unmarried women, which they'd been told to mark with a red ribbon, would be offered first and the single men could bid on those; and (3) a married man winning a container made by a married woman would share the lunch with his own wife.

Tillie and Bertha had made small containers of lunch goodies for each child, each wrapped in a handkerchief.

There were five single women: Bertha, Tillie, Anna, Olga, and now Josie, a widow. The eligible bachelors, Ole, Ernie, Orlo, Daniel Haugen (Ole's brother recently arrived from Wisconsin), and the newly arrived Nick Dokken from northern Minnesota, spent the most on their bids. They looked forward to lunch with one of the *girls*—well maybe not with Anna and they weren't sure about Olga. Bertha's container, which she wrapped in a dish towel decorated with cows, chickens, and a red barn, drew the most cash—two and a half dollars, bid up in twenty-five cent increments. Ernie won that one, hoping it was Tillie's. Tillie's came in next at two dollars and a quarter, with Ole the winning bidder, then Olga's, going to Orlo Larson for two dollars, though he had hoped it was Josie's. Anna's went to Ole's brother Daniel. Nick Dokken won Josie's.

Josie had been averse to coming to the social. Tillie had used a lot of encouragement to get Josie to agree and she eventually acquiesced for Sharon's sake. Nick tried rather unsuccessfully to engage Josie in conversation during their lunch, but when she remained pleasant but responded mostly in monosyllables or a head nod, he filled in with stories of the fishing he'd often done and now missed, since no large lakes were nearby.

Daniel looked as if he might be eating poison as he swallowed each bite of Anna's lunch. As soon as he had managed to eat the contents of the box, including the fudge, he gallantly thanked Anna, saying, "T'ank you Anna; it was good. You done bake good." Then he excused himself for "other matters" he needed to attend to, which appeared to be talking to other men who had formed a group.

Anna smiled as he left, giggling a little, "Vell, y'know, he done a right good job of stuffin' down my lunch even though he wished it had come from one of yous better-lookin' women, y'know," she told Bertha.

Most of the other lunches went for fifty to seventy-five cents, which was an awful lot of money for a lunch, the men complained. Tillie kept saying it was all going to a good cause, and, all in all, the school took in nearly twenty dollars, which pleased Tillie and Bertha.

Bertha led those gathered in "Columbia, the Gem of the Ocean" and the Pledge of Allegiance. Tillie had trained Elizabeth Aakre to recite "The Song of Hiawatha" by Longfellow and Elizabeth recited it nearly flawlessly. Loud applause followed her recitation. Then Thor Hegstad, looking adorable in new overalls and a bright red shirt, recited "The Cow" by Robert Louis Stevenson. His parents, Willie and Winnie, watched with smiles and radiant faces.

> *The friendly cow all red and white,*
> *I love with all my heart:*
> *She gives me cream with all her might,*
> *To eat with apple-tart.*
>
> *She wanders lowing here and there,*
> *And yet she cannot stray,*
> *All in the pleasant open air,*
> *The pleasant light of day;*
>
> *And blown by all the winds that pass*
> *And wet with all the showers,*
> *She walks among the meadow grass*
> *And eats the meadow flowers.*

After the clapping, the teachers thanked everyone for their generous assistance with building the school and for their contributions of the day. Orlo led a short prayer to end the ceremony. "Dear

Lord, thank you for bringing all of us together on this beautiful day to celebrate learning and our community spirit."

Tillie appreciated Bertha's presence more than usual that fall as the two women gathered the remaining potatoes and carrots and worked on chores preparing for winter, including hauling as much hay as they could into the shed for Sam, spreading straw on the floor of the chicken coop, cleaning their stovepipes, and gathering cow chips to cook with and keep themselves warm.

Tillie shot a couple grouse and cooked them for Sunday dinner. Although she had enjoyed the grouse hunt, she'd also felt some remorse when she saw the creatures lying still. After dinner, she boiled the grouse bones in water for broth, which she salted heavily and would store in the root cellar until she could let it freeze out of doors. She made up a little ditty as the bones boiled. "You've been life, you've been life; you flew the skies so high, so high. You'll bring me warmth; you'll bring me life. Yes, when winter comes a roarin' in, you'll bring me warmth; you'll bring me life. Thank you, bones; thank you, bones; thank you, bird; thank you, bird."

When school began, the teachers admitted to each other a feeling of awkwardness with the new arrangement since each had always taught independently; yet within a week or two, the new situation became quite comfortable.

Life for the homesteaders was fairly routine as their third winter in Dakota loomed. Late fall was pleasant enough with light snowfalls spreading their shimmering white on the prairie as the sun sank farther toward the south. One morning in November, as she scooped coal to bring in before school, Tillie noticed the lightening sky. The whole gray-blue canopy painted itself with filmy clouds turning gently pink. As she watched, the color deepened to rose, then began to fade as the sky brightened with the rising sun. "How beautiful you are," she said to the heavens.

The teachers continued to approach homestead schooling with the belief that practical knowledge was the most important, yet Tillie refused to neglect geography, a subject that fascinated her. The enthusiasm she displayed seemed to capture the children's sense of wonder about the world. Two of the pupils, Elizabeth Aakre and Erik Iverson, seemed especially eager and Tillie hoped they or some of the children would eventually journey to parts unknown. She also hoped to inspire appreciation of the written word by reading *Ragged Dick* by Horatio Alger, the *Adventures of Tom Sawyer* by Mark Twain, and *Treasure Island* by Robert Louis Stevenson. She introduced her students to Dickens and Jules Verne, as well.

Bertha's love of poetry drew in the small children who loved to recite with her. She, too, attempted to kindle a love of words in her pupils. She read Hans Christian Anderson's fairy tales: *The Snow Queen*, *The Emperor's New Clothes*, and *The Ugly Duckling*. Nonetheless, she focused most of her energy on basic reading, writing, and arithmetic, all with practical applications in Dakota.

———

The entire winter of 1902-03 passed without a horrendous blizzard, or perhaps Tillie and Bertha had simply grown accustomed to the fierce wind of Dakota that could make a blizzard out of just a few inches of snowfall. But early that winter, Tillie experienced a terrible fright in the middle of a night. She awoke with a start and sat up. Roger bounded off the bed and began to bark ferociously.

Bright yellow-orange light lit the room like a torch, dancing on the walls. Tillie bounded out of bed, screaming, "Fire, fire!"

Expecting to see flames surrounding her, she flew to the window where the night was lit in ominous orange.

She looked in amazement at the scene. Pillars of brilliant gold and orange amidst horizontal clouds of bright green and violet danced across the sky. Although displays of northern lights were common on the northern plain, she had never seen such a spectacular show. She opened her door to better see the display and saw her friend standing outside, gazing at the heavens with an appearance of awe.

A Tiff

Spring came in late March. Soon dainty pasqueflowers bloomed again atop their silky-haired stems. Along with their own end-of-the-year tests, the teachers gave examinations the Department of Public Instruction required for all North Dakota students. They also broke up their garden with spades, put in potatoes, and helped prepare for planting wheat, again removing rocks that had risen to the surface in the soil.

In May, the community again gathered to witness the mating dance of the sharp-tailed grouse. Just after that, most everyone helped with a shack raising after the Torgerson family arrived from Iowa with their three children. Tillie and Bertha had offered them Bertha's shack for temporary quarters until the new shack was complete, so Bertha stayed with Tillie.

It was during that time that the one serious tiff between Bertha and Tillie occurred, perhaps born of too much togetherness. A minor incident started the fight. They were washing and drying breakfast dishes when a dish with scalloped edges, decorated with delicate pink and apricot roses, slipped from Bertha's hand, sending fragments flying across the floor.

"You careless woman, you!" barked Tillie. "That was a dish my mother gave me that belonged to my grandmother!"

"I'm so sorry, Tillie, really I am," said Bertha in a high-pitched soft voice, as she began picking up the pieces.

"Sorry doesn't put it back together!"

"Well, you should have left it at home if it was that precious," Bertha pronounced loudly.

"I need some loving reminders of home here in this godforsaken land. Now you've broken the most precious one."

"Well, you broke a dish of mine once too. Remember?"

"It wasn't this precious."

"I said I'm sorry and I really am, but do you have to be such a stick-in-the-mud all the time? You get upset with the students too easily too. I see it in their eyes."

"Oh yes, Bertha. I'm strict so they get their studies done and learn. You're too weak with them, coddle them too much."

"Coddle? I'd call it understanding and helping!"

"Call it what you will! You're too easy on them."

"Well, you're too hard on 'em."

"And who bought almost all the student materials for the school? Whose parents paid for the bell? I've spent a whole lot more on this here place than you ever have, Bertha."

"Oh, yeah? And who buys all of Sam's oats? Who sells the eggs to put money in the pot? Me, not you, Tillie! You're too high and mighty for that."

"And who tends the chickens and fixes the fence and brings Sam his hay while you run around with Ole making a fool of yourself? People will talk."

"Well, then let them talk!"

Bertha left the shack, slamming the door. She walked through the grasses at a stride, not going anywhere, just walking. She walked with her head down, her jaw set, staying away from shacks. Once she stumbled on a rock jutting out of the earth. She screamed, then swore. "Damn it, damn it, damn you, Tillie!" Although she wasn't seriously injured, she had torn her skirt and scraped her knee. She continued walking, mostly going around and around, but at a slower pace.

Eventually, when the sun was past its apex and sweat soaked her blouse under her armpits and glistened on her face, and her anger had turned from tirades to tears, she walked around the perimeter of the community and reached Hans and Helen's home. She found Helen churning butter, her braids atop her head, but with some of the shorter strands of hair soaked with sweat and clinging to her face.

"Bertha, so good to see you," said Helen, stopping her churning.

"Would be good to talk to you, Helen, if you have some moments. Need to talk to someone."

"Well, my dear, you kinda look like you could use some talkin'. Looks like you've had yerself some tears you've rubbed away and like ya been sweatin' up a storm."

"Well, you look like you've done a little sweating yerself," said Bertha with a hint of a smile.

"Almost done here. Give me a few moments and we'll find some cool water and maybe somethin' sweet in the house."

Bertha waited while Helen finished, then joined her in the shack, where Helen ladled cool water into cups and set out a few graham crackers.

"Looks like you got some trouble."

"Well, just need someone to talk to. Thought of going to Ole's, but thought a woman's ear would better listen. It's really not a big thing, anyway, just a tiff between me and Tillie."

"My ears are ready to hear," said Helen. "Think you know me well enough to know I don't go gossiping."

Bertha nodded her head while she sniffed. "I broke a dish of Tillie's, a special one. She was so mad, as if I'd done it on purpose, which of course I didn't. Well, I got mad back and said all sorts of nasty things about Tillie being too strict with the children, about her being so upright all the time."

Bertha wiped away some tears. Helen waited quietly and Bertha went on. "I know it sounds like such a silly thing to get so upset about, but sometimes I feel so inferior to her. Seems to know her own mind so well; she's so prudent and capable. Guess that's what triggered my anger at her—not that I should be mad at her for being so proficient all the time, but, I sometimes feel a little dimwitted."

Bertha sniffed again, looked down at the table, and then took a sip of water. "I admire Tillie so much and yet I find myself feeling irritation at just little things sometimes, but I went too far this time."

"Oh my. These irritations between people livin' so close, like me and Hans and you and Tillie, are just a part of what happens when we spend so much time together, y'know. We ain't all the same. Little differences grow to seem like big craters between us sometimes. Just need to have at it and get the mad out of us. I've thrown a good dish across the room to shatter it on purpose just 'cuz I was so mad at Hans. Stupid thing to do, but got the madness out of me and we could go on caring and needing each other like always."

The two women talked of the crazy things they sometimes felt and soon Bertha thought she could go to Tillie's with the anger mostly gone. "Thank you, Helen. I knew I could count on you to set me straight," she said as she got up to go.

"Well, we help each other out. Got to have women friends some days. Men don't have quite the same feelin's or understandin's, y'know."

Tillie saw Bertha walking up and welcomed her in, saying, "I ground fresh beans, got the stove going. I'll make us some good egg coffee. Let's have us a cup and find some words to soothe our hurt feelings. I did wrong in yelling at you to start." Her face still looked stern, but the set of her mouth in anger was gone.

"I'm sorry for getting so upset. We both got our bloomers in a bunch." Bertha smiled meekly and looked at Tillie over the top of her glasses.

When the coffee finished boiling, Tillie put out her two best cups, those adorned with small red roses, and placed a plate of ginger cookies on the table.

For Norwegians, coffee can cure most anything—or sometimes akvavit does the trick—but akvavit wasn't called for this time, nor would the women have considered imbibing in it even if it had been available. Soon they were both shedding tears and asking for forgiveness for saying such harsh words.

———

The summer passed with only minor difficulties. A deluge during a savage storm blew off some of the tar paper, though most of the time crops and gardens thirsted for rain. A grass fire started north of Kincaid, but posed no problem for the Norwegian community. Lightning hit one of Ole's haystacks and it exploded. But his brother Daniel helped him cut more hay and eventually they got another haystack built. Bertha and Tillie aided them, glad to be able to offer a little payback for Ole's regular assistance.

As chlorophyll began leaching from the grasses, the community again worked as a whole for the harvest. When finished, the Norwegians gathered for the celebration. Blessed with sufficient rains by Dakota standards, no hail, and no serious calamities, it was the most bountiful harvest yet. Tillie and Bertha's plot of land yielded nearly six hundred and fifty bushels of wheat, at least twenty bushels an acre. "The harvest from your land is good," proclaimed Hans.

Soon school was in session again, this time with three new students, Arvid, Lillian, and Alf Torgerson. Sven didn't come, as expected.

"It's been a good year," Tillie said as she and Bertha prepared a light meal after school one warm fall evening. "No awful blizzards last winter, no fires or grasshoppers, a good harvest."

"Such a good year. I'm beginning to love this place more and more."

"And Ole adds to that love, sure, sure," put in Tillie with a broad smile. This time, Bertha didn't deny the love.

"I'm becoming quite fond of him."

"I can see that, Bertha. He's a good man. It's clear he cares so much for you."

A Brutal Winter

Fall turned to winter and December turned brutal, brutal in more ways than the weather. Little Brunhild came to school late one day, sat at her desk, and stared straight ahead. She held her mouth taut. Her reddened eyes crinkled at the corners. Tillie took over the lessons while Bertha led Brunhild into the tiny cloakroom. For minutes she remained quiet, then a tear rolled down her reddened cheek as Bertha simply held her hand.

In time, Brunhild told some of the story. "They fought last night." She let out a slight sob. "Mor's hurt."

"Is she hurt badly, dear child?"

"I dunno. Bad I t'ink."

"Is your father home now?"

Brunhild continued to look at the floor. "Went away last night. Didn't come home."

"Who's at home?"

"Sven's there with Mor. Karl and Kincaid too. Sven told me to go to school. I wanna go home, be with Mor."

"I'm going to talk to Miss Melbakken. I want you to stay here. I'll be right back."

Bertha took Tillie outside the school door. "Frank and Ellen fought last night. Ellen's apparently hurt badly. Brunhild said her father is gone."

"I must go there. At once," Tillie declared.

Bertha expressed caution. "Getting into other people's business leads to trouble, I fear. Yet we must do something, I suppose. Brunhild is so upset."

"Of course we must. I'm getting my coat."

Bertha's advice was at least to seek Ernie's help or assistance from one of the men. "Frank might come back and hurt you," she warned, "and he might take it out on little Brunhild for saying something."

"Keep Brunhild here until after I get back," Tillie ordered as she left. "And manage the students until I return. And give Roger food if I'm not home after school."

She hurried to her place as fast as she could through the snow and quickly donned warmer clothes. Then she ran to the shed, mounted Sam, and rode first to Ernie's. Not finding him there, she considered checking to see if Hans or Henry or maybe Ole were home, but decided to ride immediately to Ellen's.

She found Ellen curled up in bed. Her face was bruised and swollen. She could barely move her mouth. Tillie guessed her jaw was broken and that she was in shock.

A bit later, she'd find a broken wrist as well.

Tillie set about getting a hot fire going. Sven, his dark brown eyes darting like a captured pig's, said nothing, even when Tillie asked, "Did you see the fight?" Little Karl clung to Tillie's skirt. The baby seemed hungry and Karl said Kincaid had gnawed on a couple of graham crackers. Ellen was likely too traumatized to think about feeding him. Tillie wondered whether Ellen's soul was shattered along with her bones.

When the fire was hot, Tillie brought Kincaid to Ellen, lifted Ellen's blouse and helped hold him as he grabbed for the nipple with one hand and opened his mouth. When he finished with that nipple, Tillie took him to the other side of the bed so Ellen didn't need to move. Kincaid nursed briefly, enough to relieve the pressure that had built up as Ellen lay there impassively.

"This wrist must be set, Sven," Tillie said, "and maybe the jaw. I could try, but I might make it worse. Please, I need your help, your mother needs your help. Find someone to summon Doc Henry from Bowbells or at least get Winnie, who knows more than I do. In the meantime, I need some of your dad's liquor. Do you know where it is?"

Sven sat there, unmoving, looking at the floor.

"You—must—find—some—liquor," Tillie repeated.

Sven got up and went outside. Meanwhile, Tillie tried to entertain Kincaid and Karl with a story about bears.

A few minutes later Sven came in, bottle in hand. He handed it to Tillie. "He'll prob'ly kill you. Maybe me too."

"That's a chance we have to take, but I'm quite sure he won't. Not here in this community. Now please go get Winnie and then try to get someone to go for Doc Henry. Your mother may not last if you don't."

Sven left.

Tillie poured some whiskey or whatever it was into a small glass and fetched a spoon. She told Karl to hold the glass near her, then held Ellen's head up with one hand while holding the spoon with whiskey in the other. "You must try to swallow this, Ellen. It will ease the pain and help you settle down. Open your mouth just enough to let this go down."

Slowly, opening her mouth just a little, Ellen let a few spoonfuls of the liquor slip down her throat, coughing, and wrenching in pain when she did.

Tillie went outside, gathered ice chunks from icicles she knocked down from the roof, wrapped them in cloth, and propped one of the icy cloths by Ellen's swollen jaw, the other by her wrist.

When Ellen appeared to be resting, Tillie sat down, helped Kincaid onto her lap, and encouraged Karl to climb up. Settled in the chair, she began spinning a story.

"Once upon a time in the far-off land of Minnesota," she said breaking into a heavy brogue, "there lived a dog whose name was Molly, a large yellow dog she was, with long golden hair. One of her jobs was to guard the children, Mattie and Samuel. Samuel was an energetic boy, six years old, prone to troublemaking. His sister Mattie was a quiet girl, just four, and she loved following Samuel on his adventures. This day Molly accompanied the children down toward the small lake, just frozen over for winter. The children were dressed warmly with their coats, mittens, hats, and woolen socks inside their boots. There had been just a light, wet snow. On the way to the lake, they made snowballs. They threw them at Molly and at each other, giggling as one hit.

"Molly was nervous with the children so close to the lake. She kept watch in her serious manner while the children threw snowballs and played tag."

Kincaid fell asleep in Tillie's warm lap, as the soft, soothing sound of her voice continued. Karl's dark eyes looked up at Tillie periodically, then over at his mother who rested on her bed and occasionally emitted a slight moan.

"Adventurous Samuel dared Mattie to go out on the lake. 'It's frozen. You're little. It won't crack. Are you afraid?' he taunted.

"Molly barked in a frantic way as Mattie ventured out a step at a time—two feet, three feet, five feet. 'You're brave,' shouted Samuel.

"'Come back,' growled Molly in her own language.

"Mattie was about ten feet out on the lake when Molly heard the first crack. Mattie sensed it, though Samuel didn't recognize the danger.

"Almost too frightened to move, Mattie began turning around and at that moment the lake opened, then it swallowed her legs. She screamed. Molly dashed onto the ice and plunged into the icy water. Mattie's arms were flailing at the surface, her head still above water. Molly grabbed her near the collar of her coat and straining, fighting with all her strength against the cold, pulled Mattie toward shore.

"When they were nearly there, Samuel stepped on the ice near shore and pulled Mattie up and out of the water. He hugged her toward him. Molly shook and icy droplets flew in all directions, then she resumed her frantic barking while she galloped toward the house.

"Hearing the commotion, the children's father rushed out of the house, followed soon by their mother, who had taken time to grab a coat. Molly kept barking and began racing toward the lake with Father close behind, running as best he could in the snow.

"By the time Father arrived at the scene, Samuel had taken off his jacket and had Mattie wrapped in it, but she was shivering and her lips were blue. She mumbled but didn't talk.

"Father picked her up in his big arms and began running to the house. Mother ran toward them, screaming, 'What's wrong, what's wrong?' Samuel followed Father.

"Once inside the house, Father built a roaring fire while Mother undressed Mattie from her cold wet clothes and wrapped her in a quilt. Samuel was silent.

"Molly whined at the door. Father opened the door and let Molly enter, which he usually forbade. He found some scraps left over from the previous night's dinner and gave them to Molly, petting her smooth golden hair. Mother, too, petted Molly saying, 'You are my hero.'

"Molly curled up in front of the fire and was soon asleep.

"Mattie recovered in a short time and only then was reprimanded. But Samuel received the most serious reprimand. Father sent him to a corner to sit with his head down and then sent him to bed without supper."

"Tell me another one," said Karl. She did, after she laid Kincaid next to his mother on the bed and checked on Ellen's breathing—labored, but still regular.

Well past midday, Sven returned with Doc Henry. Sven sat down, glum, jaw set. "Thank you, Sven," said Tillie with kindness showing in her voice. "You did right."

His expression remained unchanged.

Doc set to work, first looking at the bruises on Ellen's face, then checking her jaw. "Broken or dislocated," he said. "Has she had some whiskey?"

"Some. Sometime midmorning."

"She'll need more. Bring it here."

Tillie complied, bringing a small glass of the liquor. Doc retrieved a glass straw from his bag and helped Ellen take the bitter liquid, Ellen choking and wincing as much as swallowing. After waiting a few minutes for the liquor to take effect, he grabbed her face, hoping to shove the bone into place. Ellen let out a hideous sound, unable to scream from the pressure on her jaw.

"Now bring me a kerchief, a big one."

"Find me a kerchief right now," Tillie demanded of Sven.

He found a large blue one. Doc wrapped it from under Ellen's chin to the top of her head. "She'll need broth, perhaps some milk, maybe eggnog and oatmeal in time. Use the straw. She can only just barely open her mouth until this heals. Likely it'll take a month or more."

"Yes," said Tillie.

Doc set to work on the wrist. Ellen let out a low growl when he set the bone.

"Now I need a small board and a kitchen towel or something of the sort."

With Sven's assistance, Tillie found a fairly straight, small board, about the right length. She grabbed a towel, dirty as it was, from the kitchen, and Doc wrapped the arm.

"Do you know how to make a sling?"

Tillie nodded.

"Make one. She must keep this arm in position until I return in a few days. Here's some tincture of laudanum. Give her some now and when she needs it."

"I will."

At dusk, Ernie Saue arrived, Bertha having summoned him.

"Why are you here?" he demanded of Tillie. "What business is this of yours?"

"This is my community. Ellen needed help. She really needs help." She emphasized those last words with a loud, almost staccato voice. "Doc has been here and set her jaw and arm. We can't just let people suffer because it's a family issue."

Tillie turned away from him and went to Ellen, who was stirring.

Ernie looked at the women. His stern expression began to soften. He removed his coat.

"I'll stay here in case he comes back. Brought my pistol. I'll make sure he doesn't hurt you."

Tillie turned back toward him. "Thank you." Then she turned and tended to Ellen. "Could you drink a little broth?"

Just a slight movement of her head, sideways, eyes downcast.

Night fell. Ernie brought in more coal and he and Sven kept the fire burning. Everyone slept from time to time. Tillie slouched on a chair, Ernie curled up with a blanket by the door, Karl and Kincaid slept on the bed with Ellen, and Sven lay down on his small cot of a bed.

Before dawn, but well past midnight, Ernie heard a noise outside. He stood up, gun in his hand. When Frank threw open the door, everyone awakened. Ellen moaned. The light from the stove sent a fiery glow onto Frank's face. His eyes flew to Ernie and the gun and registered shock. He reeked of alcohol. "What in the damn hell are you doing here?"

"Calm yourself, Frank. Your wife's hurt. She needed help."

Tillie held her breath.

Frank glanced at Ellen. "Well, if she could shut her damn mouth, she wouldn't need help," he slurred.

"Well, guess you saw to it that she can't open her mouth—for now. What happened between you two is for you and her to sort out. For now, she needs a woman's help and Tillie's here to help."

Tillie felt so grateful for Ernie's presence, his being there to confront Frank. Yet she decided to speak to Frank herself. She stood and looked at Frank, whose eyes averted hers. "She has a broken jaw, a broken wrist. Doc has been here. He'll be back in a few days. I'll be here until then."

Frank stood by the door, shocked into silence. "Who told you about this? Was it you, Sven?" he shouted, turning to his son.

"He did not." Tillie used her stern teacher's voice.

Frank looked around. "Where's little Brunhild?"

"She's being taken care of," said Tillie.

"Guess I'm not needed here," growled Frank. He turned, slamming the door as he left.

At that, everyone, including Sven, made an audible sigh.

Ernie stayed that night, resting in a chair, while Tillie rested on a quilt on the floor in front of the fire. The next day, Winnie arrived and Ernie left the women, ordering Sven to protect them.

Winnie brought with her some boneset she'd dried in the summer, along with dried comfrey root, and brewed tea with it.

With Tillie's assistance, Winnie helped Ellen sit up and open her mouth just a bit so the tea could trickle in. A little later she fed her a few tiny swallows of eggnog.

The two of them cared for the children and for Ellen, giving her laudanum from time to time, until Doc returned a couple days later.

"You're healing okay, Ellen. Don't try to open that mouth much. Keep food to liquids and soft stuff, but get up and start movin' round a bit. Don't use that arm. Keep it in a sling."

With that, the brusque doctor moved to the door. "If it's not healing steady, gets more puffy or somethin', send for me. Don't let Frank at ya."

Toward evening Ellen told Winnie and Tillie that she wanted to be alone with her family, that Sven would watch out for Frank and help her get some food made, that Brunhild should come home after school the next day.

Reluctantly, yet ready to be in their own homes, the two "angels," as Ellen called them, left.

A couple days later Frank returned. With Tillie's prodding, Ellen reluctantly would tell her later that Frank gave no apology and said nothing about the incident. In time, Ellen's face took on a more or less normal look, though there would remain evidence of the beating in her crooked smile. Ernie told Tillie that he, along with Ole and Willie, had a good talk at Frank. "We told him we'd run him out if he ever did such a thing again. Course most 'a the community men told me and t'others that we had no business getting involved in family matters, but we figured Frank needed a warning after what I saw." He looked at Tillie, who gave a nod. "And a'course what you and Winnie saw too," he added.

Tillie's fondness for Ernie grew after the whole affair. Soon the community recognized them as a courting pair, along with Bertha and Ole.

———

On a day late in February when there was just a hint that spring would arrive in time, Ole, who had been in town, delivered Tillie a letter, then went to see Bertha.

Dear Tillie,

The winter has been less harsh than many. Snow we've had plenty of, but the cold spells have not been long and we get a nice day once in a while.

I heard from Norway that my mother had passed in the night, no long illness, thank goodness. Even though I haven't seen her in so many years, I miss knowing that she was there and thinking of me. Now I know she must watch down upon me from heaven, and upon you, as well.

Papa is failing some. It appears to be his heart. His strength is diminished, so Peter is doing more of the chores. Papa still has a good appetite and can swing me at a barn dance, but I am a bit worried.

I wonder if you might be able to make a trip home this summer to see the family. It would do my heart good, and Papa's as well.

I hear from others that you are such a brave woman, dealing with so many things out there in what some call Brutal Dakota. Please be careful, my child, for I love thee with all of my heart.

Mama

With news of her father, Tillie began shaking. She sat down upon her bed, covering her mouth with her hand. *Papa, you must stay well. I'll come this summer, I will.*

———

As soon as school was out in early May, Tillie packed her bag. She invited Ernie for supper the evening before she left for Minnesota. It was the first time she had invited him to come without also inviting Bertha and Ole. She'd butchered a chicken the day before, washed it in several changes of water, immersed it in boiling water for several minutes, and then rubbed the cavities with pepper so its freshness would last till cooking time.

For the special meal, she baked brown bread, roasted the chicken, and served it along with potatoes, as well as canned green beans from last fall's harvest. Buttermilk pie and coffee finished the meal.

The evening was cool, but with only a breeze rustling the grasses, it was comfortable. After supper, the couple walked down by the lake, hand in hand. The sun had just set, yet displayed itself in the cottony clouds gone peach. "You vill come back, vill you not?" asked Ernie, reverting to a heavy brogue as was his manner when he was a bit nervous.

When he'd learned of her decision to go home, he'd even suggested accompanying her back to Minnesota, but Tillie had pooh-poohed that idea. "Vat vuld people t'ink if I brought home a man from Dakota, and unchaperoned even? Minnesota isn't Dakota, y'know."

After seeing his face now, she said, "I'll come back, Ernie, I will. I need to prove up, y'know."

"I know."

With that he took her in his arms, drew her close, his mouth falling upon hers, his tongue caressing the inside of her mouth. She kissed him back and lingered in his arms, yet her response was not as fervent as his. Tillie could tell he could barely contain his passion for her, but he restrained himself. She'd told him a little while back that she'd have "none of that nonsense" when his hand had gone to her breast.

Coming back to the shack, he followed her in. The two sipped on their coffee, he adding a cube of sugar. Dusk settled upon the land while they talked of the weather and their families. It wasn't until he was ready to leave that he again drew her to him. She felt his member rise against her as he continued to hold her tightly. "I'm so desirous of you," he whispered.

After a few moments, she gently moved away and looked up at him with a tender look, though he turned his face downward. When he looked up again, he simply gave a weak, almost sad, smile. "Vell, I'll be here in the morning to take you to the train," he said with a nod.

"I'll look forward to seeing you then, my dear, dear Ernie."

Roger seemed to know something was afoot and was restless that night. Tillie slept poorly as well. Ernie had offered to care for Roger during her absence and, while Tillie knew he would care for him well, ensuring he had food, she thought his offer came more out of kindness for her than fondness for the dog.

Tillie had grown to depend upon Roger's loyalty, his keen ear and ready alert. She rarely relayed her troubles to others, but she easily told them to Roger and he seemed to understand. Especially she loved his delightful antics of greeting when she returned from school and community gatherings. In fact, he often wandered over to the school just before dismissal time and accompanied Tillie home. She knew she would miss him.

The Green of Minnesota

On the long train trip home, Tillie recalled her feelings and thoughts of four years earlier on the way to Dakota. She almost laughed to herself, even let a smile cross her face, when she thought of that first night in the hut when first experiencing the lonesome landscape, when her confidence in the adventure had evaporated. Yet during those four years in Dakota, she had become even more self-assured and capable than she had hoped.

She'd even found some romance of sorts, which she had not intended. *I know Ernie will miss me, and I'll miss him. I like him a great deal. Yet though he's such a good and capable man, I don't find passion toward him. Still, any woman on the Dakota prairie would be fortunate to have him by her side.* She wondered if there was something wrong with her, something making it hard to accept love, or offer it.

She remembered how some men had ridiculed Bertha and herself on the trip to Dakota. She knew the men had doubted that the girl homesteaders would make it. There were no such taunts and glances of disbelief now. The young men on the train appeared to feel respect for her and she knew she had earned that respect. Perhaps her confidence showed on her face.

As the train traveled on, her thoughts left Dakota and turned toward home. How was her father faring, her brother, mother, and the farm? She wondered how she would feel about being in such a big house again and then how she would feel about returning to Dakota when the time came. She carried letters with her for families in the area and planned to share some of her experiences with them, as well as with her own family.

A few other travelers were heading back to eastern Dakota and Minnesota, one a family of five, having just finished proving up near Bowbells. Scottish they were, hearty thick-bodied parents with children ranging from three to ten, the younger ones born in Dakota. Tillie loved listening to tales the children told her, and she shared some of her own.

It was past dusk when the train tooted its whistle at Hankinson, where passengers were allowed off the train for a half hour. Tillie debarked and walked around the station, talking easily with some of the other travelers. Again Tillie recalled the fear she faced on her trip in the other direction. She knew full well she would never have dared to spend time alone in a railroad station back then, especially not at night. She wondered how her character would appear to the folks at home. Some would think she was too confident for a woman, of that she was sure. Some would admire her pluck. Some might even think she had become a loose woman, too forward and lacking in appropriate humbleness. She was quite sure, however, that her mother, father, and brother would admire her and those were the people who counted. *What about Jergen? Well, time will tell. And why do I even imagine an attachment is possible when there has been no courting? Perhaps I won't even find passion for him when he is no longer a figment of my imagination. He could even have a wife by now, though I think I would have heard.*

Once the train left Hankinson near the Minnesota border, Tillie's excitement grew. She tried to sleep as the train rumbled through the darkness, stopping here and there, but sleep came in snippets, along with a few strange dreams. With the first sign of dawn, she did what she could to straighten herself up. She combed her hair and fastened her bun tightly.

When the conductor came around calling "Glenwood, next stop," Tillie felt her heart beating. She peered at the green surroundings, the trees, almost endless trees, looking so strange to her brown prairie eyes. It looked like home, but home seemed almost foreign now.

As the train's whistle sounded, Tillie stood and gathered her belongings. During the final minutes of movement, she began walking toward the train door. When the porter opened the door, Tillie started down the train steps to the platform, nearly crying with happiness.

There they were—Mama and Papa. The tears now rolled down her cheeks as her family hurried to meet her. First, she embraced her mother, whose face was wetter than her own. Pulling herself away, she melted into the arms of her father, receiving a hug the likes of which she had never felt from him. In fact, she couldn't really remember any other hugs from him, only an arm wrapped around her shoulders and such. He looked frail, she could see that.

On the long ride to the farm, Tillie kept marveling at the verdancy. "How lush the trees are," she said looking at the once-familiar landscape. "Look at those tulips blooming over there!" she exclaimed in delight. "The grass is such bright green. Has it always been so?" On and on she went, her family laughing at her admiration of their familiar surroundings.

"You've forgotten already how beautiful Minnesota is in the spring," said Mama. "T'was always so; I 'spect it will always be so."

Tillie caught up on the family news. Twin boys were born to her cousin just three weeks earlier, an uncle was dying of consumption, now at a sanatorium. A cousin had skipped town on his wife.

"Just awful. Just awful. Imagine. No one knows where he went to. Someone thought they saw him in Duluth," said Mama, shaking her head.

"How long can you stay, Tillie? I hope until September."

"Nay, Mama, I must get back in August. I know how I missed Bertha last summer and how hard it was to manage chores alone. She must be missing me already. Though she has Ole," she added.

Then her mother asked about Ole and what kind of a family he came from and was he a good man and had Tillie met someone, as well? Bertha had suggested maybe so.

So, Tillie told them of Ernic, that he was an admirable man, but not likely to be more than a fine friend. "But he has been a big help and he's good to me."

"Well," said Mama, "Jergen Halverson asks of you the occasional times I see him, y'know."

"He does?" she asked trying to keep any excitement from her voice and any glee from her face.

"Oh, yeah, now and then. Anxious to see you, y'know."

"Well, it would be nice to see him too." She tried to hide her smile.

"Peter stayed home to tend to chores," Mama said, "but he has news. He's begun courting Ethel Kittelson. She's not quite seventeen, nearly five years younger than Peter, y'know, but she seems quite mature for her years. You were her teacher, as I'm sure you remember, Tillie, and she adores you."

"She was a good and serious student, and quite adorable as I remember. Long, curly, straw-colored hair."

Papa was quiet on the trip home, content with driving the buggy and listening to the family's rambling conversation. Likely he was tired since they had traveled to Glenwood the previous day and spent the night at the Glenwood Hotel. Tillie wanted to ask how he was doing, but thought it better to wait, perhaps to ask Mama alone first.

Stepping onto the home ground, Tillie wanted to reach down and caress the earth, take some grass in her hands. *All in good time*, she said to herself. The house looked so large. The red barn gleamed with a new coat of paint. The winter wheat was lovely to behold and looking nearly ready for harvest.

The aroma of Mama's kitchen hit Tillie as she entered. Her mother must have baked bread the previous morning. Loaves still stood on the counter. And two pies. Subtle aromas from years of cooking lingered there as well.

"I t'ink you've lost some weight, my dear," said Mama after Tillie removed her coat. "Ve'll need to fatten you up. You look fit, though, I do say."

"The smell, Mama, the familiar smells here, your baking aromas more wonderful than the sight of the green countryside. I forgot how much I missed it."

"Oh, you'll get plenty of the smells, sure 'nuf. But you best put your t'ings away. You should take a bath, get some rest perhaps. I'll heat some vater for a bath. You need one after the train ride, sure."

"Oh, yes, Mama, oh yes, yes."

Her mother filled the tub with nearly boiling water from the cook stove's reservoir, along with well water from the inside pump, then drew the bath and placed a tin of Yardley Talcum Powder by the tub. Tillie slipped into the warm water, an experience that had grown as foreign in the years in Dakota as a forest of trees in Kincaid would have been. There, apart from some dips in the pond, bathing consisted of sponge baths. She'd used her bake kettle, also used for washing clothes, to soak her feet. Standing in the kettle, she'd pour cupfuls of tepid water over her, rub soap over parts of her body, then rinse it away into the kettle.

The warm water encompassing her seemed to draw out the detritus of years of homesickness. Her taut muscles strung with the tension of proving herself a worthy woman relaxed and seemed to flow with the ripples of water moving about her. It was with the ease born of familiarity, the ease cemented by the unquestioned love of her family, the ease produced by her mother's pampering that she emerged from the tub.

Walking into the kitchen, clean, warm, and peaceful, Tillie proclaimed, "Oh, Mama, never did a bath feel so good! I've forgotten how it eases the spirit. And," she laughed, "I scrubbed away four years of filth. Now I smell sweetly of fragrant talc instead of like a farm animal."

"You look refreshed, sure 'nuf. We have this evening to rest and catch up on news. Company coming to celebrate tomorrow, a few relations for supper, then the rest a little later. Ve've even arranged for a little dance music in the barn, so you'll vant to dress yourself up."

The next afternoon, Tillie dressed in her nicest blouse and a long flowing calico skirt. Her brooch adorned her blouse at her throat. Her cheeks were pink from pinching, as well as from the Dakota sun, when the first of the relations began arriving, all greeting her warmly. Among the supper guests, too, were Bertha's brother and sister who of course wanted to hear news of the B&T Estate.

Tillie, all the time wondering whether it might be possible that Jergen would show up, shook hands with neighboring men and hugged some of the women as they began arriving for the celebration dance. She heard of births and deaths and marriages from her cousins and provided snippets of information from "the front" as some referred to her experience in Dakota.

While putting supper dishes on the counter, she looked out the kitchen window and saw *him* dismounting his horse. *He looks dapper, and so clean after the men I'm used to seeing. White shirt, smart black trousers, snazzy red suspenders.* She pinched her cheeks and went to the door, sighing from having held her breath at his sight.

"Well, my Tillie, how fine you look after your journey. How often I've spoken of you to friends, telling them of your escapades as I hear them from your family. How good to behold you now." He clasped her hand warmly. She knew her neck and face reddened and hoped it didn't show.

"Jergen, how well you look." She swallowed. "I've thought of you often and wondered whether you might come tonight." *And he called me "my Tillie." I think he rehearsed his little oration.*

"Wouldn't have missed it," he said, winking. Tillie extricated her hand from his and came out of the house, and down off the step. "Well, looks like Dakota's doing you no harm, You look even more fetching than I remembered," he said as he reached out for her hand, which he took in both of his. "Hope you'll tell me all about it."

"I'd so like the opportunity to give you lots of details," she said in a soft voice, unlike her usual strong one.

"Well, you've lots of company come to greet you, so I'll find you after you've had time to see the others."

"Yes, that would be nice, Jergen." Tillie felt her heart fluttering as he walked toward a couple of neighbor men.

Later, he twirled her in square-dancing, held her close for a waltz, led her by the hand down the lane for a welcome home kiss, brief, but with more passion than Tillie remembered of the kiss all those years earlier. Then he held her just inches from him, enough so that they each looked tenderly into each other's eyes. "I'll call again, and soon, very soon, if that pleases you. You can tell me all about Dakota and all I can tell you is the little excitement we've had around Big Bend."

"I'd like that. I'd like it very much."

———

Tillie involved herself in the chores of home, the soap making, the washing, the cooking, the baking, the weeding, the milking, the cleaning. She went to church on Sunday and sang hymns of praise. She chatted with her mother, worried about her father who continued to look frail, though he did his best to appear fit as he tinkered with his machinery and did what he could of the chores. "He likely wore out his heart with the work," Mama said. "That's what the doctor thought, said he'd last a while, but not too awfully long."

And the first Sunday after she'd returned home, Jergen came to call in midafternoon. Tillie was glad she hadn't yet changed out of her church dress. She invited him in, of course, again marveling at his clean and dapper looks. Mama greeted Jergen warmly, then said, "Vell, I'll get a little lunch together while you two go and renew your acquaintance."

So Tillie invited Jergen into the front room where they sat on the sofa. Jergen looked around the room, the walls hand-painted with a twirling blend of soft pastel shades of purple blended with gray, the sun lighting the room through the large window with lace curtains. "What a beautiful room," he said, "that enhances your own beauty."

He sounds like a poet, thought Tillie, and said. "Well, tell me of the excitement around Big Bend."

"Oh, not so much. I got elected to the school board, so I now understand some about what you teachers do."

"How nice. Did you know that Bertha and I are teaching in our little Norwegian community school called Meadows School?"

"Heard that from your mother, a gracious woman."

"Yes, I'm sure Mama talks of me, too much likely."

"Well, I enjoyed hearing." He paused some moments and just looked at her. "I been busy farming a'course as well as being a deacon at the church. My folks are gettin' pretty advanced in years to help out much, but Pop gives me a hand when needed with plantin' and harvesting."

"So, you're a deacon at the Big Bend Lutheran, Jergen. How wonderful!"

"And I hear you have a little church out there in Dakota."

"A small building the men put up, like they put up the schoolhouse. Orlo Larson who went to seminary for a while acts as minister until we can get one called. He's a quiet, but good man. Donated the land for the church. Lots of good people out there. Like Bertha and me, not afraid of hard work or the little calamities that happen."

"Yeah, calamities all over the country. We had a tornado come through just east of us near Milan. Had us some damage from the wind, but just some trees came down that needed cutting up for firewood."

"That's something we don't have much of in Dakota, firewood. Could use some trees, though not a tornado. Have to use coal and cow chips for heat out there."

"You don't say."

Then Mama, having called Peter and Papa for lunch, called to Tillie and Jergen. "A little lunch is on the table." She'd made little meat and hard cheese sandwiches topped with a toothpick and pickle slice. Oatmeal cake, along with spice cookies sat on little trays. She'd set four place settings with her Sunday-best china, and of course served black coffee.

So, the courtship continued on some Saturday evenings for nearby barn dances and on all Sunday afternoons. He took her on long walks and picnics. On their first picnic, Jergen said, "I worried you'd find a mate in Dakota and wondered why in the dickens I hadn't tried to court you before you left."

"I worried that you might be engaged to be married—or even married—by the time I got back. Still surprises me that our brief encounters years ago shaped dreams for both of us, dreams we held with so little encouragement."

"I realized when you left that I should have come calling. Guess I was too scared of rejection. You are so smart and accomplished, and me—just a simple farmer."

"Jergen, you are anything but simple."

He invited her to come to church with him one Sunday and stay for dinner with his parents, along with aunts and uncles. To top a roast beef dinner, his mother produced floating island meringues for dessert, a very special treat.

The following Saturday evening, while on a walk in tall grass, he produced a gold engagement band, got down on his knees, and entreated her to become his wife when she returned from Dakota.

"Oh yes, Jergen, of course, of course." Tillie did not question her decision, though in saying yes, she did think of Ernie, and felt fleeting sadness at the impending loss of that good friendship. She sensed she loved Jergen, loved him from her soul, and believed she did not have that same depth of feeling for Ernie.

While feeling such happiness at her dream becoming reality, sometimes at night she wondered at the fast happening of their engagement.

What is love? she wondered as the days in Minnesota fell away. *Why should I feel love for one good man and only friendship toward*

another who is equally as good and kind and capable? Is love an aware-
ness of the filling up of a piece missing in my own soul, a piece I don't
even know is absent? Perhaps love is a recognition that God planted.
Yet I've seen love die, or was it not love to begin with? Love includes
a need to care for someone and for the knowledge that you belong to
another. Yet the feeling I have for Jergen seems to transcend those needs.

Jergen met more of her family, though he knew most, and
Tillie met more of his. Dances, picnics, family gatherings—they
went together. Had they been younger, there may have been chap-
erones, but everyone seemed to recognize that these two seasoned
adults needed no escort. They decided they would set no wedding
date until Tillie returned from Dakota the following summer.

Tillie saw Lars and his wife Christine at some gatherings.
They appeared content. Lars asked Tillie how Bertha fared. "Oh,
she does so well. She has Ole out there now to keep her company,
along with all the rest of the neighbors, of course. And she does so
well with the children, loves them you know."

"I suppose," he said and then moved on.

———

One day Tillie wrote her second letter to Ernie, the first having
gone out shortly after her arrival. She scrapped the first versions, so
it was the third she finally brought to the Watson Post Office.

My dear Ernie,

You have been in my thoughts so often and I hope you are
faring well, that there are not grasshoppers or fires to contend
with this summer. It is so green and lush here. I wish you

could see it. Perhaps someday soon you will return to your roots near Morris and experience the wonder again of forests.

My family is mostly well, though Papa fades a bit, rests more often, looks rather pale. He tries to act hearty, though I feel it is an effort. I am so pleased to spend this time with him and worry that I may not be able to share his presence when I return to Minnesota next summer after proving up.

I must inform you that I have become engaged to Jergen Halverson. I write this with a heavy heart because I have so appreciated your care and friendship and will miss our companionship when I return. I am afraid I am causing you some pain as you read this and I feel very badly about that. You are a fine man with such good ethics and capabilities. Yet I think my place is here near my home and with the man I had some care for even before I journeyed to Dakota.

I have not written Bertha about the engagement, but feared she might somehow learn of it through neighbors getting news from home, and that you might hear of it in such a way. If you can reasonably refrain from telling Bertha, I'd like to tell her in person upon my return. Perhaps I should have waited to tell you in person, as well; yet I surely did not want you to hear of it from someone else. I hope you and I can remain friendly neighbors upon my return and it saddens me that I must convey this news to you in a letter and that our friendship will of course change.

Your friend,
Tillie

In mailing the letter, Tillie felt both relief and heaviness in her heart. She believed her decision was sound. She would prove up, enjoy her last year of homesteading in a place that she'd seen as a barren landscape when she first looked upon it, but where her eyes now delighted in the sight of abundant prairie creatures exploring their home and a place that had become populated with dear friends and neighbors during her stay. Yet she would leave that wonderful place and return to her family and to Jergen. She rather doubted that Bertha would do the same, though Bertha had not indicated her plans for after the year was up.

As August wrapped southwestern Minnesota in heat and mugginess, Tillie made her plans to return to Dakota, this time with confidence, not trepidation, with anticipation but not excitement, with thoughts of her friend Bertha and her Kincaid neighbors, but with ardor for Jergen whom she would leave behind until the following summer.

For Jergen's part, he worried incessantly about Tillie's journey west, even located a husband and wife from near Canby who were planning to journey to Dakota in late August and he suggested to Tillie that she join them on the journey. Tillie kindly but firmly rebuked his entreaty, saying she must be back by mid-August and that she was perfectly capable of journeying alone.

Four years after the first, the farewell again drew to a close at the Melbakken farm. This time Jergen would accompany her on the long ride to the Glenwood station. Papa let a tear drop from his eye as he hugged Tillie, and she entreated him, "Oh please, Papa, take good care of yourself, get your rest, and eat the good cooking from Mama. I'll be back almost before you realize I'm gone."

Mama, too, had wet eyes as she hugged her daughter. "Have a safe trip, my dear, and write to tell us of your safe arrival."

"I will, Mama, I will."

As she'd done more than four years previously, Tillie hiked her skirt and stepped up into the buggy, this time sitting next to Jergen.

Return to the Land of Deep Grass Roots

The frequency of *clackety-clack* revolutions diminished. Then the melodious whistle began sounding for the Portal stop and Tillie rose. Her journey had been long, but mostly uneventful.

As she debarked, she heard Bertha: "Tillie!"

There stood Bertha, Ole by her side, a huge smile brightening her sunbaked face.

After setting down her travel box, Tillie embraced Bertha, then shook Ole's hand; he warmly welcomed her back to "our humble, but friendly, community."

They stepped up into Ole's buggy, a new one. The two women immediately began gabbing about happenings in Minnesota, and family of course. It was while Tillie was telling Bertha about her favorite aunt that Bertha happened to glance at Tillie's left hand and noticed the band adorning her third finger.

"Tillie, you've become engaged to be married!" she nearly shouted, looking almost alarmed. Then after a moment, she said quietly with a sadness coloring her voice, "I was wondering why Ernie didn't accept our invitation to come along today."

"Yes, oh yes, Jergen and I will marry after I return next year." Tillie's face gleamed as she said this.

"So, you will return," Bertha said slowly and softly. Her shoulders slumped and her eyes displayed a gloomy and quizzical look.

"Yes, Bertha, I'll return to Minnesota. My life will be there. Though I've loved every minute—well not every minute, but most minutes—of our adventure and wouldn't give it up for anything, I belong there. I could feel it. And I believe Jergen and I belong together."

Bertha realized she should act excited for Tillie. "Well, that's wonderful for you." She gave a nice smile. "Probably what I expected, but I'd hoped that you'd find your soul here as I think I have." She nudged Ole. "Did you hear this news, Ole?"

Ole turned toward Tillie and smiled in an endearing manner. "I'm happy for you, Tillie. Congratulations." After a moment, he added, "But the community here will miss you. I think we've all grown to count on your strength and reliability."

"Oh, Ole, I shall miss the community much more, I'm sure, than you'll miss me. I've grown up here, developed that strength you speak of because of the strength in all of you."

Bertha's tears overflowed her lids at that moment in spite of wanting to hold them back. She quickly tried to hide them and wipe them away.

Quiet ensued for a brief time as Bertha reflected on how Tillie's plan would affect her own future. Then she turned her thoughts in another direction and shared news of the community. The churchmen had called a minister for their church. Pastor Fredrikson would share duties at their Norwegian Lutheran Church and the Lutheran church just started in Portal. He'd come for regular service once a month and be available for weddings and funerals.

"The Sieversons had a baby girl. Sweet little thing," said Bertha. "But the sad news . . . Sam, the youngest boy of Jorgen and

Marta, died of diphtheria and sent a shiver through the community. Many remembered the epidemic that spread through Hallack a couple'a years ago. But, although their daughter Rena became ill, and Marta as well, the Heggs confined themselves and the disease didn't spread. Marta and Rena recovered. They believe a visit to Minot infected them."

Tillie visibly shuddered and shook her head at that news as she thought about the danger there had been and the sadness that must weigh on Marta and Jorgen.

When Tillie had her first glimpse, she saw that the B&T Estate looked well kept. The summer had been kind, no grasshopper infestations or prairie fires. Though not the vibrant green of Minnesota, their land of deep grass roots was far from the parched and burned landscape it had been a year earlier when Bertha returned.

Roger, who Bertha had picked up from Ernie, came bounding up to Tillie as she departed the buggy, wagging his tail furiously and barking as if he were possessed. Tillie returned his antics, jumping up and down and then leaning down and hugging him to her.

Before even going into her shack, Tillie went to see Sam in the pasture. Just before she'd left home, a truckload of apples came from Iowa and Tillie had taken one with her. She reached in her handbag, withdrew an apple, and held it out to Sam who opened his jaw wide, grabbed the apple, and made a loud crunch, sending part of the apple to the ground. He chomped the rest, then leaned down, found the piece of dirty apple, and munched it. Tillie thought she saw his mouth forming a smile and she hugged his long neck.

Walking into her shack, Tillie felt a pang of sadness that this would not be her home much longer, that by this time next year she would be embarking upon a different kind of adventure. *Well, I'll make the most of this last year here, enjoy the families of the prairie, the little church, even the brutal winter.* She went about putting her things away, then ridding the shack of the incessant summer dust.

Bertha appeared later, having seen Ole off. The friends embraced again. Bertha wanted to know more about Jergen and the life that he and Tillie might have upon their marriage—and when was that to be?

So, Tillie talked of Jergen's steadfastness, his solidity in the community, his piousness, of his restrained but constant ardor. "He's a serious man, like me that way, not given to silliness or giddiness, though he can enjoy a good laugh. He's versed in subjects from archeology and history to the classic writers and mechanics and everyone recognizes that he is a good farmer. Frugal, but willing to invest in the newest machines. He can be tender, though he's a Norwegian through and through, not given to exhibitions of passion."

"What does Ernie know of this?"

"I wrote him." Looking down and slowly shaking her head from side to side, Tillie added, "I feel such sorrow for what likely was his sting of hurt in reading the letter." She looked up again. Her eyes looked moist, but no tears showed. "I simply hope I didn't pain him too much. I care for him, and being here, I rather long for his company, yet we can only be cordial friends now, I know."

"I pretty much guessed something was afloat when I asked him to come with me to meet you," said Bertha. She formed her lips in a taut line and appeared nearly ready to let tears flow, then went on. "Ernie took a moment to answer me and I remember his face clouding. Then he said he'd likely be too busy just then, but that he hoped to see you soon. I think I gave him a quizzical look as he turned away. Now I understand he was probably trying to hide his tears."

"Oh, Bertha, love can be so complicated. Wonderful sometimes, but can bring such sadness too."

Tillie straightened, then, assumed a matter-of-fact face, and moved her head slightly up and down a few times. "Well, and what of you and Ole, Bertha?"

"Well, Ole and I have talked about marriage, though he's not exactly proposed. I've not accepted, exactly. Yet I suppose we will be a couple after I prove up. I don't think I could abide leaving him."

"That's what I've expected, Bertha. You'll make him a wonderful wife and he a good husband to you, though won't you miss your family back home?"

"Well, with Grandpapa gone, the ties aren't so close. I'll miss my brother the most, I think. Perhaps I can encourage him to come to Dakota. Hilda I'll miss, as well, though we aren't that close, as you know. And even though Papa still lives, he was never much a part of my life after Mama died. It was Grandmama and Grandpapa that raised me up. So, I believe this community will become my family."

"It's what I've imagined for you and occasionally thought of for me as well. I sometimes dreamed of life as Ernie's wife here in Dakota. I know he'd make a fine husband. He's a really good man. Believe I could have loved and cared for him. Yet Jergen draws out something in me that I don't feel with Ernie. Perhaps it's love born of familiarity and knowledge, rather than an ardor born of loneliness and the unknown. I may not laugh as much with Jergen, but I so appreciate conversations with him, and I'm desirous of being with him. He's a really fine man.

"Too, I don't think I could abide leaving my family for a life here. Even though, more than you, I thought I had the pioneer spirit and always dreamed of coming west, it seems you may fit this life better than me. With Papa so frail, Mama will need looking after, and . . . well, it's my home."

"I understand, my constant friend." With that, Bertha slumped her shoulders, brought her hands to her face, and let her tears fall. After a few moments, she added, "While I don't have so much family I'll miss . . . well, I shall miss you deeply when you leave. I'll miss what we two have shared in this place."

"Oh yes, Bertha. I shall miss you as well. And I'll miss this place and this community probably more than I can even think about. Yet we each make choices, likely good choices, and face the consequences of those choices. Perhaps there is no calling that's meant for us, just different roads to take, each leading in a different direction." She put her arms around Bertha and let her tears fall then, not copious ones, just tears thinking of a life apart from Bertha, from Ernie, from the community.

"But we have months to share and school to arrange. We need not dwell on our eventual separation," said Tillie, wanting to break the uncomfortable melancholy.

"Sure, sure. And I came to tell you that I have side pork and cornmeal mush ready to make for our supper, so join me whenever you have yourself organized here."

Tillie saw Ernie at church that first Sunday upon her return. "Hello, Ernie," said Tillie in a quiet voice, her statement sounding almost more like a question.

"Good to see you back to Dakota," he said with a slight smile.

"It's good to be back," she responded in a firmer voice, returning a feeble smile. With that, they each found a seat on the pews. When they departed after the service, they gave each other a nod with a warm smile, but sad eyes.

On their way home, Tillie told Bertha, "I don't want it to end like this with Ernie, without being able to express to him how much I care for him."

"Well, then don't let it end that way. Find a way of being alone with him and tell him what you need to say," her friend replied.

"Ummhmm."

The summer began its ending, the evenings growing cooler, the days shorter, the sun coming up a little more southerly while its intensity weakened. The migratory birds put in their appearances, the wonderful whistle of the tundra swans being the most beautiful to hear, and the swirling and twirling of the cranes winding toward the heavens the most striking to behold.

The wheat harvest looked to be magnificent that year, and when the harvest crew came with the reaper, Ernie among them, the girl homesteaders shocked the wheat to prepare it for drying. Later, after threshing, they'd find that their bushels would total around seven hundred, nearly twenty-three bushels per acre. It would yield three hundred and seventy-five dollars to share with each other and Hans and Henry.

The two women prepared a special meal for the crew at harvest's end. While Tillie was mashing potatoes, she saw Ernie mounting his horse, apparently planning to leave. She rushed outside.

"Ernie, Ernie."

He turned around.

"Please stay for the meal, Ernie. Please."

He nodded his head, but didn't dismount at first. Then he swung his leg over the horse.

She went up to him as he stepped down. "I hope we can find some time to talk, Ernie. Our formal treatment of each other is hard on both of us I think, and I do so care about you." The two looked deeply into each other's eyes, each of them nodding their head, and Ernie displayed a very slight smile.

"You'll stay, will you not?"

He began walking with her toward the group that had gathered.

Roger bounded up. He wagged his tail energetically as Ernie petted him with obvious affection.

The ice broken, he joined the others at the makeshift picnic table and joined in the frivolities and celebration. And he and Tillie were occasional partners during the square-dancing. He stuck around when the others left and Bertha had wisely gone to her shack. He and Tillie both remained quiet as he helped Tillie clean up from the gathering, and then the two walked down to the lake, slowly strolling hand in hand.

"You've been the best support and companion I could have hoped to have in this place," she said. "And there were indeed times I thought we could make a life together, and I think you thought that too."

"So, so," he said quietly.

"You are such a good man and will make some woman a wonderful husband, I know, I know. And I wish I could explain to you without hurting you more why I must return to my family . . . and to Jergen." Tillie kept trying to hold back her tears. "Hurting you more is the last thing I wish. I can't even quite explain it to myself, except that it seems I am meant to return to my roots."

"There was a woman where I came from, a good and honest woman. Yet I couldn't find a place in my heart deep enough for her.

I know it pained her when I left for Dakota. For you, that place in my heart is there, but I understand that for you, that place is not there for me." He said this while looking at the lake, then turned to her and said in a soft and shaky voice, "Yet, I so wish it were different."

Tillie closed her eyes and reached out again for his hand.

They walked along as the sky deepened to a majestic purple, the wonderful image of the cranes just a shadow in the darkening sky. "Look, they're on their way south," Tillie said softly, pointing upwards.

He looked up as many moments elapsed, then turned to her. "Might I hold you once again, my dear Tillie?"

She simply nodded her head and he took her. He clung on and on and she allowed it, even let herself warm to it as she imagined the hug might last a lifetime in his dreams. She felt his desire keenly against her abdomen, and felt some of her own response, until finally he released her.

"In my thoughts I will always be your friend, Tillie, and you will always reside in my heart. Please let me help in any way I can, especially as winter comes upon us."

"And I will be your friend, dear, dear Ernie."

They turned then, walked toward the shack where he had tied his horse. He let go of her hand, nodded his head a few times, mounted, and spurred his horse for the trip home.

Winter Events
at the Shacks

Tillie had seen little of Ellen since her return, but Karl was ready for school this year and came along with Brunhild. Karl, like his sister, was eager to please, though more boisterous than she was. Too, he had a solemn look on his face, especially when caught staring out at nothing. Although Frank sometimes showed up at community gatherings, and frequented the Pig, Ellen usually came to Sunday services with the younger children in tow, but without Frank. Occasionally Sven joined them. Ellen always greeted Tillie and passed some words with her; yet, as usual, she seemed reserved. Tillie saw no bruising, which she hoped meant the couple was faring better now, and Ellen didn't look to be with child. Perhaps Winnie and her herbs had helped with that.

As fall turned to winter, Tillie became more and more homesick, yet she tried to approach her final winter in Dakota with appreciation and gratitude for all she had learned and come to respect. She knew her experience in Dakota would fortify her for hardships as well as enhance her appreciation for any amenity of modern life she might receive.

Her sight would linger on the hoarfrost producing glittering wraps on the bushes near the lake, the brilliant frostings of crystals on the windows when the sunlight hit them, and huge snowflakes looking like fluffs of cotton as they softly drifted upon the wide-open Dakota plain. She loved the sea of white with new-fallen snow where not a human track was visible as far as her eyes traveled across the flat plain, broken only by shacks with smoke rising in tendrils or billows usually drifting southeasterly.

Most late afternoons after returning from school when it was still light enough to see well enough, she worked on a quilt, which she would give to Bertha and Ole for what Tillie assumed would be an upcoming marriage, although there had been no clear declaration. With careful stitching, she pieced together cloth from her own tablecloth, one of Bertha's torn and discarded blouses, and other remnants, along with some flannel from one of Ole's shirts, which she had surreptitiously acquired.

She and Bertha ate many suppers together, especially on school evenings when they would review the day or plan the next. Bertha usually invited Ole for supper on Saturday or for dinner after church on Sunday. Sometimes she invited Tillie to join them.

At night, Tillie missed both Ernie and Jergen and wasn't sure which one she missed most. That thought disturbed her. *I should no longer be thinking fondly of Ernie*, she told herself. *Jergen's to be my husband. He's a good and thrifty man who will make me a fine husband and our children a good father.* Yet Ernie's easy wit and good nature, his little sayings like "golly man," his comfortable bear hugs—all these she longed for when sleep was at bay.

On Sundays when the weather was decent enough for services, she attended. She and Ernie greeted each other warmly and exchanged superficial talk. "Isn't it grand to have such a sunny day?" she'd inquire. And he would respond, "Yeah, yeah, sure is nice after last week's blizzard." He inquired about Roger, and Tillie responded that he was getting fat from too much lying around. She'd joke, "Course I could feed him less, but then I'd feel guilty eating."

During service, Tillie would pray for forgiveness of her continued longing for Ernie and she'd tell herself such thoughts would fade as soon as she returned home and no longer coped with the homesickness of Dakota.

The coming of Christmas was joyful for Tillie, if a bit melancholy. She especially awaited opening the package from Jergen, small and exquisitely wrapped in blue paper. *Has he wrapped this himself?* she wondered. Too, she imagined him opening the gift she'd sent, a hunting knife, which Nels Iverson made. Nels was a superb scrimshaw artist, having learned the art from his grandfather who'd been a whaler. The knife handle was made of deer antler, onto which Nels had finely scratched a scene, then polished it with ink so a tar paper shack revealed itself, with a woman washing clothes next to it.

The day of Christmas Eve was sunny without much wind. Bertha had invited Ole and Tillie for dinner. Coming into the shack, Ole exclaimed, "Could smell Christmas cooking as I rode in! Brings back memories of home with all the odors of Christmases past concentrated right here."

Ole hung his coat on the peg, gave Bertha a big grin and a peck on the cheek, and sat down. The three sang carols together—both women again marveling at Ole's voice—while the women finished meal preparation: a roasted goose, mashed potatoes with plenty of gravy, and lefse of course.

"Read in the paper a while back that the Wright Brothers out east kept their flying machine in the air for five whole minutes," said Ole after they finished singing. "This morning when I looked up at da moon, I thought about them brothers and figured we just might make it to the moon yet."

They all laughed. "You have quite the imagination, Ole," Tillie said as she shook her head.

While they ate they reminisced about Christmases in their early years. Ole remembered yule log hunts, especially the year he found the log. Tillie and Bertha told him about julebukking, which he'd heard of, but never participated in. "Was lots of fun," said Bertha. "We'd dress in some kind of disguise, go from neighbor to neighbor and make our voices sound different until they guessed who we were. Usually got some coffee and cookies or *julekake*, which filled our bellies to the brim."

"Have to get that tradition started 'round here," he declared.

After the rommegrøt, Ole took out a small package, though it was a little bigger than Tillie thought Bertha was imagining it might be. He tenderly handed it to Bertha, whose wistful face briefly displayed a look of disappointment.

She carefully opened the package, discovering a small silver sugar dish. "Oh, for nice," she said, then quickly exclaimed, "How lovely! It'll add such a touch of elegance to this plain-lookin' shack. Thank you!" And it was lovely. Intricate little roses adorned the perimeter. She planted a little kiss on Ole's lips.

Ole gave Bertha one of his bear hugs when he received a knife similar to the one Tillie sent to Jergen.

The gift exchange left Tillie feeling kind of like a third fiddle and longing for Ernie's company. She wondered if he, too, was hungering for her companionship.

Even while they were eating, they'd heard the wind begin to wail and by the time the gift exchange was over, it began to beat against the shack. So Ole left for home soon afterwards.

By Christmas Day, snow started falling and the wind's shrieking grew by the minute. Tillie brought food scraps to the chickens, filled the bucket with coal, and brought it inside the shack. Roger bounded in behind her. Soon she could barely see Bertha's shack, but Bertha arrived minutes later, having secured the door to Sam's shed after bringing him water and throwing him more hay and some oats.

Bertha brought with her a gift of pillowcases for Tillie to take home for her marriage bed. She had beautifully embroidered them with two overlapping rings and lovebirds. Tillie gave Bertha embroidered flour-sack dish towels. One said, "Friends forever;" another, "Christmas 1904;" and the third, "Kincaid on the Dakota plain." On the first, Tillie had portrayed two hands clasped; on the second, a Christmas tree; and on the third, a depiction of a shack.

Wanting to keep her anticipation going, Tillie had waited until now to open the package from Jergen. With gentleness, she removed the wrapping paper that contained a small wooden box, a box she assumed Jergen had made. Inside the box with a velvet cloth lining, she found a locket. "How beautiful!" she exclaimed as she gazed at the locket engraved with a delicate flower pattern and, near the outer edge, three rubies, her birthstone. "What a sweet, sweet man he is," she said softly to Bertha, a lone tear spilling onto her cheek.

"It's a beautiful locket, Tillie, yes a very sweet gift."

"And your little dish from Ole was lovely and sweet, as well."

"Lovely, yes." Bertha tightened her mouth. It was hard to see whether it was a smirk or a smile or just a way of controlling her emotion. "I'd rather it had been a smaller gift . . . like a little band for my finger." The way she said this, it almost sounded like a question. A few tears then spilled onto her check. She sniffed her nose.

"Oh, my friend. Ole seems so in love with you. Don't know why he hasn't quite asked you to marry him yet, but . . . well, I can see that he will. I'm sure he will."

"Suppose so. It's just that your time with Jergen was so short until he asked you to be his wife. Seems like it's taking Ole a long time to decide or something. Maybe it's like it was for you with Ernie."

"I don't think so, Bertha. I really don't. Maybe he's just waiting for the right time."

"Could be, I suppose. Most of the time I seem to know that I'll be his wife in time and we kind'a talk that way."

"Sometimes hard to figure out men's notions, that's for sure."

"Sure, sure. And the little dish is very special. I hope I didn't show I was disappointed when I got it. Did I?"

"I don't think so. I think I kind of expected you to get an engagement band, too, so I was even a little disappointed. But many men don't even give engagement bands, you know, just wait for a wedding to give a ring. Who knows, but I can see he loves you dearly."

The wind cooled Tillie's shack almost as fast as the fire warmed it while the two reflected upon previous Christmases in Dakota, especially remembering the night of Kincaid's birth. And as the evening turned to night, they blew out the candles and extinguished the lantern and snuggled into bed with Roger, sharing his warmth between them. Getting a whiff of his breath as she burrowed in, Bertha turned away from him and his reeking scent.

The storm raged overnight. By morning, after getting the fire going, fixing dishes of oatmeal, and sipping on their coffee, the two worked to open the door until they could see that the blizzard had created drifts up to four feet high while it swept other areas of the prairie clean. The two worked periodically through the day, shoveling paths first to Bertha's so she could light her fire, then to the shed to feed and water Sam. Tired, ready to relax in front of a fire, they stopped by midafternoon and decided to spend another night together at Tillie's, especially since the paths were already filling in.

The wind died down by late afternoon and Ole made it to the B&T Estate near dusk. He checked Bertha's shack first, then went to Tillie's. With Tillie pulling and Ole pushing, the door opened enough for him to get his rounded belly in, sending Tillie backwards. She almost fell on her bottom side.

"*Uff da mayda!*" he exclaimed upon entering. "Another bad one. So glad to see you both okay."

"Come by the stove and warm up, Ole," Tillie said. "You shouldn't have braved the blizzard yet, but we'll soon have rice mush ready for supper. Been cooking it for hours. You'll stay, of course. Warm you up, it will."

"My, does rice mush sounds like a bit a'heaven after the trip here."

"Heaven, it may not be. No harps playing or angels hovering, but the mush should be good for sure," said Bertha with a wide grin.

"Well, I'd say there be a couple angels hovering 'round," Ole laughed.

After saying grace, each of them ladled the mush onto their plate, then floated a large pat of butter in it and sprinkled it with sugar and cinnamon. Ginger cookies and egg coffee completed their supper.

When they finished, Bertha said, "You'll not be leaving tonight, will you, Ole?"

"Well, I got . . ."

"You'll stay," said Bertha definitively.

Ole looked at Tillie, raising his eyebrows as if to ask her permission.

"That's a good idea," she said, with a bit of a smile.

The three chatted on as the night blackened with not even much of a moon, while gusts of wind tore at the shack and blew in a little snow through the seams of tar paper.

"Perhaps Ole and I ought to see if we can get to my place and get a fire roaring before things freeze over there," suggested Bertha after a while. "And it'd be a bit crowded here," she added sheepishly.

Again, Ole looked to Tillie with raised eyebrows. Eventually she nodded. "Yeah then, I won't say a word to anyone."

And so the two lovers spent a night together, huddled together for the physical warmth, allowing their passions to reach fulfillment. Although it was their first time together, it wasn't the first time for either of them (though it had just been the once before for Bertha, the last time she'd been with Lars). Yet both admitted worrying about Tillie's disapproval.

"Will she t'ink we're sinners, den?" he asked her.

"Well, I s'pose she don't need to know the whole of it, Ole." Bertha smiled weakly; yet a look of anxiety crossed her face. "Not much else we could do, but have you stay the night in this weather."

"Well, I s'pose it'd been more proper for me to sleep on the floor at Tillie's or to leave you there and come here myself. You won't t'ink the verse of me now, will you, *min lille kjæreste?*"

"Oh, Ole, would I try, I couldn't think less of thee."

He drew her into his bear hug, then reached for his coat. "Left my dog Sandy in the barn with the cows for some warmth, but best get home and check on her and the cattle." He left soon after the day dawned sunny.

Eventually Bertha appeared at Tillie's door.

"Come in, come in."

Tillie set out coffee, along with bread toasted in the oven and spread with gooseberry jam.

"And how was your night?" queried Tillie with a soft smile.

Bertha seemed unable to look Tillie in the eyes, so looking at the table, she answered, "It was a good night, Tillie," and then burst into tears.

"Oh my, oh my, did he hurt you, then?"

"Oh no, not at all. He was very gentle. I just so fear your disapproval, and am not quite sure what I think of myself. Here I am, a teacher, expected to be upright, and we're not even engaged, though he keeps hinting that might be coming. Maybe I've been duped."

Tillie waited some moments before replying. With a firm, almost teachery voice, she responded, "Bertha, you may think I'm a stick-in-the-mud, that I don't understand human desire and urges, but you are wrong. I feel it myself, even though I don't seem much able to express the passion." After a moment, she added, "I don't think Ole is deceiving you; he just doesn't seem like that kind of man."

Bertha looked directly at Tillie then, trying to rub the tears away. She gave a wan smile.

"Oh yes, Bertha. I understand and I do not condemn you, though others might. Let's drink up our coffee. You can trust me to have my lips closed about this."

"I just hope I don't find myself in a family way." Bertha looked down at the table again, but moved her eyes upward to glimpse Tillie's reaction. "Think I know enough about biology to say it's unlikely," she added quietly, "but I don't know that much."

"Well, time will tell of course, but do tell me if your sickness doesn't come on time."

Although Bertha and Tillie had rarely hugged, Bertha stood, moved to Tillie's chair, and bent down for a gentle hug. "Thank you, Tillie, thank you for understanding and not judging me too harshly."

"There, there. Drink some more coffee now and eat up your toast."

Two weeks later, Ole asked if he could accompany Bertha home after church. The two women had walked together to church that morning of a January thaw, so Tillie glanced at Bertha. "You go with Ole. I'll spend a little time here with the women and I'll hike home in a bit."

When they got inside Bertha's shack, Ole bent down upon one knee, produced a gold engagement band, and looked up at Bertha. "Will ya be my wife, my love?"

"Of course, of course. Now get off the floor and put the band on my finger." Her smile seemed to light up her whole being.

He slipped it on her, gently moving it back and forth to get it over her knuckle, swollen from years of hard work. "I wanted it for your Christmas gift, but couldn't get it by then . . . or guess I didn't t'ink of it soon enough." His face grew red.

With the pure joy of those initial phases of unrestrained love, the two waited for Tillie, to give her the news. With smiles and laughter, they told her they would marry as soon as the two girl homesteaders could prove up, hopefully by the first part of June. "We'll get hitched before you leave so you can be my bridesmaid. Yes?"

Tillie hugged the two of them together and said of course she would stand up for Bertha.

———

A couple more serious blizzards occurred that year, but by then the two women handled Dakota blizzards with aplomb. They called school off those two times, but otherwise, classes continued.

Their teaching style and lessons had changed so much from that first year. No longer were they quite as concerned with making sure the children knew history and geography, good manners, or proper grammar. Although Bertha would read the children stories of faraway places, the skills she taught were to read words such as *milk* and *pudding*, *lath* and *coal*, and *fox, badger, skunk*, and *pronghorn*. Tillie taught the girls to read recipes and sewing directions. She helped the boys learn to read well by giving them text about raising hogs, harvesting wheat, and shoeing a horse. Arithmetic was heavy on learning how to pay for items at a store and how to figure charges for items the students might eventually sell.

Yet both teachers worked more worldly ideas into their lessons. Tillie delved into national and world events, such as the work proceeding on the Panama Canal. She taught civics and encouraged all of the boys to vote and suggested that likely one day girls could vote as well. "In fact," she said, "in Wyoming, Colorado, Utah, and Idaho, women can vote for state offices now."

With their classes joined, the teachers talked about the nickelodeon, a place where one could go to watch a moving picture; the Wright Brothers' flights and the possibility of other flying machines; and the coming age of motorcars, even to Dakota. Tillie used that idea to talk about arithmetic, how much a motorcar might cost, what gasoline for it could cost, and how the expenses might compare to the costs for a horse and buggy, including feeding the horse.

Calamity

It was past mid-March, a sunlit, though cold and windy, Saturday morning. Tillie was working on Bertha's wedding quilt when she heard a knock on her door. Expecting Bertha, she quickly hid the quilt under the bed. Opening the door, she discovered Sven. "Well, Sven, do come in."

He came in without speaking.

"Are you thinking of getting some lessons?"

He shook his head. "Mor needs your help."

"What's wrong?"

"She's hurt perty bad."

"Oh dear. Give me just a minute and I'll ready myself." She quickly stashed the quilt in her trunk, then got her medicine kit. "Is your father at home?"

"No, he left. He's gone."

"How bad is your mother?"

"She's perty bad."

"I'll be along in just a minute. I'll put on some warmer clothes. Wait for me outside, if you wish, or head right home."

Sven left the shack. Tillie pulled long woolen underwear over her bloomers and put on her coat, hat, and mittens. She ran to Bertha's, told her what she was doing, asked Bertha to try to get word to Doc Henry and to Winnie, and perhaps see if Ole or Ernie were willing to come check on her and the family. Mounting Sam, she spurred him into a gallop.

Entering the shack, she saw Ellen on the floor, a small amount of darkened blood near the side of her face. Silently, the younger children got up from the floor near their mother and went to stand near Sven, who'd arrived home just before Tillie got there.

Ellen's face was pasty. She lay there, mouth hanging open, not moving, not appearing to be alive; yet her chest moved up and down, if weakly. Tillie felt Ellen's arms and legs for signs of breakage. She found no obvious breaks and no sign of a gunshot or knife wound. She positioned one quilt around Ellen, tucking it under without moving her much, then covered her with a second quilt. Ellen's head was turned to the left. When Tillie moved Ellen's head slightly, she saw that her hair on that side was matted with blood. Black rivulets ran from her ear down her cheek. Tillie talked softly to Ellen, telling her help was coming soon. "Just breathe in and out, Ellen. No struggle needed. We'll take care of you."

Tillie had never been more frightened as time slowly moved on. She told the little children to sit quietly near their mother. "Just hold her hand, perhaps." She asked Sven to keep the fire going nice and hot. Tillie sang softly, encouraging the children to join her. From time to time, she'd speak to Ellen. "We all care about you. You've borne so much, too much maybe. Your children are here with you, loving you."

As the moments crawled on, she tried to comfort the children and told them how brave they were. "You're helping your mor by touching her, holding her hand."

Finally, she thought she heard a horse approaching. Moments later, Ernie walked in, not bothering to knock. He looked at Ellen and his face went white. "Oh my God!" he exclaimed. "What happened here?"

"I don't even know. Sven has been quiet about it, but it looks like her head was hit hard. She breathes, but . . ."

"Ole went to get Doc. They should come soon, I hope. Winnie's gone to Portal, I guess, but word was left for her."

Tillie nodded and again sat on the floor next to Ellen and softly told her that Doc was on his way. "He'll know what to do." She wasn't so sure there was anything to do, though. She simply ran her fingers over Ellen's face, caressing her gently.

"Thanks for coming, Ernie," she said in time, then returned her gaze to Ellen, occasionally placing her hand under the quilt to feel the rise and fall of Ellen's chest.

"What happened?" Ernie asked Sven.

"Not sure. Dad was mad at her for burnin' the bread. He told me to get out, get some coal, so I went. Couple minutes later heard her scream and ran in. He stomped out when I came in. Had the fire poker I think."

While they waited for Doc, Tillie saw that Ellen's hands had turned white, white with a tinge of yellow, like a corpse.

Long after Ernie arrived, Doc came. It felt to Tillie as if a whole day had passed since she'd come, but in truth the afternoon was just waning. Doc kneeled down, checked Ellen's breathing, checked her head, saw that her hands and feet had gone white. And cold and hard to the touch.

He glanced at Tillie and shook his head slowly, then looked again at Ellen.

After a while he said quietly, "You've done what you can. We just wait now. Maybe she'll recover. Some."

Tillie was quite sure there would be no recovery. "Why don't all you children come down here and tell your mother how much you love her, how you want her to get better soon."

Sven said, "I'm going out. I'll be in the barn, tending cows."

The little children followed Tillie's suggestion. Stoically, Brunhild rubbed her mother's face, "I love you, Mor. Please get well." Karl and Kincaid seemed unable to speak. Karl's tears dripped slowly down his cheeks, then fell upon his mother, but he made no sound. Tillie took the two little children and cuddled them to her. It was then that their sobs began.

After comforting the children as best she could, she found the family's Bible and began reading from the Psalms, hoping her voice would bring some comfort or maybe would bring God's presence among them.

Doc motioned to Ernie and the two left the shack. When the door closed, Doc said, "She'll not make it, I reckon. Blow to her head was too much."

Ernie just looked at the ground, shook his head.

"I'll stay for a while," said Doc. "See how long it might go. Nothing to do but keep her warm, I reckon. The children will need caring when it's over."

"I suppose Tillie and Bertha will handle it as best they can. I'll stay here until we're sure Frank doesn't come back, though I 'spect he'll be gone for good now."

"I 'spect."

Doc went to find Sven. The boy was in the barn, sitting on a bale of hay and staring at the wall. Doc sat down next to him and told him his mother likely wouldn't live. "I'm sorry," said Doc. "Wish there was something to do. Ya might want to go in and say somethin' to her." The boy continued to stare at the wall.

The vigil went on and then went on some more. Tillie sat on the floor most of the time, reading the Bible, making up stories, sometimes just sitting quietly holding Ellen's cold hand. Doc again went out to find Sven.

Eventually Sven came in, slowly taking off his coat and over-shoes. Then he bent down by his mother and whispered so Tillie could barely make out the words. "Wish I could'a protected you better, Mor. Ya' been a good mor."

Tillie put a hand on Sven's shoulder, touching him lightly. He didn't flinch; Tillie had feared he might. "I'm so sorry, Sven. I'm sure you did what you could."

"Maybe," he said, then got up.

Ole came along at some point and was as shocked to see Ellen as they all had been. After understanding the situation and seeing he wasn't much use waiting out the vigil, Ole said, "I'll head back. Tell Bertha and the others, I reckon."

Doc stayed till the end, when Ellen's shallow breaths slowed so that each one she took seemed unexpected, then stopped with barely a sound. After several moments, Doc nodded to Tillie. It was the first time Tillie felt impressed by the usually gruff doctor. His brusque demeanor had been absent during the watch and Tillie felt his compassion by the very fact that he stayed when his doctoring could no longer help.

When it was over, Tillie did her best to console the children. Doc took Ellen away, laying her over his horse before he mounted. He rode to the church, then went to Orlo's shack to tell him. Together, they brought her into the cold church. Orlo said he'd summon Pastor Fredrikson to plan some kind of a funeral.

Tillie and Ernie helped the young children onto their horses, then mounted themselves.

Sven refused to come. "I need to be alone."

"We'll handle the little ones. Someone will check on you tomorrow," Tillie offered.

Although it was midnight or after, they could see Bertha's face in the glow in her window as they approached. As they dismounted,

Bertha opened the door. "Come in, come in." She hugged the silent little ones to her. "I'm so, so sorry about your mor. All of you can stay with me for now."

To Tillie she said, "I kept your stove going, stoked it just a bit ago, so should be warm over there. Took care of Roger. Left him nice and comfy in the shack."

Exhausted and bereft, Tillie nodded. "I'll see you and the children in the morning."

Ernie accompanied her to her shack and she invited him in. "Should have known this was comin', I s'pose," he said.

"Yeah, I suppose."

She stoked the fire, put on coffee to boil, and when it was ready, she brought out flatbrød and lard. "It's all I have."

"It's good."

The two drank coffee, mostly silently. Ernie ate a little. Tillie was too forlorn even to try.

When they stood up, he brought her to him and she crumbled into his arms, letting out a deep sign but little other emotion. "I'll stay the night if ya wish," he said. "Just sleep on the floor."

"Please come to the bed and just hold me, if you can."

And he did. He stroked her hair and stroked her face, now moistened by the few tears that spilled.

Both slept fitfully, reaching for the warmth and comfort of each other each time they awakened. Although their bodies touched, neither reacted with passion. Tillie was spent from the ordeal, drained by the dark suffering and heinousness they'd witnessed, but also guarded of the potential of their passions erupting out of some animal need for release from the wretchedness of the day.

If one could observe the two lying together in the bed, one would see such tenderness in Ernie's features and his gentle, respectful touch, and one would know he felt a depth of love he longed to express and knew he couldn't allow himself to demonstrate.

He left early in the morning, after coffee and oatmeal. Tillie would remember that night and his care for the rest of her life.

Tillie put on her coat then and went to Bertha's shack. The two youngest children still slept, but Brunhild was awake. She sat staring at the wall, mute even when Bertha asked her if she could drink a little cocoa or eat a rusk.

Tillie climbed onto Sam, then went to Orlo's. She told him she would wash Ellen's body and dress her. She then rode to what now seemed to be Sven's shack, bringing him potato *klub* and bread, which Bertha had provided. He looked stoic and serious, though not angry or agitated. He accepted Tillie's dish and thanked her for it. "I'm so sorry for all that has happened," said Tillie. "I so wish we'd been able to prevent this."

Sven nodded his head.

"I need to find a dress for your mother's funeral, Sven. Do you have any suggestion?" He shook his head, just moved his hand in the direction of where Ellen kept her clothes.

She found what she hoped was appropriate and took the dress back to the church. Orlo had lit a fire, so the place was cool but not freezing.

Tillie had never cared for a body before, but she did her best, holding her emotions inside. She washed away the blood from Ellen's hair and combed it, often talking to Ellen as she cleaned her up. "I wish I could have helped more, Ellen. I'm preparing you for God now. At least now you will have peace. The community here is good, as you know. We'll care for your little ones the best we can, I'm sure."

Tillie continued to talk to Ellen from time to time as she clad her in the dress she'd seen her wear to church, a homespun calico print with a high collar and long sleeves. When the dress was on, she wrapped a half-apron around Ellen's tiny waist, brown to match the gold and brown in the calico.

While Tillie readied Ellen, Ernie and Ole, who'd come to be of help, finished putting together a rough coffin, then laid a blanket in it. Pastor Fredrikson would not arrive until the next day, so Orlo asked Tillie to help him position Ellen in the coffin and she did. "Be at rest, Ellen. You are in God's hands now," she said after she positioned Ellen's stiff hands one on top of the other across her abdomen.

Pockets of snow lingered on the prairie. The cold ground had barely thawed enough for Ernie and Ole to dig through the frost-laden soil deeply enough to accommodate a coffin. Even with all of their strength, their arms felt like putty when they finished.

The entire community gathered the following day for the funeral. All of them were solemn and feeling the guilt of not helping more; yet for the most part they believed there was nothing appropriate that could have saved Ellen, that family life was private. Perhaps Tillie was the only one with the throbbing belief that she could have done more, the guilt of not having done enough. "I should have at least offered my shack to Ellen and the children."

"That's nonsense, Tillie," Winnie said. "Ellen would not have dared accept more help and, even if she had, you might be dead along with her."

That didn't diminish Tillie's shame, a shame that included the possibility her attempts to help had contributed to the disharmony in the family, a belief that was shared widely in the community, mostly among the men. When Tillie confessed her fear of this to Bertha, Bertha responded, "Tillie, you did more than any of us to prevent this. You didn't contribute. Was likely inevitable given Frank's violent streak when he drank, or maybe even without drink."

Sven was stoic at the funeral. Frank, as expected, wasn't there. The sheriff, who Doc Henry had summoned, would have him taken away if he'd shown. The little children remained in Bertha's care and she and Tillie held the young ones during the short funeral, with Brunhild sitting next to Bertha, her little hand clutching the larger one. Pastor Fredrikson, who didn't know Ellen at all, simply followed the funeral service, read "The Lord Is My Shepherd," and commended Ellen's body to God. It left Tillie feeling it would have been better had Orlo led the service, even if he was short on words.

Following the service, Sven, Orlo, Ernie, and Ole carried Ellen's coffin out behind the church where the ground was open. The men used ropes to lower the coffin. "Dust to dust," proclaimed Pastor Fredrikson. Several men took up shovels. The first thud to hit the coffin gave Tillie a deep shiver, then other shovelfuls filled the grave. Sven said he would make a wooden cross to mark her resting place.

That evening Tillie and Bertha huddled together in front of Bertha's fire after the children were asleep. "I wonder what allows a man to do such a monstrous thing, whether it's demons that possessed him or some brutality that broke his soul." Tillie's face was creased by her anguish.

"Can't imagine," said Bertha softly. "Knowing the rough treatment these children have seen, it likely will affect them forever, Sven especially, but these sleeping darlings as well. Maybe someone brutalized Frank when he was a child and he had no one to care much for his pain."

"Maybe."

Tillie offered to manage school so Bertha could look after the little ones until they could make some other arrangement.

Through Sven, Bertha learned the names of Ellen's sister and brother, and the town in which each lived. She sent telegrams, telling of the unfortunate circumstances and the four orphaned children. More than two weeks later, a letter came from Ellen's sister. Her name was Delores.

> *I have five children and am expecting a sixth. I am sorry to hear of the death of my sister and the circumstance of the children, but I don't know how I can help out, except perhaps with Sven should he desire to come here. He could help on the farm. Ellen should not have followed Frank to Dakota. We told her not to go.*
>
> *With regrets,*
> *Delores*

So, the community gathered to try to figure out what to do. Bertha talked with Ole and the two decided they could raise up Brunhild, if someone else could take Karl and Kincaid. Some of the families said they would consider it, but didn't make a commitment. Tillie knew that if no one stepped forward, she'd feel obligated to send a letter to Jergen and consider bringing them to Minnesota. Yet she knew it would be better if the children could all be near one another, and although she felt obligation, she didn't want her marriage to begin with two orphaned children to raise. *Yet we can't abandon the children to an orphanage after all they've experienced. They require a family's love and care.*

Days later, Olga and Anna announced they would take in Karl and Kincaid and care for them together as best they could. Most of the members of the community said, among themselves, that it was an odd thing. Yet no one else expressed willingness to take the children. Most of the mothers promised to do what they could to help, as did some of the men, including Ernie. Tillie felt such admiration for Ernie, and his offer added to her respect.

She also felt great relief in not needing to try to get Jergen to understand and in not having the difficulty of incorporating two wounded children into a new marriage. While Tillie looked forward to her upcoming marriage and knew, or certainly believed she knew, that she and Jergen would do well together, she also recognized she could not be too forward in her suggestions and ideas. Bringing home two young children Jergen had never even met would probably be more than he would tolerate.

She had seen enough of marriage to know that it often became a life of menial work, of usually submitting to a husband's rule and ideas, of not having much time or encouragement for one's own talents and interests. She had seen her own mother, an intelligent woman, allowing her husband to determine how the family would live and direct much of what she did.

Tillie's adventure in coming to Dakota was proof enough of her independent streak, and her sense of self-sufficiency had grown in Dakota. She knew her married life would often require submitting to Jergen's wishes, yet she was determined not to completely lose the confident demeanor and strength of character that gained vigor during her Dakota experience.

She also saw that Ole was not overbearing with Bertha. He seemed to value her spunk and ability to make decisions. Certainly, he never interfered with any of Bertha's ideas about caring for Brunhild. Of course, they weren't married yet and Tillie supposed it could change.

While Brunhild was a quiet and well-behaved child who followed rules well, Tillie clearly saw that her short life had damaged her deeply. And now she was in effect an orphan. Though not prone to tears, she easily turned sullen and rarely laughed or looked joyous. *How she must long for her dead mother!* thought Tillie. Bertha and Ole would certainly have struggles raising her up, she believed, and Bertha easily acknowledged this. Yet both she and Ole committed themselves to providing the child a good home. Ole's avuncular good spirits would hopefully help the child heal.

One could see Brunhild's love for Bertha in her warm eyes as she looked at her and in the way she tried to help her with chores, seeming to mimic Bertha's actions. Tillie hoped Bertha had already given Brunhild the strength to survive the pain, scarred as she was. Tillie saw the love in Bertha's eyes, too, such as when Brunhild would come to greet her and Bertha would take the child's soft little hand in her already work-worn and callused one, and when Bertha turned down the quilt for Brunhild at bedtime and nestled her into bed.

Proving Up

Proving up required filling out the Homestead Entry, generally known as the proof document, getting neighbors to vouch for the accuracy of the person living there and the improvements on the land, and paying six dollars. Once the homesteaders submitted the document, the official at the land office would arrange for publication of the "proof" to run five consecutive weeks in the *Bowbells Tribune*, which was an opportunity for anyone to contest it. Finally, the applicant must appear at the land office, along with the two neighbors who had signed the application as witnesses.

Ole, along with Hans, agreed to make the nearly one hundred-mile journey to the Minot Land Office to vouch for Tillie and Bertha. Henry would help out with Hans's chores and Daniel would take care of Ole's.

The travelers decided to take the train because they wouldn't need to worry so much about the weather and could limit the trip to three days, two of travel and one day to spend in Minot. Olga and Anna volunteered to care for Brunhild while Bertha was gone.

Riding on the train, the four reminisced about the early days. Tillie and Bertha remembered when they first saw the land. They recalled how foreboding it looked with no trees and also remembered twirling around on it with excitement and trepidation about their dream.

"Bertha and I feared you and Henry wouldn't show up when we came through to stake our land, that you wouldn't be there to help. You surely proved those fears were pointless, Hans." Tillie grinned at him.

"I remember that first *hallo* of yours, thinking I'd never heard a word sounded so good," admitted Bertha.

"Well, Henry and I weren't at all sure you girl homesteaders would show up, that's fer sure. Then when you got here, we figured you'd last till the first snowstorm hit, then head out. No way did I imagine I'd be going with ya five years later to get ya proved up." Hans let out a loud chortle. "And that one of ya would be gettin' hitched to Ole here."

The next morning, Tillie and Bertha excitedly awaited the opening of the land office. A pleasant clerk greeted them and, after examining their papers and checking his files, he determined that everything was in order. Ole said, "Ve'll vouch for the women," as Bertha had told him they wanted to be called, and he and Hans did just that. Tillie and Bertha each signed a Final Affidavit of the Homestead Claimant. The clerk congratulated them and told them that in a few weeks, they should receive their homestead patents from Washington DC.

Then the men headed to the Charlesbois Blacksmith Shop, and the proved-up women homesteaders to Ellison's Fair Store to purchase fabric. The bustling city of around three thousand inhabitants seemed both exciting and intimidating to the homesteaders so used to open spaces dotted with people they knew.

In late afternoon the four met at the Waverly Hotel, where they would again spend the night. After washing up, they checked out the fancy dining room at the Leland Hotel. There they saw stylish dresses and suits decorating the chairs, then decided to eat supper at a small and less expensive café, where their overalls and plain blouses and skirts better suited the simple surroundings and the prices better fit their pocketbooks.

After that journey, all that was left was waiting to receive the land patent, a document with the signature of the president of the United States of America. They hoped it might come before Tillie left to go east. While awaiting the patent, the two women, along with Belle and Helen, made plans for Bertha and Ole's wedding to occur on Saturday, June 17. As well, it would be a celebration of proving up by the girl homesteaders and a farewell to Tillie.

———

On June 12, 1905, upon returning from the general store and post office, a beaming Eleanor delivered the patent documents, certificate numbers 5379 and 5408, with President Theodore Roosevelt's signature. That evening, while Brunhild remained in Bertha's shack putting together a jigsaw puzzle, Tillie and Bertha celebrated by sitting outside Tillie's shack, reminiscent of sitting outside the hut five years earlier. Again, they shared a glass of Vin Mariani they acquired for the occasion, not quite as adventuresome a thing as it seemed back then.

While drinking the wine tonic, a bit more than they drank five years earlier, the women watched the sun slowly shifting from a brilliant orange orb to a muted ginger hemisphere, casting its pink glow across the western sky. A few peach-tinged, gauzy clouds floated above.

The two officially proved-up homesteaders laughed at times as they remembered their first sip of wine the first night on their homesteads, sleeping in the tiny hut, the shock they first felt at

Olga's coarseness. They remembered the panic of blizzards and the grasshopper invasion. Tillie retold the story of the fire. Their celebratory mood sobered while talking about the recent heartache of losing Ellen and the sorrow showing in the eyes of her four nearly orphaned children.

A little later Bertha broke the somber mood. "We did it!" She twirled around, sending her skirt flying, then grabbed Tillie's hands and both skirts went whirling. They sipped the last drop of wine and hugged each other while tears streamed down Bertha's face and formed in Tillie's eyes.

Teaching had ended a few weeks earlier and a new teacher would arrive for Meadows School before the start of the school year. Bertha was headed for marriage and parenthood, not just for little Brunhild, she thought, though she wasn't quite sure yet and hadn't told Ole of the possibility. She confided in Tillie, though, that her sickness was just over a week late. She didn't know if the lateness was a result of all the excitement or something more dramatic, both frightening and exciting.

"Well, so you might have a child just a wee bit early," Tillie said with a glimmer in her eye and a soft smile showing on her face.

"Oh, Tillie, you are the best friend I have ever had or ever could have. I'll miss you deeply."

"And I shall miss you more than I can even imagine. From girls we've grown into women—strong women—and have each other to thank for all of this. Not so many women have land in their own names, but as of a few days ago, we do." Her arms opened in wide expanse as her eyes looked eastward.

"We did it as one. And now we face new undertakings without each other." Bertha restrained her tears.

Then, when the mauve dusk moved in, each retired to her own shack.

On the evening of June 16, the last together at the B&T Estate, the two again sat outside, again reminiscing. Brunhild joined them in time and all three hugged. Brunhild was adjusting to this new life and she and Ole got along famously, he often joking with the little girl, trying to keep her spirits up. The grasses hummed a lullaby in the gentle breeze as they retreated to their own shacks, Bertha and Brunhild for the last time. But, for some years to come, even as she saw her shack begin to crumble, Bertha would periodically wander over alone, find a place to sit and reflect or to lie down and look up at the clouds. "This is still land in my own name," she'd whisper.

Earlier that day, Ole brought Sam to his own place, where Sam would become part of his team. Bertha's shack would be empty when she and Brunhild went to live at Ole's. In a couple of days, Tillie would abandon her shack as well while wondering whether she would ever return and what would become of her land.

The two friends promised each other they would keep in touch, writing often, for the remainder of their lives. Their deep friendship had been forged by similar experiences and values, cemented by adversity and accomplishment. Distance, new challenges, and novel pleasures would alter their bond, of course, but their friendship would survive through the years.

On June 17, the community gathered at the church for the wedding. Bertha looked gorgeous in her traditional celebration dress—white puffy-sleeved blouse with traditional hardanger stitching, black-and-red vest, black skirt topped by a white apron with intricate needlework—with her grandmother's brooch at her neck. Ole, with such twinkles in his eyes, looked handsome in his new black suit with a white tie as the two said their vows. Tillie stood up for Bertha and Ole's brother Daniel was a fine-looking best man. Brunhild of course was the flower girl and Karl the ring bearer.

The community women had prepared open-faced sandwiches, hot dishes, meatballs in brown gravy, sandbakkel cookies, *kranselkake*, and of course good egg coffee for the celebration. Ernie toasted the two women homesteaders on their proving up. "Skål," said everyone, raising their glasses of punch. Daniel toasted the new couple, saying he was honored to have Bertha as part of his family. Anna toasted Tillie, bidding her a wonderful journey home to begin a new life. "Skål."

As the festivities were ending, Ernie took Tillie's hands, looked into her eyes—his a bit teary, as were hers. "I hope you will have a wonderful life and many children. And, although I'll long for you on cold winter nights, and probably on summer ones too, I'm glad I found a place in myself for such love as I've felt for you."

Tillie nodded. "I shall often think of you, my dear, dear friend Ernie. I shall remember all of this with such fondness. Thank you for all you have been to me." She didn't withhold her tears.

Ernie had offered to take Roger, to care for him as his own. "I'll try to care for Roger half as well as you did," he told Tillie in halting words. He nodded, turned, and tears began spilling. Then he walked away.

Roger, who had waited obediently outside the church during the service, trotted off with Ernie, with a backward glance at Tillie, who waved him a good-bye.

Back to Her Roots

Just before Tillie left her Dakota land, she tried to paint an indelible photo in her mind to inform the days and years to come. She scanned the landscape: barren of trees, but filled with creatures she'd come to know; wildflowers, some hidden in deep grass and others with long stems displaying subtle hues and fragrant scents; and prairie grasses that yielded nutritious food for her gentle horse Sam. Her eyes rested upon her own acres with their shack, chicken coop, and shed, now empty, but which harbored so many memories. She captured her schoolhouse, which had held all the children she taught and from whom she learned so much. Finally, she lingered for a time on the nearby shacks that held her community and, with a pensive stare, gazed at the shack where her best friend Bertha now lived with Ole and then at the one of her supporting and loving friend Ernie.

It was at that moment that Tillie's mind clouded with doubt. She sat in the grass, wet with the morning dew. Not muffling her sobs, her chest heaved while her hands covered her wet face.

After a time, she rose. With resolve, knowing she must return to her roots and commitments in Minnesota, she turned her mind to the coming years. With plans for marriage, she knew her teaching days were over as married women were not allowed to teach in those days. She hoped for children of her own and planned to be active in her church and community.

The sound of an approaching horse broke her reverie. Turning, she saw Hans and Helen, who greeted her and helped her load her trunk onto their buckboard wagon. Then Tillie stepped into the wagon and sat next to Helen, hoping to create a cheerful countenance.

Leaving Dakota was bittersweet. So many friendships, so much accomplishment, and so many hardships had strengthened her and left enduring features on her body and soul. Learning to make-do with so little was a lesson that would serve her well when the Great Depression hit some twenty years later. So much of proving herself had happened in the proving up on her homestead. She would remain a strong woman, determined and capable.

As the train rumbled toward Minnesota, Tillie's mind at first remained in Dakota with memories, both wondrous and horrendous, though mostly rewarding and inspiring. She let her care—*was it love?*—for Ernie fill her soul, then eventually turned her thoughts to home, especially to Jergen. Yearning to see him again, she imagined their life together, each reading by the light of kerosene lanterns in the evenings, he tending to farm chores, being a deacon and perhaps a school board president, while she managed the chickens, the cooking, the butter churning, and perhaps the milking of cows. She imagined children, maybe a boy and a couple of girls, teaching them, reading to them, sitting next to them in church. She saw their farm growing larger with Jergen's ingenuity, having the finest of farming equipment, and building a new home.

Yet, from time to time, her mind still lingered on Ole, Bertha, and Brunhild, on Hans and Helen and Henry and Belle. When she thought of Dakota, her mind easily turned to Ernie, his skillful carpentry, his intelligence formed by the physical world near him, and too, his deep care for her.

As the train neared the Glenwood station, she powdered her nose, pinched her cheeks, and fastened her hair into a tight bun, and imagined her joy upon seeing Jergen again.

Stepping off the train, she saw him hurrying toward her and calling her name. Her heart quickened at the sight of him with his fashionable straw boater and tailored suit. "Jergen!" she exclaimed in a shaky voice, some combination of excitement and anxiety. He kissed her outstretched hand. "Velkommen, my wife-to-be, welcome home." His eyes were warm, his smile tender.

Her brother then stepped out of the train station and came to greet her. After the hugs and greetings, Tillie asked of her father.

"He's poorly, dear sister. He so wanted to welcome you home at the train station, but he knew he was not up to the journey. But both he and Mama are so anxious to see you."

"We should hurry then, but I must collect my trunk."

Jergen asked for her trunk slip and, along with Peter, went off to retrieve the trunk. After loading it into Peter's wagon, Jergen and Tillie set off in his buggy, with Peter pulling the cart behind them.

Again, the green of Minnesota seemed so brilliant, the kitchen aromas so alluring, and the warm bath so luxuriant. The comfort of home seeped into Tillie's pores as she involved herself in the routine of daily life on the farm.

Jergen came to call on Friday evenings, and sometimes Saturday ones when a barn dance was taking place in one of their communities. Most Sundays he joined Tillie and her family for church and shared Sunday dinner with them. Sometimes the two would walk into the prairie that bordered woodlands, find a shady stop for a picnic, and share romantic longings and future hopes. They talked of setting a marriage ceremony for the coming spring.

"I hope to make you the happiest of wives," Jergen said. "You'll see how our farm grows and I'll buy the best equipment. I'm already successful in farming, but with you by my side, I'll flourish even more. You'll be envied by the church wives, my Tillie."

Sometimes in the evening Tillie and Jergen sat on the porch swing and read, Jergen often reading magazines such as *American Agriculture* and *Popular Mechanics*, but also the *Atlantic Monthly*. Tillie would look at the *Saturday Evening Post* or read a book. She especially enjoyed Helen Keller's *The Story of My Life*. "What a brilliant and admirable woman Helen Keller is," she said to Jergen.

Sometimes they'd walk down the road or into the woodland, hand in hand. He'd turn to her and give her a peck on the cheek and occasionally they'd engage in penetrating kisses and warm embraces. They sometimes took evening coffee with Tillie's parents, the men talking mostly of farming issues or church events, and the women chiming in with their thoughts about those issues from time to time, but chatting more of happenings in their community or news of friends and family.

"He seems to adore you so," Mama told Tillie one evening after he left. "What a praiseworthy man he is. So learned and all."

And Tillie? What were her thoughts? She admired Jergen so very much and believed she loved him and also knew that her thoughts kept returning to Ernie, to the deep warmth she felt for him on that night of Ellen's death. Of these thoughts, she spoke to no one and chided herself each time they arose. Yet she found herself in a place she had never traversed—deep indecision. Rarely had she questioned her own decisions once she made them and never had she done so on such a serious issue.

What is it about Jergen that I am unsure of? Was my decision to come home more for Mama and Papa than for Jergen? And, isn't that reason enough? I have no question about whether Jergen will be a steadfast partner in life, a father who will provide for me and our children in ways I can only dream about. His values and beliefs are such honorable ones. When I was in Dakota, the longing for all of these things filled my heart. Yet perhaps I long for the spontaneity of Ernie, who is so decent and upstanding and yet given to splurges of enrapture in the flight of a bird and who reveals deep pain and sadness at the tragedies of life. I don't see that sense of delight in Jergen, nor do I see the same degree of sensitivity to the pain of others. Oh, that I could feel my own confident self again, that I could lose this uncertainty!

———

Regularly, Tillie received news from Bertha of the Norwegian Dakota community. The most recent letter was short.

> *The harvest season is upon us, so I'll limit my words out of tiredness. First, though I do not feel the movement of life within me yet, I know I am with child, so much excitement awaits our little family. Brunhild is doing quite well, though of course still harboring wounds from her mother's death. I've grown to love our pigs and, especially the little piglets. I feel such anguish when a pig is slaughtered, but yet am grateful for the lusty flavor and heartiness of their meat and for the lard they provide in abundance for pies, for frying, for lamps, candles, and soap-making. Ole is a tender and caring husband and a good father to little Brunhild.*
>
> *These cool nights of autumn draw me inside for warmth and reflection. It is then that I often think of you and our adventures that brought me not only land, but such a good*

husband and family. I hope for your happiness with Jergen
as your marriage draws closer.

Your forever friend,
Bertha

As the fall season settled upon western Minnesota, the grasses
began losing their chlorophyll and luster while the beauty of the
trees intensified, some displaying rust among the green, others yellow, yet others maroon. The harvest usurped energies while it filled
grain bins with swollen kernels of wheat and golden, dented corn.

And in that season of retreat to an inner life, Papa's heart slowly
drummed its last beat while Tillie and Mama each held one of his
cool hands and Peter stood at his side. His ending was peaceful, for
which Tillie was grateful. Yet, an ending is always wretched—even
when expected and when there has existed a hope for an end to
suffering—when that moment of aliveness is followed by the gulf
of stillness and quiet, when the inert body that you love seems no
longer to hold the cherished person.

During his final months, Tillie had grown closer to Papa than
she'd ever been, had even confided her indecision to him, a wavering
she withheld from Mama. He had looked deep into her eyes and, in
his frail voice so quiet she had to lean close to hear, he'd said, "Tillie,
my girl, you must follow your instincts in matters of love. Pay attention to the leanings of yer heart. Then let it lead you in the direction
its wisdom reveals and don't go judgin' yerself when you follow it."

Tillie's energies, though dimmed by her sense of loss, were at
first directed at supporting her mother and providing what comfort
she could. Jergen of course attended the funeral and stood at Tillie's
side when the family men lowered Papa's body into his grave on
a cool late September day. He held her hand and she was grateful

for his palpable warmth and his tender, restrained smile, and words of comfort. Yet, she couldn't help but fleetingly think of the deep warmth she felt from Ernie when Ellen died and knew Jergen's care lacked some of the emotion and recognition of the burden she carried, which Ernie had demonstrated. *Since Jergen hardly knew Papa, perhaps he simply doesn't have his own grief to share*, she told herself.

Jergen's fall work was upon him, so their courting time diminished while Tillie helped Peter with the harvest and, with Mama's help, provided food for the harvest crew. It gave Tillie a bit of distance from Jergen, a time to reflect upon her feelings toward him. *What so compelled my dreams of him? Do I still feel that sureness of love for him I felt in Dakota? What is this confusing thing called love?*

She judged herself harshly for her wavering of sureness. Such thoughts often prevented sleep. So one night by candlelight, she composed a letter to Bertha.

My dear Bertha,

I need your thoughts and counsel. I feel so confused. I felt so sure of my love and commitment to Jergen when I left Dakota, and of my friendship and care for Ernie, but not the depth of love I thought I felt for Jergen. What do I know of love? Perhaps I am unable to love when faced with its reality, rather than its dreams. Jergen is adoring and most clearly wants me for his wife. Yet his restraint is so different than Ernie's restraint, which I knew was due to respect and concern for me, for not requiring more of me than I seemed able to give. Perhaps much of my need to return to Jergen was out of a need to be here with my family, to be with Papa in his last moments, to help Mama through her transition to widowhood and into her future life.

I know Jergen will respect my need to have Mama with us as our life continues if that is her desire, and that is important to me, but I continue with this sense of something missing within him. I recognize that most men have cloaks that protect them from much emotional expression. Papa had that in him, though it seemed to fall away as he came close to death. I see it in Peter. Perhaps that is what I see in Jergen and it is simply usual and to be expected; yet, I don't believe I saw it in Ernie.

What is wrong with me, Bertha? Perhaps it would be best for me to remain a spinster and continue to be a teacher. You know me as so strong in my decisions. I must seem quite strange to you. I so miss your constant companionship.

In deepest friendship,
Tillie

While Jergen and Tillie's courtship continued with regularity and plans for marriage remained formed for June, the ardor seemed somewhat diminished for both of them. *Perhaps it is simply the season when each of us is drawing our energies inward like the bears who retreat to their caves, the chipmunks to their underground lives, and the trees to their trunks and roots.*

Soon Bertha's response came and Tillie eagerly opened the envelope and smiled at the sight of Bertha's penmanship and the three-page letter. Bertha shared news of the community, how little Kincaid and Karl fared, said that little Brunhild seemed more adjusted as the weeks flew past, and told about the harvest celebration. She wrote that Roger seemed well adjusted to his new life, though he often wandered over to where Tillie's shack stood, that Ernie seemed fine though more pensive than was his nature. And she noted that her own tummy was becoming rounded and her breasts fuller. She thought she might have felt the miraculous flutter of her child moving within her just a day ago, but wasn't quite certain yet.

> *I'm sure your questions are not uncommon among those plan-*
> *ning to marry. Such choices are almost always for a lifetime.*
> *Yet, I cannot help but wonder, given your previous words of*
> *sureness of Jergen, that you did not know him well enough to*
> *make a firm choice. Only you can discern the answer to your*
> *vacillation. I hope you will talk with your mother or with*
> *others close to you, especially the women, but perhaps Peter,*
> *as well. Be not afraid of admitting your wondering mind. It*
> *is likely that many others have faced such wavers.*

Tillie wept as she finished the letter and two evenings later asked Mama and Peter to sit with her at the table after dinner. She poured coffee and poured out her quandary. At first her mother was aghast, "Oh, Tillie, you can't break an engagement to such a fine man. The community will judge all of us!" she exclaimed.

After some moments of reflection, Peter looked at Mama and said with a soft, soothing voice and warm eyes but a firm expression on his face, already weathered from his years of farming, "I think we should listen to Tillie's difficulty without first worrying about the reaction of others. She is our kin; we must support her in this most important decision."

Tillie felt such deep love and admiration for her brother at that moment and looked at him with thankfulness showing on her face. She then turned to Mama and said in a faint voice because she was nearing tears, "I want to share Papa's words . . ."

Mama said, "Speak up a little, dear child. My old ears don't hear so well as they used to."

Somewhat louder, Tillie said, "Mama, I told Papa about my indecision not long before his ending came. He told me to heed my own instincts and to follow my own heart. I hope you can understand."

With a look of surprise registering on her deeply lined face, Mama said, "I see." She closed her eyes then and, for some moments, gave a sense of being disappointed while lost in thought. She then opened her eyes and gave a slight nod to her head. "Of course Papa's counsel was wise, as it always was. I will support your decision, whatever it is; I only wish for your happiness. Jergen just seems to me like such a good match to your seriousness and mind, but love doesn't always follow the mind. It has its own ways."

Tillie stood and opened her arms for her mother. With weakness and stiffness showing, Mama stood and embraced her daughter. Both let some tears wet the other's face.

Tillie continued to struggle with her indecision over a number of days.

The night before a courting call from Jergen, she couldn't find the rest of slumber as she weighed her thoughts. Finally, toward morning, she made her decision, then slept for a couple hours at last.

At breakfast that morning, after her mother had poured hot coffee and sat down to eat, Tillie gave the grace. "Come, Lord Jesus, be our guest. Let these gifts to us be blest."

Tillie took a sip of steamy coffee. "Mama, I have looked at my decision in as many ways as I am able, for love is indeed a complexity. Jergen is indeed a fine man, and learned as you say, so upstanding and respected in the community. I could marry him and, I think, make him a good wife." She took another sip of coffee. Mama looked at Tillie with an intensity or sense of anticipation that, for her, was uncommon.

"I don't quite understand what holds me back when I was so sure of my decision to marry him a year ago. But, that seems now to have been more a fantasy and dream of him than the reality I feel as I grow to know him. He's good, kind, probably will be wealthy, but somehow my desire for him has waned and become uncertain. I think it is simply something about his rather stiff personality and maybe I sense a lack of understanding of human frailties in him. When I told him of many of the people in Dakota, he seemed to judge them some, not give recognition to their different circumstances and customs." She took another sip of coffee. Neither she nor Mama had touched their food.

"I'm not sure I can cherish him for a lifetime, so it would be wrong to agree to this marriage. Yet, I know I will cause him pain, like I caused Ernie pain." She began to weep softly and Mama patted her shoulder.

Then Tillie took out her hanky, dabbed her eyes, and blew her nose. In a stronger voice, she went on, "Perhaps I'm not able to love a man like most women can and should simply be a teacher and a spinster. I will ask Jergen for forbearance and tell him I am unable to be his wife."

Her mother simply nodded her head. Then mother and daughter ate their breakfast without words.

Late that afternoon in early December, while Tillie and Jergen walked in the woods, rustling the dry leaves under the newly fallen snow, she said, "Jergen, I don't know how to express what I must. I've come to an almost unbearable decision." They had continued a few steps, the leaves crunching under their feet. Tillie stopped and turned to Jergen while he turned his head to face her.

"I've decided it best that I not become your wife." She began sobbing then and when she had brought herself under control and wiped off her eyes and nose, she went on. "You are the very finest man I know and I admire you so very much. You're a deacon, a school board member, an excellent farmer, and you are so knowledgeable about so many things. I can't even explain what holds me back, Jergen." She began visibly shaking.

He took her in his arms and held her while her shaking and quivering subsided. "Tillie, it's almost unbearable to think of losing you. I will hang my head in grief and shame. I beg you to change your mind." He continued to hold her for some moments and when he released her, she looked up into his pleading eyes that appeared to be holding back some tears.

Tillie didn't find any words to say as they continued to look at each other.

Then Jergen seemed to girdle his emotion. His face became impassive. "I know you well enough to believe it is not likely that your mind is changeable. However, should you rethink your decision, I will be waiting and hoping, at least for a time."

She nodded her head faintly. "Thank you, Jergen, for all of the good times we shared, the picnics, the walks, the dances. I felt proud and happy to be by your side." With downcast eyes, she added, "Perhaps I am simply not ready to be a wife, if ever I will be. I ask your forgiveness for causing you discomfort, pain, needed explanations to family and friends, for all the difficulties I am causing you. I wish I could simply feel happy to proceed with our marriage plans, but it seems I cannot." Her voice became halted and shaky again. "I only hope . . . you will find someone . . . to love deeply . . . someone who will love you just as much."

He gave a slight nod and they turned to leave the woods. She held his hand firmly as they slowly shuffled back through the light snow and sun left the land. Tillie slowly removed the ring from her finger as they neared the house and then placed it in his hand. He took the ring with a look of dismay and planted a small kiss upon her cheek, then turned, slowly walked to his horse, and mounted. Tillie watched him with deep sadness, feeling responsible for his pain, and hoping he would recover and, in time, find a suitable wife.

Tillie Shapes a New Life

During the next couple of weeks, Tillie tried to occupy her days. She asked Mr. Larson, the teacher at the school where she had taught, if she might assist with the Christmas play and sing-along, which she did. She went to choir practice at church and participated in Ladies Aid, which, among other things, involved assisting with funerals. The death so near the holidays of Rena, the seven-year-old daughter of Karl and Matilda Roderson who lived just a mile from the Melbakkens, was such a sad affair. Tillie brought a hot dish for the family as soon as she heard the news. She stayed with the younger children while the parents met with the undertaker and the pastor. She helped, too, with preparing sandwiches, cakes, and cookies for lunch in the church basement after the service. Little Rena had seemed rather unwell from the start, had never gained weight well, and during the last couple of years had begun severe coughing spells, which Dr. Smith was unable to cure.

Christmas festivities seemed muted to Tillie that year, but of course making cookies, julebukking, decorating the tree, and preparation for a family dinner all occupied much of her time.

Just before the year turned to 1906, Tillie received a letter from Bertha, who after the initial words of greeting, wrote:

287

I think of you so often as the holidays approach, and miss you so it makes me shed tears at times, especially when I yearn for someone to whom I could confide my deepest thoughts. Ole is so good to listen, but, as Helen once said, sometimes we need a woman's ears.

We've decided to try julebukking out here, so Ole has made each of us a wooden mask and he has become quite the wood carver with this project. Mine is the likeness of a cherub while his mask is an ugly ghoul. He's still working on a mask for Brunhild. I don't know how I'll hide my big belly, but maybe I can add a pillow and pretend it is part of my disguise.

Brunhild, of course, continues to miss her mother, but always calls me Mama and Ole, Papa. She has quiet moods sometimes, but is looking forward to the birth of her little sister or brother. I will be glad to rid myself of my full belly, for it is indeed uncomfortable now, but I fear the birth itself. Winnie will help of course. And I joyously await hearing the little one's first cry.

I see Ernie from time to time. He's lost the look of anguish I could see on his face when you left, though he seems more reserved and less jolly than in years past. Along with Orlo, he helps out with Josie and Sharon. I think he visits with and helps Sven quite often, who is out there alone, rather removed from the rest of us. Roger is often by Ernie's side and Ernie treats good Roger with care, not like most men treat their dogs.

We had one good blizzard, but we all managed fine. Sam of course is more of a working horse now, helps pull the

*cultivator and hay wagon, among other chores. He seems
glad to have more of a job than he had with you and me.*

*If this gets to you by Christmas, I wish you and your family
a wonderful Christmas and I hope you find peace and happiness as the new year comes.*

Tillie spent most of her evenings reading and sometimes simply
sitting deep in thought. She felt very lonely in spite of the presence
of Mama, who was abiding her own loneliness. Especially after
receiving Bertha's letter, Tillie often imagined what might be happening in her Dakota community and even wondered if it might
be possible for her to return there, though usually she put that
thought aside. Sometimes Peter sat with Tillie in the evening, but
often his courtship with the young neighbor girl, Ethel Kittelson,
occupied him.

During the lonely hours of New Year's Eve, Tillie remembered Ole joining Bertha and her as 1901 came, and she let her
thoughts drift again to Ernie, as they often had. She had considered writing to him to tell him of her change of heart, but she
restrained herself. *I have caused him so much pain. What if, again, I
find that I cannot love him? What if my thoughts of love only feel real
at a distance, not when walking by the side of a tangible man with
a firm body?*

Eventually, she came to some peace with the likelihood that
she would remain a spinster. Still, she harbored a dim hope that
Ernie would send her a letter after he heard of her change of plans,
about which Bertha certainly would have told him.

Soon the winter began in earnest. In the latter part of January,
the teacher Mr. Larson took ill and needed to go to his home near
the village of Hazel Run. Tillie took over teaching duties at the

nearby school, and she was delighted to be a teacher again. Her face and quickness of step showed that, as Peter said to Mama, "She's got her old spirit back."

One evening she reread the letter she'd received from Bertha that day and hadn't had time to absorb.

My dearest friend, Tillie,

January was almost over when a ferocious blizzard began. So did my labor pains, a little early I believe. Ole rode for Winnie and brought her back on Sam, who is strong as a horse. Haha. After much screaming from me and lamenting from Ole, who thought I'd never stop yowling, little Tillie came through my legs and gave her wondrous cry. What an astonishing thing it is to birth a child and this one, of course, is named for you. Ole agreed with me that it is a good name. I hope that sometime you can have such an experience. Brunhild is smitten with the little infant, as is Ole. I find her suckling at my breast more heartwarming than anything I have experienced in life. When she cries and I can't determine why, I berate myself, but sometimes Brunhild will take her and rock her and put her to sleep and I smile.

Ole tells me Sven seems to have disappeared without a word to anyone, perhaps heading for Minot, where he might be more anonymous and escape a brutal winter alone on his lonely farm. Brunhild's younger brothers continue to be a handful for Olga and Anna to manage but I'm sure the two women try to do their best. The teacher, Mr. Swartz who hails from the German community, not wisely uses a switch on Karl from time to time I hear. Karl hardly needs more cruelty than he has seen. Next year Kincaid will begin schooling and I hope we can get a more caring teacher.

I hope you continue to enjoy your teaching. I miss it, yet I have plenty to teach Brunhild who learns a little slowly, but I am patient with her. I'll have much to teach little Tillie over the years. Just like when you and I learned from our pupils, I'm sure I'll learn from Tillie while she learns from me.

Your always friend,
Bertha

Taking in the news, Tillie felt such joy for Bertha and Ole and shed a few tears for herself, thinking she would likely never have the thrill of hearing her own infant give its first cry. She remembered, too, the amazement she felt when little Kincaid made that first wail.

As Mama became a bit less hardy, Tillie took over many of the household chores, although Mama still did most of the baking. When Tillie didn't have lessons to prepare or papers to correct, she and Mama often spent the dark evening hours knitting and crocheting, sometimes darning socks. One such evening Tillie said, "You know I feel such deep satisfaction in teaching the young'uns. I doubt if marriage and my own children could provide as much fulfillment."

Mama smiled. "Nice it is to hear you say that. I worried 'bout ya, but I can see you're finding pleasure in being a school teacher and I'm proud of you for that. I hear from the parents and grandparents that the children seem happy to go to school. They say 'twasn't always that way when Mr. Larson was there." After a few moments she added, "Yet I still carry some hope of you being swept off your feet by someone and giving me grandchildren."

"Oh, Mama."

———————

By spring, Tillie was asked to stay on as teacher. She happily agreed. She had become recognized as an excellent teacher, and School Superintendent Saunders asked her to assist a young teacher, just graduated from normal school, who would begin teaching in Milan in the fall. So, over the summer Tillie met with Miss Lilly Thompson a few times and helped her prepare lessons. She also agreed to meet her as needed after the school year started.

The big change in the Melbakken household came with Peter's marriage after harvest the following fall. His wife, Ethel, was welcomed into the home. She was young, had just turned eighteen when she exchanged vows with Peter, but was well versed in the chores of farming life. She took over much of the animal care, collecting the eggs, separating cream and churning butter, and of course assisting with the other seasonal chores. Tillie had taken over most of the cooking when Mama became stiffer in her joints. But Ethel said she could do some of the cooking and Tillie appreciated relief from the daily chore. She found most of the meals made by Ethel quite tasty and enjoyed some new dishes, although a few meals had turned out poorly, either undercooked or burned.

Occasionally Ethel's rather childlike exuberance felt a little hard to bear, so Tillie would quietly retreat to her room. She might read, do handiwork, or prepare lessons.

The winter passed, and a welcome spring arrived on the Melbakken farm, then a fall, another winter, and another spring. On a hotter-than-usual early summer day, Tillie was using her hoe to dislodge carpetweed, bindweed, and pigweed in the garden when she saw a man walking up the path, a dog trotting beside him. After watching him for a moment or two, with a gasp, she recognized the gait. In that moment, the dog left the man's side and began sprinting toward her. She barely had time to push the hair off her sweating face and wipe her soiled hands on her apron before Roger, barking with such happiness, began licking her hands. As she bent down to greet him, his tongue swept across her face.

As the man slowly walked toward her, she dropped the hoe and rushed toward him, exclaiming, "Ernie!" He took her soiled hands in his rough but clean ones. She wanted to lean in for a hug, but she resisted the urge. Yet he clung to her hand, and her fingers closed tightly around his as they looked in each other's eyes and held their gaze for several moments. Finally, choked up, her voice barely audible, she asked, "What brings you here?"

His voice sounded shaky and weak as he began. "My older brother who ran the farm has contracted consumption." He cleared his throat. "Likely won't live. He's entered the sanatorium near Walker. Family needed my help. And . . . " he added after a moment, hesitated again and turned his eyes downward. "And I hoped to see you."

After more questions and answers from each of them, with his hand in hers, Tillie led him to the house where Mama had been watching from the kitchen window in some amazement. Following introductions, Mama made coffee and put out cookies while they talked of Dakota, especially of Bertha and Ole, of Ernie's family near Morris, of Tillie's school, of the greenness of Minnesota that Ernie had seen upon his return, which brought laughs from Tillie and her mother. Ernie said his younger brother Karl had come to Dakota the previous year and would watch over his land and tend to his crop and animals. "Karl didn't want to come back to Minnesota, partly 'cuz he found a woman from Bowbells, Synneva's the name, and they got hitched just this spring. Don't know if I'll return out there or not."

Before he left with Roger to walk down the path where he had left his cart, he asked in a quiet voice, barely daring to look at Tillie, "Would it be okay for me to call again?"

"I'd like it very much," Tillie said with Mama smiling behind her.

So it began again. He came the next Sunday afternoon, Roger again by his side. Tillie showered affection on Roger, then showed Ernie around the farm and introduced him to Peter, who was fiddling with the reaper. He and Ernie talked amicably of farming, how the crops in Dakota compared with those in Minnesota.

"Vell, the wheat is better in Dakota, least when we get 'nuf rain, but corn will hardly grow, a'course," said Ernie.

"Would love to see that land sometime," Peter admitted. "Kind of hoped I'd make the journey when Tillie was there, but farming chores keep me busy until winter when snow and blizzards kept me from going, and then Ethel and I were seeing each other and I guess that stopped my dreaming of Dakota. Come on to the house and I'll introduce you to my wife."

After coffee and a light lunch, Ernie and Tillie walked out through the grove of trees, again hand in hand. It was then that he took Tillie into his arms, held her in a warm embrace, and gave her a light kiss on the lips, seeming too shy or restrained or nervous to do more than touch her lips. Likely he didn't know how forward he dared be. Tillie, for her part, would have welcomed a deep and lingering kiss.

The courtship continued as summer turned to autumn, when farming chores limited their time together, but Ernie never failed to arrive sometime on Sunday, even if it was late afternoon before he could make it to Melbakken's.

"Hard for me to know just how you feel about me, Tillie," Ernie admitted during a late afternoon picnic on a cool, but sunny and calm, late October day. "I don't want to push you to accept me and don't feel worthy of your attention, but during your absence from Dakota, I felt a hollowness in my life. I could busy myself in activity and talkin' with the men, but sometimes at night, I'd pretty near shed tears with the ache." He looked at her with wistful eyes. "Perhaps we should decide now if you would be unable to find a deep place in your heart for me."

Tillie had never heard a man be so forthright about his feelings and she knew a part of her care for Ernie, which she had decided was love, came from sensing that warm and vulnerable emotional place in him.

"I love you, Ernie," she said simply. "I hurt you before when I didn't know my own feelings. I don't want to hurt you again. There were so many times after I broke off with Jergen that I wanted to write you. Yet, I feared there was something amiss in me, that I didn't know how to love, and that I might pain you even more, that being with you I might not feel the depth of care or love I felt from afar. But, that fear is pretty much gone." She opened her arms and again said, "I love you."

He wrapped her in his embrace and held her in a long and passionate kiss. When they eventually pulled apart, she could feel that her cheeks were moist from his tears.

As winter came, the couple saw each other as much as weather, distance, and chores allowed. Ernie and his mother came for Christmas Day dinner with Tillie and her family. Tillie continued to feel what she believed was deep love for Ernie. Although she didn't feel any reticence about the potential of being Ernie's wife, she knew she had jilted Jergen after first believing she loved him, so she wanted to be very sure of her love for Ernie before she made a commitment. She suggested as much to Ernie. "I can wait as long as you need me to wait, Tillie, but golly man, it's not easy." He grinned then, showing the smile that narrowed his eyes, a look that Tillie loved.

But when school ended the following spring and the care each of them felt for the other continued without showing any sign of abatement, Tillie accepted his proposal of marriage without reservation, and she advised the Chippewa County superintendent of schools that it was time to find a new teacher.

In late October, after Ernie completed fall farming chores, the couple said their marriage vows at Zion Lutheran Church in Watson. Unlike Bertha, Tillie decided not to wear the traditional Norwegian wedding outfit and chose to wear modern American apparel instead, a white gown and veil. She and her mother had sewn the lovely dress made mostly of taffeta. They made the long sleeves of lace, as well as the bodice that attached to the dress just above her bustline and covered Tillie onto her neck. For some Norwegian flair, Mama had made a hardanger insert for the area that covered Tillie's cleavage. Near the top of her silk stocking, Tillie wore a blue garter, which she would later laughingly show Ernie. Around her neck Tillie wore a locket her mother had received from Papa and happily gave to Tillie for her wedding gift. Ernie was more handsome than Tillie had imagined he could be when he appeared in a starched white shirt, black suit, and white knit tie with a hardanger insert his mother made. The church filled with relatives of both Tillie and Ernie, as well as friends and young people who had once been students of Tillie's.

They began their lives together near Morris with Roger, whose energy had dimmed but seemed so glad to again be by Tillie's side every day. Ernie's mother, a lively and warmhearted woman in her early seventies, lived with them and the three regularly visited Mama where she preferred to live out her later years with Peter, Ethel, and their children. Yet, as Mama's end came, Tillie spent her last week with her, providing tender care.

Ernie received letters from his brother Karl periodically, and Tillie got news of their community in Dakota from Bertha regularly. Bertha and Ole with their gaggle of children, including Brunhild, then sixteen, once visited Minnesota to see what was left of Bertha's family, but especially to spend time with Tillie and Ernie and their three children. The two women reminisced about their salad days when they developed the kind of strength that grows from hardships and accomplishments. They caught up on each other's lives, conversing as if they'd been next-door neighbors the entire time. Bertha said Sam was still active, though slowing down, and was the gentlest horse in their stable.

From time to time Tillie learned of Jergen's life with his wife Hilda. He was known as a successful farmer, and as his wealth grew, he and Hilda enjoyed many fineries of the time. They had one of the first automobiles in Chippewa County.

Ernie's farm was smaller and less productive than Jergen's, but Tillie never doubted her decision. When young she had sometimes dreamed of having riches and fine clothing, but her years in Dakota had demonstrated that the things one can buy to pretty up a place and show off one's prosperity to a neighbor don't replace the important values and care that underlie a satisfied life. While she and Ernie experienced tragedies, including the death of their second child in infancy, and the travails, irritations, and difficulties common to family life, their deep care for each other remained strong. With Tillie's help, Ernie built a fine new home for the family. Their frugal, inventive, and hard-working ways, strengthened by their homesteading years, would help them survive the coming '30s with less trauma than most city folk and farming families.

As their love matured, the small kindnesses they showed each other, the help they gave each other in projects around the house and farm, the comfort of being able to depend upon each other in hard times, and simply basking in the other's familiar ways, replaced the passion of their early years. When Ernie would bring in a small bouquet of prairie flowers, including her beloved pasqueflowers, Tillie felt joy. When he would happen to look up at Tillie with her dripping brow and flying hair while she was helping pound in fence posts, he'd smile to himself in appreciation of his wife.

Some of the hardships of farming diminished as new inventions of the twentieth century eased the work. Although their life together was fulfilling and both enjoyed the rewards of creating a family and building the farm, Tillie and Ernie admitted to each other that they treasured memories of proving up and sometimes longed for that time that was simpler, albeit harsher, a time that taxed their emotions and stretched their skills. "I don't think I have ever felt quite the satisfaction and sense of soul fulfillment as in those first years," said Tillie to Ernie as they sat by the fire on a cold winter evening, and Ernie said he felt the same way.

In her strong but never strident way, Tillie supported the Minnesota Woman Suffrage Association through letter writing and by encouraging her friends, church women, and neighbors to do the same. She cheered the passage of the Nineteenth Amendment by the United States Congress in 1919, which when ratified gave women of all the states the right to vote in national elections. Upon hearing the news, Ernie joined in Tillie's celebration and raised a toast, "To Tillie, my strong, courageous wife who will now be able to vote. Skål."

———

And once, in 1928, Tillie and Ernie, along with their three children, visited the land of their Dakota dreams. The village, first called Kincaid, had become Lignite. Leaving Lignite, now grown to a population of 216 with a café, blacksmith shop, grocery, post office, hardware store, and general store, they bumped along toward their homesteads in their newly purchased Studebaker. "I remember my first visit in 1900," Tillie said with a laugh. "Sitting on the wooden cart-seat on the bumpy path jostled Bertha and me to the point of bruising, and on the way back to Portal we got soaked even beneath our skin, I think. You young'uns ought to be grateful for padded seats."

Feeling delight in being so close again to her little community, she told them about her sense of being lost or orphaned that first night in the hut, though neglected to tell them of the Vin Mariani she and Bertha had sipped. "And I remember first meeting your papa at the harvest gathering. He asked me to dance, which we did. He's become a little better dancer since back then," she said with a laugh.

Years back, Bertha had written Tillie that a number of homesteaders new to the community put up shacks in the Norwegian section after Tillie left, but that many of the homesteaders eventually abandoned their shacks and went back to their origins or moved westward, while retaining ownership of their properties. Most eventually sold their land to neighbors.

As Tillie and Ernie approached their old homesteads, awareness grew that most of the homesteads had grown into larger farms, and the farmers had plowed up much of the prairie and built bigger barns and houses. The era of homesteaders, before electricity, before automobiles, before the land was plowed up for large expanses of crops that eliminated most of the pasqueflowers and harebells in the process, was gone. Perhaps it hadn't changed the lives of dwellers of the Dakota plains in the same way it changed those in large cities, but a new era of invention and industrialization was upon them.

When the homesteaders had first come, the land had shaped them. Those who stayed shaped the land, not necessarily for the better—as would be apparent a few years hence, when the wind during the dry years blew the topsoil into huge, dark clouds.

Approaching Ernie's land, which he had deeded to his brother Karl years earlier, Tillie and Ernie saw that his barn still stood and looked newly painted, while remnants of his shack lay crumbled on the ground. Karl and his wife Synneva saw them arriving and hurried to greet them, followed by their children, all nephews Ernie and Tillie had never met. After conversation over coffee and muffins, Ernie said they would return to spend the night, but that first they must see Bertha and Ole, and that they felt anxious to set foot on Tillie's land.

Bertha was hanging clothes on the line when she saw them walking toward her house, a frame structure Ole and she had built not long after the arrival of their first child, little Tillie. She dropped a shirt back into the basket and ran to hug Tillie, then Ernie, and then greeted the children. She invited them in, but Tillie said she first wanted to show her children her own land and would return within the hour.

Tillie's shack had collapsed; the grass, still mostly virgin prairie, was brown and dry. Even though most of her land had been free of the plow, as the dry years of the Dust Bowl approached, it appeared thirstier than when Tillie and Ernie put up tar paper shacks in those years long past. Yet, it still held deep grass roots and their abiding affection and memories. "My God!" exclaimed Harold, their eldest. "How did you ever manage?"

Tillie simply gave a broad smile. She twirled around and around, sending her skirt flying and amazing her children. She set about showing them her own land, still in her own name. She pointed out where Bertha's shack had stood and showed them Sam's shed with its roof caved in and dirt walls collapsing. "There," she said with twinkling eyes, "was the garden and there the chicken coop. And here," she said laughing, "was the outhouse."

Stories slipped from her that she thought had been long forgotten. "One day," she said to her children, "this will be your land."

Afterword

Perhaps I wasn't born a century late. Perhaps, I . . .

Although I've lived in modern times with computers and iPods and smartphones, I've resisted technological advances, for a while at least. Microwave ovens became available for public use in 1967. It wasn't until 1983 that I consented to using one. My childhood home didn't have a television set, so it wasn't until 1968 that I first had one, only to give up watching TV for good some twenty years later. In 2018, I have a flip-top cell phone, not a smart one. However, I embrace computers—at least some of their functions—finding writing and design so much easier than with typewriters and press type.

Riding my own motorcycle from Minnesota to Alaska to California and back to Minnesota in 1990 certainly wasn't as adventurous as Tillie's journey to the wilderness of northwestern Dakota in 1900. Yet, my journey displayed some of Tillie's courageous spirit and grit.

While in my late forties, I assisted my husband in building a thirty-by-fifty-foot pole structure that became our home for over twenty years. When we first moved in, we had no running water, so I used a solar shower for bathing and washed my hair under the hand-operated water pump. Since my twenties, I've gardened using organic methods, the only method Tillie ever knew. During much of my adult life, I split wood with an ax to heat my home, although in later years a gas-powered splitter eased some of the work.

As a nurse, as a guardian ad litem, and as a person, I've assisted and befriended those who were shunned, downtrodden, or abused. When a friend died of AIDS in the late 1980s, my husband made a pine casket for him and I lined it with velvet fabric. When our teen-age son died in 1992 after a heart and lung transplant, I dressed his body for the celebration of his life, as I did for an aged aunt who died several years later.

Perhaps, just perhaps, I remember a time on the plains of Dakota, a time that certainly was not simpler in a physical sense, but a time that, for me, seems more tangible, more genuinely human than the gadget-driven world of the twenty-first century.

Acknowledgments

Ream Team, my writers' group in Saint Cloud, Minnesota, deserves significant credit for bringing this novel to life. Bill Morgan, Bob Roscoe, John Roscoe, Jeanette Blonigen Clancy, Marilyn Brinkman, Arlys Krim, and Margaret Mandernach encouraged and motivated me as I worked to complete this novel. Their critiques and suggestions enhanced my writing craft.

My friend Nancy Overcott, an author and editor who lives in Preston, Minnesota, provided skillful editing on my first drafts and encouraged me to seek publication. I deeply appreciate her expertise and care, as well as her friendship of over fifty years.

My husband, John Neely, encouraged my writing and listened to me talking of Tillie and Bertha as if they were my friends. My brother Doug Pederson, an artist from Montevideo, Minnesota, created the front cover and other artwork. Hal Stoen of Oxford, Mississippi, who is now deceased, provided background on the actual Tillie, his great aunt. Billy Thompson, a historian from Milan, Minnesota, and Duane Essen of Powers Lake, North Dakota, each read one of my first drafts and provided helpful input. The staff at the *Bowbells Tribune* opened their old files to me, which provided good historical detail. Jim Davis at the State Historical Society of North Dakota answered many of my questions. I'm grateful to all of them.

My perceptive and gifted editor, Angie Wiechmann at Beaver's Pond Press, provided comments and suggestions about places to improve my writing, create more dialogue, and bring out more detail. She also noted places of excellent writing. She encouraged me to change some segments of the last couple chapters, which I'm sure enhanced the narrative immeasurably. My project manager, Alicia Ester, assisted me through the entire publishing process. She also provided careful proofreading and caught some significant errors. The entire staff at Beaver's Pond Press deserves much credit for bringing this novel from initial manuscript to book form.

Finally, I am grateful to my adopted father Ernest Stoen, now deceased, who told me about his mother whose homestead experience stimulated this novel. I am also grateful to my mother Mae (Pederson) Stoen, also deceased. With limited education, she was a skillful writer and encouraged me in all I did.

About the Author

Marcia Neely worked as a public health nurse and nursing supervisor during her younger to middle adult life, then joined her husband as co-publisher of the *Granite Falls Tribune*, a small-town newspaper. After five years of publishing, and following the death of their seventeen-year-old son, the couple purchased five acres of land near Benson, Minnesota. Moving down the ladder of success, as defined by society, they discovered a love for an organic lifestyle informed by their natural surroundings.

While living in the country, Marcia published essays, stories, and information in the *Honey and Herbs Newsletter*, and wrote feature stories for the *Swift County Monitor* in Benson. She also authored and published the following two books: *101 Herbs with Essays and Stories* (2007) and *Cooking with Herbs and Spices* (2009).

Marcia now lives with her dog Snicklefritz in Saint Cloud, Minnesota.